Praise for

KEY TO CONSPIRACY

"Talia Gryphon is a master at making the impossible seem real. Her diverse group of characters lives on in your heart and your imagination long after the last page has been turned. Her women are strong and independent, and her men are alpha enough to be led. Talia is a developing master of the word who has an amazing grasp of human nature and the ability to craft tales that will engage the mind as well as thrill the soul."
—Stephanie Burke, author of *Keeper of the Flame*

"Fun and imaginative, this rock-'em, sock-'em vampire tale puts a hard-as-nails military twist in the old wooden stake. Oh, you want some erotic spice? Here's a whole rack!"
—David Bischoff, author of *Farscape: Ship of Ghosts*

KEY TO CONFLICT

"A kick-ass blond vampire-therapist, two sexy vampire brothers and an evil Dracula looming in the offing. I dare you to put this book down."
—Rosemary Laurey, author of *Midnight Lover*

"A fast-paced adventure tale set in a fascinating new alternate reality."
—Robin D. Owens, author of *Heart Dance*

"Kick-butt attitude, sassy dialogue and steady action make this a light, fast read. Gryphon puts a refreshingly different spin on Anubis, Osiris, Dionysus, Jack the Ripper and elves, while giving a nod to J. R. R. Tolkien."
—*Monsters and Critics*

"Urban fantasy readers will welcome Talia Gryphon, whose thriller will appeal to fans of Charlaine Harris and Kelley Armstrong."
—*The Best Reviews*

"With a story that is just complex enough to be attention grabbing, rich locales, vibrant characters and multifaceted mythology interwoven with current cultural icons, this book will draw you in and not let you put it down. It is impossible to pick which of the two heroes you like best, both are so intriguing. I hope this is the opening volume in a series, not a one-shot. It is familiar, but new, and quite fascinating."
—*The Eternal Night*

"Gill is a wonderful character, full of conflicts . . . interesting twists and turns . . . The story was strong, the characters were intriguing and . . . the prose really took off. I think that we'll see some really great writing from this author in the future."
—*SFRevu*

"A great story. I found it an enjoyable read and was hard-pressed to put it down . . . Talia Gryphon's take on vamps and other paranormal creatures is interesting and different."
—*The Romance Readers Connection*

Ace Books by Talia Gryphon

KEY TO CONFLICT
KEY TO CONSPIRACY

Key to Conspiracy

TALIA GRYPHON

ACE BOOKS, NEW YORK

THE BERKLEY PUBLISHING GROUP
Published by the Penguin Group
Penguin Group (USA) Inc.
375 Hudson Street, New York, New York 10014, USA
Penguin Group (Canada), 90 Eglinton Avenue East, Suite 700, Toronto, Ontario M4P 2Y3, Canada
(a division of Pearson Penguin Canada Inc.)
Penguin Books Ltd., 80 Strand, London WC2R 0RL, England
Penguin Group Ireland, 25 St. Stephen's Green, Dublin 2, Ireland (a division of Penguin Books Ltd.)
Penguin Group (Australia), 250 Camberwell Road, Camberwell, Victoria 3124, Australia
(a division of Pearson Australia Group Pty. Ltd.)
Penguin Books India Pvt. Ltd., 11 Community Centre, Panchsheel Park, New Delhi—110 017, India
Penguin Group (NZ), 67 Apollo Drive, Rosedale, North Shore 0632, New Zealand
(a division of Pearson New Zealand Ltd.)
Penguin Books (South Africa) (Pty.) Ltd., 24 Sturdee Avenue, Rosebank, Johannesburg 2196,
South Africa

Penguin Books Ltd., Registered Offices: 80 Strand, London WC2R 0RL, England

This is a work of fiction. Names, characters, places, and incidents either are the product of the author's imagination or are used fictitiously, and any resemblance to actual persons, living or dead, business establishments, events, or locales is entirely coincidental. The publisher does not have any control over and does not assume any responsibility for author or third-party websites or their content.

KEY TO CONSPIRACY

An Ace Book / published by arrangement with the author

PRINTING HISTORY
Ace mass-market edition / May 2008

Copyright © 2008 by Talia Gryphon.
Cover art by Judy York.
Cover design by Annette Fiore DeFex.
Interior text design by Kristin del Rosario.

ISBN: 978-0-441-01576-4

ACE
Ace Books are published by The Berkley Publishing Group,
a division of Penguin Group (USA) Inc.,
375 Hudson Street, New York, New York 10014.
ACE and the "A" design are trademarks belonging to Penguin Group (USA) Inc.

PRINTED IN THE UNITED STATES OF AMERICA

10 9 8 7 6 5 4 3 2 1

With my love and my thanks, to:

Jill Marrinson, beloved friend for all my life, and her husband, Rick, who understands the intricacies of girlfriend-sisterhood and loves us anyway.

Lisa Deller, cartouche sister, godmother to my children— we have survived so much together, and it was worth it.

Hilly Dubin, for your help in the research of the book, for taking care of my eyes and for being a great godfather to my children.

Don Akina, convention comrade and fellow rebel. Rock on, Kahuna. Thank you for everything. You know why.

Megan Bershon, my wise and wiseass, hilarious, stabilizing rock. Woot for the Tennessee Gal.

Sharie Young, your unshakable faith is a precious gift.

Karina Beattiger, part of the Axis of Evil Brilliance.

Brenda Edde, you are an inspiration—a wild woman in her prime with class.

Rachel Mincey, convention goddess and a great friend.

Manda Clarke, for every thoughtful thing you do.

And to my ex-husband, Heinz: I will always love you for giving me our boys. I'm glad we managed to remain friends. Thanks for the support whenever I was struggling.

Special thanks to my military advisors: Charles Randolph, Sgt. U.S. Army Special Operations Command, Retired; Jon Eppler, Sgt. U.S. Army Reserves Intelligence Analyst; Steven Mills, Sgt. USMC, Retired.

As always, to Ginjer Buchanan, my wonderful editor, and Joe Veltre, my fabulous agent.

Talia Gryphon

CHAPTER
1

THE first sign of trouble came on the huge C-130 cargo transport plane. It had been commissioned to carry Gillian Key, newly recalled United States Marine Corps Captain, Special Forces field operative, and clinical Paramortal psychologist, and her handpicked Re-Con Team from London to Northern Russia on a historic mission. *Historic* because it was a very public but very necessary operation intended to bring positive public opinion to the Paramortal community at large.

Their actual assignment consisted of rescuing indigent, orphaned children from child traffickers after a major Russian earthquake. That last detail wasn't for public disclosure at the moment. The powers that be didn't want the perpetrators tipped off, so Gill and her group were officially going in as part of an assessment and tracking Team to help search for and rescue missing persons in the area. The camera crew already seated in the plane's enormous cargo area was a dead giveaway that this was actually a PR assignment, something that didn't sit well with one individual in particular.

"Oh hell no! I don't think so! Aristophenes!" Captain Key was obviously annoyed as she glared at the documentary squad. Anyone watching could tell exactly how she felt by the way she stopped dead in her tracks, then turned to snarl up at the handsome and photogenic Major Daedelus Aristophenes, who was dogging her heels up the ramp into the plane.

The diminutive, curvy blonde stepped up to her much taller commanding officer, shifted her assault rifle to her other shoulder then poked him in the chest with a rigid index finger.

"We are rescuing children from the clutches of sick and twisted fucks. This is not a photo op for you to show off your leadership skills and artificially whitened teeth."

Daed gazed down at the little fireball, adopting the look and tone he generally used when explaining something complex to a subordinate. "Gillian, this is not for me, this is for your Team. To show the heroic rescue efforts of a Human-Paramortal group who cares more about the safety and well-being of Human children than about rampant political issues."

His large hand found her shoulder and he squeezed it in what he thought was a warm gesture. "Think of the good PR you're about to buy everyone."

She mirrored his gesture, reaching up to clap her hand on his broad shoulder, leaning in conspiratorially. "I am about to be very insubordinate and on camera, *sir*."

Her whisper increased in intensity. "You keep those shutter bug shitheads away from me or else."

Turning and leveling a chilly green glower on the hapless docudrama boys, Gillian reiterated her point. "This is not a game, people. Children's lives are going to be at stake as are those of my Team. One camera, one fucking camera, gets in my face or interferes in what we're trying to do and you will pay dearly for it."

There were gulps, gasps and faces paled as she went on, utterly merciless in her rhetoric, "I mean it. You can take all the pictures you want for background and again, when we're the hell out of there. Then, it had better not be of the kids or of us. *Just* pictures of the Major announcing a job completed.

"Anything else and I will consider it a hostile action with an intent to thwart these special ops soldiers in the performance of their duties."

She leveled her gaze at every single pair of wide eyes, locking looks with them, making sure they understood her. "And at that point, because you are interfering, I will shoot you. So before you take off a lens cap or load up any film, you ask yourself, is that the hill you want to die on? Clear on that? Good."

Without waiting for a response but satisfied they got the point, she moved off to sit with her Team, strapping herself in next to Trocar, her Grael Elf lieutenant, and Humans Kimber Whitecloud, a light weapons expert, and Jenna Blaise, demolition guru, all of whom applauded unnecessarily.

"Oh, shut up," she said offhandedly, closing her eyes and trying to think of what to do first when they got where they were going. Not of Aleksei Rachlav, the breathtakingly handsome Master Vampire she'd left behind for the time being. Nope. He never crossed her mind. Yeah, right.

Luis Clemente, their Vampire pilot Team member, was safely secured in a shielded coffin near the rear of the craft with Pavel Miroslav, budding Alpha Werewolf, watching over him. Humans would be flying them today since takeoff and landing would occur during daylight hours. Besides being a pilot, Luis was also one hell of a soldier, which was why he was along for the adventure. Daedelus wisely kept his distance from the rest of the Team after seeing that Gillian was pissed off. He settled for sitting by the now rattled camera crew.

Gillian relaxed against the side of the aircraft, focusing on whom to speak with in the area they were going. Her natural empathy would be a help in the process of liberating any children they found. Sometimes, if the exposure to a captor had been long enough or in some cases pleasant enough, Stockholm syndrome could develop—a situation where the hostage becomes sympathetic toward his captor, often impeding rescue efforts or defending his jailer.

That empathy also allowed her to pinpoint a lie with nearly the accuracy of a Master Vampire or a high-level Fey. Truth was in short supply in black market trafficking but she'd done this before and had confidence in her own abilities and the expertise of her crew. Unbidden, her thoughts did turn to a pair of magical silvery eyes beneath elegantly arched ebony brows. *"I am with you, angelica."*

She jumped. *"Stay the hell out of my mind, Aleksei."*

A low reverberating chuckle stroked through her skull like the finest fur pelt drawn across sensitized skin. *"I will not intrude, cara, I simply want you to know that you are not alone."*

Instead of pissing her off, Gillian felt strangely comforted by Aleksei's shadow in her mind, a side effect of him receiving her blood through the fang nick during the last kiss they shared. It was very intimate and very erotic to know he was only a thought away from her. Their relationship had been strained owing to the monumental attraction they'd shared, which had started when he was still her patient.

Until he had officially *not* been her patient for a long enough time as dictated by her Code of Ethics, they had not been able to act or think on it. His little erotic display with her before they left on this mission had only piqued her curiosity more. He was waiting for her back in Romania, with the same anticipation she felt about the promise of culminating their relationship.

Wordlessly, Aleksei sent her the sensation of his arms around her, holding her closely against a heavily muscled chest offering comfort and his strength for the trials to come. Gillian relaxed in those phantom arms and allowed herself to sleep.

Landing hours later, Gillian woke and knew the Vampire slept, though it was dusk where they now were. There was no ghost in her mind, no feeling of warmth and well-being around her. Shaking herself mentally, she got over it. She'd done her job for years without a big, fanged Romanian teddy bear hovering over her, and she'd do it again.

The Team organized itself with no help or direction from her. It was second nature—her people knew their jobs and would do them well. Right now, being somewhat unobtrusive was the best route. By the time they were ready, the sun had dipped below the horizon and it was safe to let Luis out of his box.

Gillian commandeered an extra camera, lights and recording equipment from the docudrama crew with the intent of posing as a part of their group, only there to shoot the aftermath of the earthquakes. They were only too willing to let the little blond powerhouse have whatever she wanted if it kept her attention off them. Daed watched approvingly; this might just work.

The damage from the massive earthquake was already apparent as they stood looking around. Lights from the airstrip let them see that the tree line was broken in places where huge, gaping tears in the ground were evident. The forest was thick, ancient and foreboding. The huge trees that the quake had felled lay like giant matchsticks over the landscape. There was a raw smell in the air from the open earth, broken trees, the still unlocated bodies. The gashes in the countryside, which spread from the airstrip to the horizon, were like open wounds, the devastation from the crushed houses, buckled roads and crumbling buildings in the little village adding to the horror. In fact, towns within a hundred-mile radius had sustained varying degrees of damage.

They'd seen death before, dealt with it in battle and on missions, but the bleakness of the situation, the stark terror from the natural disaster radiating in the air, set Gillian on edge. Her empathy screamed at her to help, to nurture the frightened and wounded, to destroy those who were taking advantage of the situation, but she approached it warily, with caution and determination. It was a trait that made her a good leader and an exemplary psychologist. She never let her feelings overwhelm the necessity of the situation.

Still, Gill felt inexplicably renewed. This was a situation that had nothing to do with Dracula, Fang Wars, historical serial killers or Sidhe protocol, at least not as far as they knew at the moment. This was a crime scene, the whole area; they were the new sheriffs in town to help solve the dilemma. They had perpetrators to find, an area to investigate, victims and a rescue mission to carry out. It was a job she and her Team did well.

Realizing just how powerless she'd felt over the last year sent a jolt to her sensibilities. As familiar as she was with military procedures and Paramortal psychology, she had been living under a very big cloud for a long time.

Nothing she'd studied or put into practice with her clients could have prepared her for what they'd all come through so far. She grasped that she'd been second-guessing herself, trying to keep a sharp division between herself as a psychologist and herself as a soldier, and it just wasn't that simple. It felt good to be in a situation that was new but completely familiar to her. The person inside her who she'd been trying to come to terms with embraced it and reminded her that she was still herself despite everything.

She took a deep breath of the crisp Russian air. Even loaded with the scents of uprooted vegetation, diesel, un-hygienic conditions, burned structures and the faint aroma of decay, it smelled like freedom. It felt outstanding to have a measure of personal proficiency back in her hands.

As they prepared to mingle and investigate, they all dressed down, not a hint of a uniform or rank about them. Luis wore a ribbed green turtleneck, jeans and hiking boots and carried a rifle over his shoulder, surreptitiously posing as a bodyguard for the group. Trocar and Daed mirrored each other, both in black on black fatigues—the Elf with one of his famous capes, Daed with a black leather jacket.

Trocar was looking very official with a clipboard and satchel; he would be armed from head to foot, nothing visible until he willed it, his inherent magic just another defense system he put to very good use. Daed stood holding the lighting assembly and extra batteries, his weapons hidden on him somewhere if he carried any, which Gill was betting he did.

Jenna and Kimber managed to look cute and dangerous respectively. Kimber in a pair of hiking shorts, boots, heavy turtleneck and down vest; Jenna in a dark leather duster over her own olive drab fatigue pants, combat boots and a long-sleeved T-shirt that announced, DON'T MAKE ME GET MY RING, complete with a picture of the "One Ring" from Tolkien on it. Both women were armed—sidearms, knives and UV flashlights, capable of producing enough of the sun's rays to damage any Paramortal's vision briefly.

A black sweater, thigh-length leather jacket, black cargo pants and boots covered the weapons Gill had on her person: her trusty Glock, a UV flashlight, mini–grenade launcher and twelve rounds strapped around her stomach, her silver stiletto in its familiar position in a spine sheath, hidden by her braided hair.

Since they didn't know what or who was perpetrating the child trafficking, going in as a camera crew from a popular exploration television program, highlighting the devastating effects of a massive quake on both the environment and the people, was a brilliant cover. Human or non-Human, the monsters who were preying on the tragedy of the children orphaned by the quake had to be stopped.

Daed briefed them quickly. Intelligence had filtered through that there was a pedophile ring operating soon after the devastation of the area became clear. It was unknown who or what species was stealing Human children from infancy through midteens but the children were disappearing from hospital beds, orphanages, temples, even police stations, within a hundred-mile radius from the epicenter of the quake. At least two hundred children had gone missing and it was up to their Team to rescue and recover the kids alive. Treatment and placement with appropriate homes or shelters would come later.

Making friends with the local magistrate was Gillian's and Kimber's job. Accompanied by Luis as their "guard," they asked for and received permission to film and research their cover story. Jenna went out to mingle with the community, setting up interview times for families to speak of their losses and concerns. An expert networker, she would have an opportunity to pinpoint some of the families who were missing kids and gauge their reactions. There was the possibility that some could potentially be involved. Pedophilia was possible even within family units. They couldn't afford to miss anyone who might be a perpetrator of a heinous crime.

Trocar and Pavel melted away into the thick forest now partially leveled and scarred by the devastation of a quake that measured an 8.8 magnitude on the Richter scale. The Grael Elf could make contact with any local Fey or Elf population faster by himself and a lone Lycanthrope would hook up with other Shifters better without an audience.

Staying at a Red Cross shelter was an obvious choice. Most of the rescue workers, regional residents and medical support crew stayed there. They had connections to surrounding area hospitals, clinics and staff. The mortuary detail stayed off by themselves, retrieving and numerically tagging bodies, taking pictures of the deceased found and posting them, to make identification faster.

Within two days, owing to their stellar investigative work, Gillian's Team had everything they needed to know. Older children had simply vanished from the various facilities during the night; the little ones under the age of three had been claimed by couples who by their descriptions could only be Lycanthropes of some kind in Human form. All of them had appropriate documentation but some of the workers had misgivings about the so-called parents. Their fears were realized when the real parents of a few of the kids showed up and demanded their children back. By then it was too late.

It didn't take long for the local police department to put all the clues together. The children were being intentionally stolen, most likely for nefarious purposes. The consensus was to stake out some of the likely areas and follow the perpetrators when they actually claimed a child.

Daed was pacing, diagramming the village and surrounding area on a white board. It wasn't the first time Gillian noticed his liquid movements. Normally she didn't think about it much, being in a group of Paramortals, but watching him apart from the rest, his unnatural grace was more evident. Kimber echoed her thoughts, whispering, "What is he?"

"Shifter of some kind, he's never told me and I never asked," Gillian murmured back.

She hoped that whatever Daed was, it would count for something if they got into a real jam. Wouldn't help to have him turn into a Werebunny or Werehamster when muscle counted. As she dismissed her errant thoughts, something did occur to her. She unknowingly and reflexively reached out for Aleksei.

"Why can he be in my mind when Tanis wasn't? Tanis took blood but he never used his ability . . ." Her thought trailed off and was answered by a deep, familiar, comforting Romanian-accented voice in her mind before it completed.

"Something has happened here which has allowed my powers to blossom fully. A shift in the very fabric of magic. I suspect Tanis's will as well. He had been weak for a time because of the torture but is becoming stronger. I do not know what it is, but I am glad I can simply feel that you are all right, dolcezza.*"*

Gillian thought about that a moment. Deliberately keeping the link open between them, she asked Trocar, "Hey, is it possible to put up, like, a magic-dampening field, specific to geography?"

"You mean which will prohibit magic from being used?" Trocar was puzzled.

"No, more like one that might keep a Master Vampire from knowing he was a Master Vampire," Gillian said.

"A nullification field?" Trocar asked.

"Yes."

He chuckled. "It is possible, Gillyflower. All things are possible within the Fey."

"What Fey could or would do that?"

"Any who were loyal to the Dark Prince's cause."

"Wizard caliber?"

"Not necessarily. A potent spell does not need a potent caster. It may take the skill of several mediocre practitioners and require"—he searched for the word—"bolstering of some kind to ensure it stays in place."

"Hear that, Aleksei? You and Tanis may have been rendered impotent by our fangy friend and his pals."

Amusement from him flooded her and she shivered at his warm mental touch. *"I would hardly call myself . . . impotent, cara. But your analysis and deduction with the Dark Elf is very informative and would be the most reasonable explanation for why Tanis's and my own powers had never exceeded a certain level. It may also explain how I am able to contact you in this way, thousands of miles from you."*

"Shit."

"Pardon?" Trocar asked.

"Nothing, it just seems that this coup we're in has been planned for a very long time."

Aleksei again: *"If that is true, piccola, I must ask you to please hurry back here where we can gather our resources and put a stop to it. Tanis and I may not be the only Vampires or Paramortals who have been affected this way. It is essential that we understand what kind of powers we may have inherited. I shall contact Osiris and gather information."*

"You do that," Gillian said out loud. "Let's move, people, we've got assholes to catch. Lock and load."

Being a real psychologist, Gillian had used her time wisely and resourcefully. She sat in one of the makeshift hospitals, doing what she could for the survivors, both children and adults. Most were dealing with post-traumatic stress disorder and grief and loss issues from their ordeal. She and Jenna managed to make contact with a number of families who had children missing, possibly due to foul play rather than the quake, and found out about scads of families that had been wiped out and now had one or more missing orphaned children according to non-abducted siblings. A high-level Red Cross worker confirmed those suspicions and gave her a list of missing children and infants from the surrounding and immediate areas.

The female worker told her off the record that she suspected inside contacts within either the medical staff, the police or the military assigned as disaster aid. Gillian and Daed caucused over that possibility. It made sense in a very sick and twisted way. Someone in authority would have access to all sorts of information such as which children were orphaned or had missing adult family members or who were not being claimed—those who wouldn't immediately be missed. Like a labyrinth, the plot was twisting in all sorts of spectacularly inconvenient directions.

Stealth would be their best offensive. They couldn't

afford to risk the lives of the kidnapped children by blasting in like storm troopers. Pavel returned with news late that night. Rumors abounded as to who was responsible in the Paramortal community but the most persistent rumor was of a rogue Shifter who was spearheading the operation.

The rumor among the locals was that this individual had been fairly twisted before being turned and preyed now on the Human children whom he had found delectable while still Human. No one was sure what flavor of Shifter the man was since he was a loner who had not been in the vicinity more than a year, but those who had tried to investigate early on had come up empty. Nothing was ever traced directly back to him; he had used several aliases and lived in a very remote area to the North of the village. No one was even sure of his actual name.

There were also reports of a strange couple who had claimed several of the children in the area and had finally been turned away when a worker had recognized them from another camp. Pavel melted away to find Luis and Daed, leaving the rest in the buckled street.

"Great," Gillian muttered, "just fucking lovely," upon hearing the news. "Even more sick twists than originally determined, and no one has a goddamned clue as to anyone's identity. This has FUBAR written all over it."

A new allegiance came from an unexpected source. Trocar glided back into town shortly after Pavel delivered his news. Kimber noticed and motioned to Gillian. They watched the tall Grael Elf melt out of the trees. Trocar apparently had some sort of a misshapen lump on top of his shoulder. The moon was full, bright, and visibility was good, but they still couldn't quite make it out. Until he got closer.

Jenna and Gillian chorused, "Oh hell no!" bringing a look of puzzlement to his ebony features.

"You object to those who offer to help us, Captain?" His voice was level but there were the beginnings of anger in his tone.

"To those, yes, I do. They're not reliable. They're like Pixies, for Crissakes, Trocar, undisciplined and noisy."

Trocar gently lifted the small being off his shoulder, setting it on the ground, where it scampered over to Gillian and shook a tiny spear at her. "You ungrateful *Big*! You do not accept the help of the Brownie Nation? Those who are already allied with you?"

"Big?" Gillian processed that. Apparently whatever language the Brownies spoke had limited vocabulary for a larger size.

It was small, less than eight inches tall, with darkly tanned leathery skin, a tiny nose, snapping black eyes, clothed in an owl-skin hood, cape and bright clothing made of woven, dyed thistledown fabric. "I am Ignacious, I am Herald of the Brownies, and I came to offer help." He waved a hand back at Trocar. "I came knowing he is of the Fey Bigs, knowing he is with Human Bigs. You insult us!"

The Brownie's voice was raspy, his cadence and dialect sounded like it was coming through a translator, but Gillian could feel his sincerity with her empathy. Oops. No sense in making enemies. Time for a tactic change.

She knelt before him to come more to his level. "I am sorry, Ignacious. I have had no direct dealings with the Brownies and did not realize your dedication to our cause."

Formally she offered a fingertip, and after a moment, he placed his tiny hand on it and said, "We oppose the Dark Lord and his plans. The Brownies are independent and do not wish the Councils of Elf or Fey and Fairy to speak for us. We honor our word, even to the Human Bigs."

"Then I apologize for my candor, Herald. Apparently

what I learned about your people is wrong. We would welcome your help in finding the lost children." Gillian rose and elbowed Jenna, who was snickering behind her. "Shhh. We can't afford to piss anyone off."

"I know . . . but Brownies!" Jenna giggled. "We're getting help from Duncan Hines and Betty Crocker! Snack food for the win!"

That elicited snickers from Kimber, and Gill bit her lip to keep from joining them as the Herald turned back toward the forest. The Brownie unhooked a small horn made from the tooth of some woodland creature from his belt and blew into it. The noise was abrupt and sounded gaseous.

Jenna and Kimber degenerated into laughter. A sharp look from Gillian and they tried to maintain decorum. "Sorry, but that sounds like a mouse fart," Jenna gasped between guffaws of laughter.

Kimber giggled helplessly. Gillian palmed her face, hoping the Brownie wouldn't pay attention to her blunt companions. No one had time to debate her; there was an outcry from the woods, and suddenly Brownies, thousands of them, poured out to surround their little group. They were all dressed in various small bird or animal skins and similar brightly colored clothing, and they held tiny weapons: spears, bows and miniature quivers. Torches made with fireflies captured in some form of delicate silk waved about in tiny hands. It was rather amusing hearing the small but mighty crowd and their ferocious determination.

Ignacious shushed them all and then spoke. "The Elf Big has explained that Human children are being used by Others for pleasure."

There was a rippling of angry squeaks and shouts from the Brownies. Ignacious continued, "This female Big is going to tell us how to help. She is their leader. The honor of the Brownie Nation will be known to all!"

There were cheers, spear wavings and general bouncing from the assembled Brownies. Gill, Jenna and Kimber managed to keep straight faces; Trocar was looking down at the little beings with what could only be described as a kind expression on his lovely face. Who knew? The Grael apparently had a soft spot for small beings. *Wait a minute . . .*

Louis, Pavel and Daed, hearing the commotion, walked up to join the group, Brownies hurriedly scattering out of their way. Gillian briefed the newcomers on what had been happening. She was a little concerned being out in the open with people coming and going, back and forth, but there was nowhere to meet with a thousand Brownies and not attract attention. Workers, military and body detail were all passing them and staring with great interest.

Finishing her assessment and her thoughts, she said gravely, "Forgive us . . . Bigs, we are not used to seeing so much courage in ones so small but we thank you for your gracious help. We must find these children before more harm can come to them." That was so diplomatic it made everyone's teeth hurt.

"We shall help you. We will join with your cause, Gillian Key," Ignacious proudly announced.

Gillian took a little more time, explaining the presence of the Vampire, Elf and Lycanthrope in their party and who Daedelus was, then went over the Turf War in more detail with them as well. The Brownies had a right to know all that they were committing to. It took less than an hour. The little people were bright, and determined to listen and understand.

"The Brownie Nation is loyal to the one you call Osiris and we will state so."

This was from a new voice, a female Brownie, a little taller than the others, dressed in a bullfrog skin. "We know of this War already. It has spread to all parts of Fey and Fairy. We are noisy and undisciplined as you have said, Gillian Key. To most Bigs we are of no use, but we will keep strong the ties between Brownie and others of like minds."

Ignacious, the Herald, announced her. "This is our Brownie Illuminati, our Light, our Queen, our Wellspring."

The female was taller and more slender than the other members of the group, who seemed to be all male. She was pretty, her features more defined than the males. Nut brown hair hung to her ankles in waves. She carried a scepter and a very nasty-looking knife.

"I am called Sanovia Tanichka," she said in her dulcet little voice.

Gillian nodded in acknowledgment, then introduced all of them, adding, "You are to help keep these Bigs safe as well when we go on our mission."

There were nods and murmurings of assent among the throng of little beings. *Good*, thought Gillian. *At least we might stand a chance and everyone will be all right.*

Pavel stepped close to her and whispered in her ear, "Her name means strange Fairy queen. I do not believe it is her correct one."

"Thanks, Pavel," Gillian whispered back. "But we'll take allies named and unnamed for now. Maybe it's a ritual where they have to know us or have fought with us before we get to hear the name of their Queen."

The handsome Werewolf nodded. "This may be true. I am not from this region so I do not know the customs of the Fey here."

Turning her attention back to the assembled masses, she ordered them to move out and track their quarry. The light was good tonight and there was no sense in wasting an opportunity. Everyone snapped into movement. The Brownies melted into the trees, Ignacious and Sanovia going with them. Apparently Brownie Queens and Heralds weren't exempt from fighting.

Trocar moved up to her elbow. "I am worried about Luis, Gillian. He is too quiet and still even for a Vampire."

"He's been through a lot in a short time, Trocar," Gillian replied softly, sparing a glance at Luis, who stood silently by the trees, gun in his hands, waiting. "He'll be all right."

"I hope you are correct. Nevertheless, do not be alone with him, you or the other Humans," Trocar said firmly.

Gill watched his perfect features and saw the slight frown flicker across his perfect brow as he looked at Luis. Trocar never told her what to do, never second-guessed her. He rarely used her real name.

"You're serious." She was amazed.

"Indeed I am. I do not want to contend with trying to intervene for your safety while we are rescuing the children. You, Jenna and Kimber are the weak links in this particular chain." At her offended look, he laughed softly. "I mean you no disrespect, Captain, but you are more easily killed than the rest of us."

"Maybe, maybe not, Trocar, but I thank you for your concern." She smirked at him. "I'll watch my ass, you just watch yours."

"I believe watching yours will occupy my time much more judiciously." His grin was absolutely wicked.

"If you two are through seducing each other, we need to get moving." Daed's imperious voice grated on both of them. Gravelly and Southern, his accent was pure Virginia money, despite his family coming from Greece only a generation before.

"Stuff it, Daed," Gill remarked good-naturedly. "Lock and load, gang." But she passed on the information about Luis to both Kimber and Jenna. It was just too out of character for Trocar for her not to act on his suggestion. They were a Team, after all.

CHAPTER

2

GILLIAN moved through the trees taking point, flanked by Trocar and Pavel. Kimber and Jenna followed while Daed and Luis brought up the rear. They spread out, treading quietly, weapons poised and ready, noticing the smaller shadows running silently with them.

It felt good to be productive, out on an official mission again, she had to admit. Being so long under the watchful eye and curtailing thumb of the Vampires she'd left in Romania, she'd been worried about her own abilities to reengage her command and survival skills. Apparently they were right there where she'd left them, in working order.

Daed suddenly whispered to her to wait, moved up next to Pavel then motioned Gillian and the rest back. She nodded and signaled the others. It made sense to let the Shifters go first. Lycanthropes of any flavor had a better sense of smell.

While Trocar's and Luis's hearing and eyesight were on

par with or better than theirs, Shifters could pick up scent long before any audio or visual clues emerged. It was interesting to see Daed surreptitiously displaying his Shifter status. She had never seen him allude to it in any way before.

Abruptly the uneven ground gave way to a solid flat surface; they were on a road. The forest was bathed in moonlight, but there were sinister shadows and shapes in the darkness. Gillian, Kimber and Jenna followed their paranormal colleagues with complete trust. Vampires, Elves, Fey and Shifters could see in the dark much better than they could. No one needed flashlights or other illumination unless they wanted to see what they were shooting at. Hopefully they wouldn't be shooting. Gillian was optimistic about a peaceful detain and contain.

Thinking about the fact that the pedophiles they were searching for might be, or might have ties to, Lycanthropes of some kind, Gillian reached back and removed the twelve-inch knife from its spine sheath. The bullets in her gun would blow a hole in whatever she shot at, mortal or not, but wouldn't kill a Shifter unless she blew its head off. The blade was pure silver and had been a gift from Trocar. It would bring true death to any Shifter they tangled with, if she wound up that close. She was hoping they wouldn't have to get that close. Unfortunately, she was wrong.

In the darkness the roar of a hunting predator shattered the silence. Everyone froze. Looks were exchanged all around but no one appeared able to identify the type of sound.

Pavel and Daed were scenting the air. It looked a little unnerving to watch them sniffing around in Human form, but if anyone could decipher their adversary, they could. There was no telling what was out there. Most Lycanthropes outside of large metropolitan areas tended to settle in geographically compatible locations specific to their type—that way the Shifter didn't stand out as much. This was Northeastern Russia, home to Siberian brown bears, Siberian tigers, lynxes, snow leopards, eagle owls, gray wolves, moose, boar, a host of heavy-bodied, powerful beasts and birds. Goddess only knew what the hell was stalking them.

Pavel loped back to where Gillian and the other women stood. He had partially shifted and it was a bit unnerving to see his six-foot-three bulk looming in the darkness.

"Shifterrrrrr," he said with difficulty through his muzzle. Then turning, he placed himself squarely in front of the women.

"Pavel," Gill hissed. "Don't stand in front of any of us." She didn't want to risk him being caught in the cross fire, if it came to that. Pavel wasn't up to speed on fighting with projectiles. It didn't hurt to remind him that he was just as squishy as they were.

He moved obediently but remained close, noticing Jenna shifting her trusty fire cannon away from his back and Kimber releveling her crossbow. Trocar was suddenly behind them with Luis, who had his rifle on his shoulder. The Dark Elf wizard-assassin could kill with his bare hands or even spell damage, but he held a short bow with an arrow nocked and who knew what else hidden in his clothing. They all noticed that the Brownies had flanked and surrounded them.

There was a crackling in the bracken some distance away. Something large and heavy was moving toward them. Everyone braced themselves. Kimber brought out her UV flashlight and affixed it to a top mount on her crossbow. She'd flip it on if they needed it.

Pavel growled but Daed motioned him to be silent, his own body coiled and poised. Trocar motioned to Gillian;

there was a side trail off the main road that was where the noise was coming from. Soon they heard a rough, deep, gravelly voice, accented in Russian, accompanying the crunching and crashing noises. "We guide you in."

Everyone lowered their weapons but didn't put them away. Out of the gloom came two creatures, both massive in their dimensions, and again the voice spoke. "Ah, you bring assistance to supervise your new prizes."

Then laughter, low and mocking. Gillian's stomach clenched. She could feel the sickness permeating from the speaker, the depravity, the self-assurance that he was providing a service. Her analytical mind wrapped around it. Generally with most Paramortals she'd dealt directly with, there was not this sense of "unrightness." Well, with the exception of the Dracula Vampires she'd worked with and Jack, though she hadn't actually worked with him. Even Dante hadn't been this bad when he was pissed off. Fighting to keep her control and temper in place, she waited.

Emerging from the trees was a huge man, followed by something even bigger with some sort of misshapen branches above its head. The first man was as tall as Aleksei and Tanis but much, much bulkier and heavier. The Shifter trait of good looks held true. The man was strikingly handsome, but any attractiveness he had in the long dark brown hair and intelligent liquid brown eyes was lost since they all knew what lurked in his heart.

One massive hand held a leather leash wound into a heavy chain. Said chain was attached to a harness on a . . . Moose? The look was all wrong, the antlers were twisted and bent, not the flat heavy rack of a true animal. As it became more visible, they could see it was bipedal.

To their horror they realized the Moose was a Shifter too or had been magically torqued into Shifter form. Held in place by the heavily chained leash, the creature looked woeful and lethargic. Only its melting, pleading brown eyes displayed any life and that life had been hard. It was radiating distress and Gillian shielded frantically. In her mind she felt the now familiar brush of Aleksei's touch.

"I am with you, piccola."

Gratefully she sent him her equivalent of a warm fuzzy thought then focused on the scene in front of them. It was nice of him to try to comfort her, but she couldn't afford the distraction.

Daed looked relaxed, calm even. Pavel moved a little to the right, opening up a corridor in case the women's heavier firepower was needed. The new Shifter eyed him warily. Pavel was still partially in Wolf form and looked intimidating as hell. Unfortunately, the other didn't look intimidated, he looked interested. *"Ew!"*

"You come early. Our scout scented you or we would not come now." The man spoke again, jerking hard on the leash unnecessarily and causing the Weremoose to flinch.

"Easy, Kemo Sabe," Kimber murmured to Gillian, who was reflexively fingering her knife. Their Captain's temper was well-known. Gillian was a bully to bullies. She hated deliberate mistreatment with a passion and had been known to do very bad things to someone over just such an act.

"I'm fine," she whispered back.

"Gillyflower." That was a quiet warning from Trocar.

"Fine."

Shit, everyone else collectively thought.

Gillian's shields were firmly in place. She was blocking everything except what they had to do, even Aleksei's gentle touch. Right now, getting in and getting the kids out was top priority. Maybe she'd get to hurt one or two of the perpetrators in the process. Yeah, it was good to be armed and dangerous again.

No, no, stop thinking like that. If necessary she would come back later and then hurt them. Yup, that was the ticket. Come back, bring silver weapons, make it a Marquis de Sade Free for All. A little pain, a little torture, a little dismemberment . . . The bastards would pay if they'd hurt any of those kids and this pitiful moose-like creature. Satisfied with her thoughts, a slight, chilling smile crept onto her face, scaring the hell out of the members of her Team who could see her.

"I am Boris and dis is Natasha." The pervert laughed at his own humor.

"I was thinking more like Bambi-zilla and Thumpersaurus Rex," Jenna muttered.

"I was thinking 'Kill squirrel, save moose.'" Gillian was already moving forward to stand beside Daed and Pavel. Kimber and Jenna followed with Luis bringing up the rear.

"Please don't let her kill him just yet," Kimber prayed to no one in particular.

Her Captain wasn't thinking about killing at the moment. Dismemberment, torture maybe, but killing, no. Bad, wicked, evil thoughts for a psychologist who helped heal minds and souls. Still, she was a soldier right now, and a Special Ops Expert. Assassin. Executioner.

No. NO! Psychologist! Think Gestalt thoughts! Bad Captain Key! Good Gillian and Bad Gillian were currently at odds in her psyche.

Gill watched Boris's eyes. There was no direct threat. He obviously had expected to meet someone and didn't know whom. This could be turned to their advantage. They could nail the traffickers and also their supplier at the same time. She glanced at Daed and, with the camaraderie born of years of working together, saw that he mirrored her thoughts.

"Lead on," Daed said pleasantly.

His Team watched his back nervously. Daed, like Gillian, had a short fuse with situations like this. The more charming and cooperative he was, the more dangerous for their adversary.

Boris turned the shifted Moose and moved down the pathway with more assurance than when he'd arrived. He was thinking about the money, thinking about the others like him who believed children in their innocence were perfect to train as sexual toys. He wasn't thinking about danger or subterfuge. That was their leader's job. He was the muscle not the brains behind the organization.

Boris led them unerringly another mile into the forest, where there was a surprisingly big compound; there were at least seven buildings they could immediately see, probably barracks of some kind, an office and a mess hall, positioned in a crudely formed circle around an open courtyard. Uncomfortable thoughts of Auschwitz, Sobibor and Treblinka crossed Gillian's mind. It looked like a concentration camp.

She felt herself go into mental lockdown—cold, empty and without feeling. It was automatic. Her empathy, as much as she blocked, couldn't help but leak through with the enormity of emotions emanating from the children in this terrible place, so her mind took over and shielded her. It was as inherent within her as the Paramortal's magic.

Then she saw the crates. They. Had. Crates. Huge, ugly, air-holed wooden crates. For shipping. Rage started to rear its very ugly head and she forced it down with effort. Now wasn't the time.

A door opened in one of the closer buildings and another large, imposing man came out, walking toward them. Human from the look of him, red haired and bearded; his walk was arrogant, confident, authoritative.

"Hello, you are a bit early."

The voice was level, with a Russian accent. He walked straight to Daed, hand extended. Daed took it and shook it, applying a bit more pressure than necessary and causing the redhead to grimace a little. The man continued, assuming they were who he thought they were.

"The merchandise is almost ready," he looked behind them curiously, "but I do not see a vehicle for transport?"

"It's coming," Daed said in a noncommittal tone.

"Where are . . . is the merchandise?" Gillian asked, her voice level and calm.

"Of course," Red Hair said, and barked a command in Russian.

Pavel nodded to Daed and Gillian that the redhead had indeed called for the "cargo" to be brought out. Dozens of children streamed hesitantly out of two of the apparent barracks, followed by armed adults, both Human and Paramortal by the way they moved. They lined the children up in front of the Team; the youngest was a girl who looked about three, the oldest was a boy who looked about fifteen.

Gillian did a quick head count of the kids, the adults and the weapons, knowing the rest of her Team was doing the same. There were about twelve adults not counting Red, Moose and Squirrel, er . . . Boris. Red had a sidearm and the rest except Boris and Moose had rifles. Probably because Boris didn't need one and they weren't absolutely sure which side Moose was on yet. That thought wasn't comforting. Two thousand pounds of battle tank deer meat had better indicate real damn fast which side of the fence it was on if things went South or there would be a venison barbeque at the end of this.

A thought suddenly occurred to Gillian. There were more kids on their missing roster than were visible.

"Where are the rest of them?" she asked softly, taking the time to smile in what she hoped was a reassuring way to the kids.

"The rest?" Red seemed confused. "But your order was only for these forty. Our message was no babies, nothing under the age of three and nothing over sixteen."

"That order has changed," Daed growled, his voice deepening.

Pavel, Gillian and Kimber flinched almost imperceptibly. Daedelus sounded like a Shifter who was about to let loose a can of USMC industrial-strength whoop-ass on the perpetrators. Jenna was either scanning the surrounding forest wondering where the hell the Brownies had disappeared to or she'd seen something interesting to look at and wasn't tuned in to current events.

Gillian hoped that her dingbat ass would focus so she wouldn't flame anyone on their side by accident. Trocar was listening with half an ear but still keeping Luis in his line of sight. The Vampire had been moving almost mechanically, hadn't spoken unless spoken to and had gone entirely too still.

"Certainly," Red said, backing up a little from Daed, his face going curiously blank, "we will show you everything we have."

He barked another order in Russian. The others in the compound responded by leveling rifles at the group and jacking bullets into firing chambers as Pavel simultaneously whirled back to his Team with a howl of warning.

CHAPTER
3

PAVEL snarled, "Kill themowwwooooo!"

His voice changed to a howl as he dropped and shifted fully, clothes shredding and dropping off the massive body. Suddenly a blond blue-eyed Wolf the size of a pony stood in everyone's midst. A shot rang out from the other side, the children screamed and all hell broke loose as Pavel launched himself at Red. Gillian and the rest of the Team dived behind the crates, which were the only cover in the yard. Everyone but Luis, who stood trembling in the open.

Trocar's slender black shape was a blur as he slammed into the Vampire, taking him to the ground and partially behind a crate, where Kimber dragged him the rest of the way. Luis looked horrified and threw his rifle away from him. Shots were zinging around their heads and putting more holes in the crates, the kids were still screaming and Gillian knotted a fist in Luis's sweater, yanking him to her.

"What the fuck is wrong with you, Clemente?" she snarled savagely in his face, completely disregarding the fact that he could dismember her easily. She was his commanding officer, he had just royally fucked up and she wanted answers.

Luis shook his head then grasped it with both hands, mouth opening in a silent scream as he bucked against the ground, jerking out of her hand. Fury gave way instantly to fear as Gill watched her trusted friend twisting in obvious agony at her feet.

Frantic with worry, not knowing what else to do to stop his apparent torment, Gillian punched him in the jaw with the side of her gun, hoping to render him unconscious. He didn't lose consciousness but curled into a near fetal position, still holding his head tightly. Apparently you couldn't knock out a Vampire even when it was for their own good. Pity that. If he'd been Human, she would have shattered his jaw. As it was, there was a red mark where she'd belted him but otherwise he appeared uninjured.

Barking orders, Gillian positioned everyone as best she could behind the crates when a thousand little voices shrieked as one and the Brownie horde swarmed over the compound. The bad guys all reacted, trying to aim at Gill's Team and at the throng of tiny beings who were grabbing children and dragging them to safety while stabbing feet and legs with very sharp little toothpicks of death and twanging miniature arrows into soft bellies.

It was too much for several of them, mostly the Shifters, though one Human broke and ran. All at once there were six, no, seven Wolves (counting Pavel, who was somewhere chewing on Red), a Snow Leopard and a Lynx—all oversized, all standing next to discarded weaponry and clothing. They began batting Brownies around like footballs, trying to separate the remaining children, who were shrieking in terror at the toothy faces coming after them.

Jenna was muttering, "Wereleopards and Werelynxes and Werewolves, oh my!" while torching anything furry that moved close to their area.

Mentally Gillian was compartmentalizing her thoughts. *Shit! Guns! Kids! Post-traumatic stress disorder! Sexual abuse! Lycanthrope trauma! Guns! Brownies! Bullets! Shit!*

That wasn't helping so she found something to do: shooting the new Shifters in vulnerable parts like the knees and hips to cripple their escape while yelling at the kids to stay down. It was a futile attempt since none of the kids spoke English to any degree, but she couldn't help it.

Trocar was making some arcane motions in the air and murmuring softly in some esoteric magical dialect. The children simply vanished from sight. Picking up Luis's gun, the tall Elf drew down on the Shifters then started firing back at the remaining Humans who had stayed to fight.

The crate in front of Gillian shattered on one side. She looked up in time to roll left, avoiding a massive Bear paw coming at her head. Jenna's flamethrower carried searing orange fire toward the paw and set the crate on fire.

Kimber was commando-crawling toward where the kids had been and feeling around. She'd noticed that the Brownies hadn't stopped pulling things into the forest, even if she couldn't see them. Several of the little beings pointed toward the wood and she crawled there. Hopefully whatever spell Trocar had thrown would wear off quickly and she could help get the kids away from there while the rest fought.

"Jenna, go! Take Luis out of here! Help Kimber!" Gillian snapped.

Not bothering to look at her companions, she was shooting the enormous Werebear from point-blank range. It was coming through the fire and smoke toward her, crunching the crate pieces like matchsticks under its one-ton bulk.

Jenna obeyed her, firing the flamethrower to give them cover, grabbing the prostrate Luis by the collar and unceremoniously hauling his ass back and away. Gillian couldn't spare the time to see if they made it. She danced around another crate, the Bear right on her heels, hot breath on her neck, when she heard a reverberating bellow that nearly stopped her heart.

What. The. Hell?

She froze; the Bear froze; Jenna holding Luis froze; everyone in the compound froze except the Brownies, who were still frantically reabducting children. Some had made it to the compound buildings, thanks to Trocar, who was, amazingly, across the yard with them. He was keeping the remaining child traffickers busy by having them continue to try to kill him, while the Brownies persisted in sneaking kids out the back of the barracks.

The bellow came again. The remaining Humans in the yard suddenly panicked, scrabbling backward, over each other, never taking their eyes off the yard. Even the enemy Shifters were backing up, turning their guns from Trocar toward whatever it was.

What the hell would spook a Shifter? Gillian had only a moment to wonder.

Boris, and it had to be Boris as the Bear bore a striking resemblance to the man, appeared to get over his shock more quickly than the rest of them and growled. His face was twisted in a parody of Human expression. Smirking at Gillian, he began to stalk her again.

She bolted, trying to put some distance between them. Once she made it away from the fiery crates, she could turn and fight him in the open with the silver blade. Her gun wasn't having much effect against his sheer bulk. She had to hope that her speed and utter gall would keep her in one piece until she could shove the blade into his eye, ear or other vital spot. Hopefully before he clawed her to ribbons or bit off her face.

The crate she'd maneuvered behind exploded into fragments as his huge paw crushed the wood. Gillian rolled to the right and clear. Bouncing to her feet, she leveled gun and knife at Boris, then stopped and stared openmouthed, much as Boris was now doing.

Both of them gaped in disbelief as a colossal Minotaur, straight out of Greek legend, formed through the smoke like a demon from the Gates of Hell. It was all of eight feet tall, bipedal, broad shouldered, heavily muscled and black as pitch from nose to tail. The eyes were black on black, the red flames of the fires reflected in them, giving the bull-man a hellish look. Above its ebony-furred face, curving horns as thick as Gillian's thigh rose from its immense skull, arcing forward to wickedly sharp points, gleaming like hematite in the firelight. The great beast kicked the remainder of the crate which separated him from Boris away with a huge black cloven hoof, its long tail swishing in agitation.

"Daed?" Gillian asked hopefully, taking a quick mental headcount of who it could possibly be.

If it wasn't Daedelus, they were all seriously screwed, starting with her and the Bear. Minotaurs were legendary for their brute strength, short tempers, sharp intelligence and supreme dedication to tearing the living shit out of whatever got in their way. They also happened to have rows of sharklike teeth, being flesh eaters, and they weren't picky about whether their prey was still moving or not when they started to bite chunks out.

The massive, horned bull head swung briefly toward her on a neck as thick as a tree trunk. A disturbingly Human but mammoth hand came up in a brief salute in acknowledgment, before it turned back toward the hulking Werebear. Actually, the Bear didn't look quite so hulking while being faced with over a ton of pissed-off walking hamburger.

Gillian breathed a quick sigh of relief then got the hell out of the way as the Minotaur and Werebear launched themselves at each other. Deciding she would be of better use getting the kids out while letting the behemoths fight, she started to run for the barracks when a movement to her left got her attention.

The Weremoose, or whatever it was, was cowering by the burning office building, its chain leash tied to one of the support beams. It was honking softly, great tears running from its liquid eyes, foam around its muzzle as it strained at its chains in an effort to get away.

Swearing, Gillian banked left and raced up to it. It jerked back from her approach, its misshapen hoofed hands pawing at the air with fear. Its eyes were ringed white with terror as it nearly overbalanced owing to the weight of the horns on its head. Steeling herself, Gillian pulled up short, lowered her gun and tried speaking to it.

"It's all right; just be calm."

She forced herself to open her empathy to the creature and its terror nearly overwhelmed her. Only her iron will to help the pathetic creature kept her focused as she allowed her empathy to work, while inwardly cringing at the thought of a bullet finding her back. She projected goodwill toward the beast, murmuring to it softly despite the bellows and roars behind her and the shots still ricocheting in the buildings. It was working but much too slowly.

"Piccola, *look at it. Look directly at it, and let me try to help you.*" Aleksei's black velvet voice rumbled through her head.

She didn't argue about his mental intrusion. There was no way she could subdue the damn thing unless she shot it and she wasn't a hundred percent sure that it wasn't a victim here too. There was also no way she would let it burn to death.

Looking directly into its eyes, Gillian concentrated, letting Aleksei see what she saw, feel what she felt. At once she felt his support, his arms around her . . . No, he was embracing the Moose, the feeling only spilling over onto her. She could hear him speaking softly in Romanian and Italian to the creature, using her as a bridge. It didn't matter what he was saying, only that he was saying it, and the creature was apparently responding. It seemed to relax, looking at Gillian so piteously that it broke her heart.

Aleksei again: "*It does not understand you, or me for that matter. It is a captive also,* bellissima. *Speak softly to it, get it away from the flames and the noise. It will go with you.*"

"*You're really quite handy to have around, you know?*" she sent appreciatively back to him. He chuckled in her head: deep, warm and comforting before he withdrew.

Slowly, Gillian reached for the chained leash wondering how the fuck she could break that without scaring the thing to death. Pavel trotted up at that point, blood on his muzzle and chest and no sign of Red. He looked up at her, panting, a doggy grin on his face then shouldered her out of the way, taking the chain in his mouth and snapping it cleanly.

The Moose nearly bolted at the Werewolf's appearance but Gillian soothed it, reaching up to unweave the leather strap from the chain so she might remove the halter around its hideously ugly face. She shooed Pavel back and pointed him toward the barracks to help the others. Grabbing the Weremoose by its forelimb, she pulled it out of the compound and into the forest. White eyed and sides heaving, it was still terrified, but it trusted her and was trying to calm itself. Patting its neck distractedly, she watched to see where her Team was.

Her heart nearly stopped again when a small voice next to her leg spoke. "Her Majesty says the children are safe, Gillian Big." A Brownie she didn't recognize stood by her shin.

"Jesus, don't sneak up on me like that." Gillian had her gun leveled at the Brownie, who cocked its head and looked at her disdainfully.

"Do you have a message for my Queen?"

"Yes, tell Her Majesty thank you, and that after we return, the Brownie Nation will be known for their loyalty and bravery." That seemed to satisfy him and he disappeared again.

Waiting in the woods for everyone else sucked, so Gillian gradually began to move back toward the compound. Stealthily, quietly, so as not to give away her position. The Moose bounced in front of her, abruptly blocking her path and honking worriedly. It—or rather "she," as Gill noticed after seeing it up close—didn't want Gillian going back there.

"It's okay. I have to see if my friends are all right," Gillian soothed, gently pushing it aside.

The Moose wasn't happy but it moved and let her pass, following her like a huge, horned puppy on two legs. It was rather disconcerting.

Edging up to the compound, Gillian saw that the Brownies had recovered the Humans who had run away. Most of the Shifters were wounded and being tied up by Kimber and Jenna, who was thoughtfully loading a .357 Magnum with silver bullets. "Now, you all can either shift back and let us secure you or I can shoot you right now, then we'll take the shifted body back. Your choice." Jenna always did have a way with words.

Trocar was kneeling next to the Minotaur, apparently bandaging him up. The Bear was gone but Boris was there, dead, with a very large hole through his middle, which she could see as she approached them. Once again the massive head swung toward her and she greeted him.

"Thanks for saving my ass back there, Daed." She knelt next to the enormous creature, the Moose hovering worriedly off to the side.

Daed and Trocar looked at it. "New friend?" Trocar asked. Daed snorted derisively.

"She was a prisoner too, a victim like the others. We're taking her back, but I need Pavel. She apparently doesn't speak any Human language but Russian."

"How are the children?" The baritone voice rumbled out of the Minotaur's huge chest.

"Fine, I think. The Brownies, Trocar and Kimber got them out. Does anyone know where Luis is?"

"Right here, Gillian."

They all spun, Daed as much as he was able, still in the huge Minotaur form and on the ground. Luis stood there, hands at his sides, eyes glittering dangerously.

"What's wrong, Luis?"

"Kill me, Gillian. Do it now while I still have control." His voice was agonized and his eyes flickered with pain.

"Trocar . . ." Gillian asked, backing up from Luis and motioning the Moose behind her. "What's wrong with him?"

The Dark Elf closed his eyes for a moment, seeking something. When he opened them, he relayed his information. "His will is not his own. He wants you to kill him so he will not endanger all of you."

"Hell with that," Gillian snapped. "You're a Marine, Luis. One of our own. We leave no one behind."

Luis looked at her gratefully for a moment, sanity back in his eyes, "I am grateful for that, Captain. But I am a 'plant.' A danger to you all. Kill me. Do not force me to kill my friends." His lovely face contorted in pain.

"They're trying to control him even now. Trocar, put him out, do something." Gillian was frantic; she didn't know how to fight this, and she wasn't about to just kill Luis if there was any other option.

Moving up to Luis, Trocar whispered a few words, made some symbols in the air that made Gillian's stomach lurch and Luis's eyes widen. Elf and Vampire stared at each other, wills clashing, each trying to override the other one. Whatever was left of Luis inside his body rallied and, with an apologetic look to Gillian, slashed his own throat with his nails. Ignoring Trocar's warning shout, she caught him as he fell, blood spraying everywhere.

Lowering the Vampire's body, Gillian was furious. "No! No, he is not going to have you."

They all knew who "he" was. "Not in this lifetime, mister!"

She desperately tried to staunch the bleeding, Trocar handing her a cloth he'd produced from somewhere on his dark clothing. Fortunately, Luis was attuned to her, as his friend and commander, and he listened, ignoring the huge bull's head that bent concernedly over him.

"Shut down your heart, Luis, sleep and we'll get you to Dionysus," Gillian ordered. Luis was of the Greek Lord's bloodline and he might be able to save him.

In her arms, the Vampire sighed, shutting his system down and "dying" as she held him. Quickly, they bandaged the terrible wound in his neck. A noise made them look up but it was the others joining them. Daed filled them in, his voice echoing and hollow sounding coming from the huge chest. He was exhausted from the fight with the Bear and didn't have the strength to shift back yet.

The Moose wandered up, curious. Gillian nearly pushed it away impatiently then thought better of it. "We need to figure out how to get all these kids, the Vampire, this Moose and any wounded back to the village." Her voice sounded tired even to her.

"Ignacious!" she called out and was rewarded by a scurrying in the bracken.

He appeared with a small contingency of Brownies. "Yes, Gillian Big?"

"The kids are all safe, right?"

"Yes. They are most amused to find beings smaller than themselves."

"Great. Look, we need some help. While we get the kids back to the village and the police station, we must get this Vampire back before the sun comes out fully and he melts. Can you help?"

Ignacious shook his tiny head. "The children we can help with and keep safe. They are uninjured but hungry and very frightened. The Vampire is too big for us."

"Fine, then organize your group and get those prisoners in line to march back. Any of them breathes wrong and you kill them, understand?"

"Yes, Gillian Big." He scampered off, yelling orders to his people.

Soon the four remaining prisoners were lashed together and amid hundreds of Brownies who had very disagreeable expressions on their little faces. That done, Gillian turned back to the problem of transporting Luis.

"I will carry him," Daed rumbled, his voice still sounding very otherworldly coming from the giant bovine chest.

"You're exhausted and wounded; don't even think about it," Gillian objected.

"I can carry one of our own," he insisted.

With the Brownies providing twine of spider silk and Trocar's healing skill, Luis was soon prepped and tied to the broad back of the Minotaur. Daed had a massive gash in his side but insisted he'd heal faster with the Elf's help and if he remained in shifted form.

"Fine. Everyone alive?" Gillian spoke up when it looked like everyone was ready. "Jenna, torch it. We're not burying these assholes." She pointed to the dead in the yard. Her dear firebug friend cheerfully went about setting the entire place ablaze. Gill meant the destruction to be a definite warning.

Kimber had obtained the hard drives from the computers in the compound's office and had a folder with manifests, receipts and schedules in it. With the kids and themselves as witnesses, hopefully they had everything needed to topple the entire structure of the ped ring. All of the perpetrators there were either dead or prisoners, but the Team and children were all still alive. Not good as far as investigations went, but as a rescue, it was stellar.

As they trudged back to the village, exhausted but happy, they came upon several dead bodies that were trussed up with Brownie twine and who had been summarily killed. It seemed the original buyers for the kids had tried to make an appearance after all and their fierce little allies had done their job very well. No one had a camera and no one wanted to pack the bodies back with them, so by mutual consent, they left them there. They'd notify the authorities when they got back and let the locals handle the paperwork.

CHAPTER

4

THE trek back was slower. They moved at a less frenetic pace with the children along and the Moose dragging behind. She was still very sad and honked to herself as they went along. Gillian walked with her for a time, then asked Pavel to speak to her and find out who she was and where she was from.

True to their word, the Brownies accompanied them, singing to the traumatized kids, feeding them bits of Fey delicacies. Kimber was alarmed at first but Gillian assured her that the legends of being locked into the world of the Fairy for eating or drinking from a Fairy's hand were just that, legends. After that, Kimber relaxed and even joined in the singing and snacking.

After discovering they had only a hundred seventy children with them, Gillian was furious. The original number had been a little over two hundred, but Daed reminded her that the villages in the area were still sorting out who was dead and who wasn't so it was a sad fact that some of the children might already be dead but still missing. Sighing, she agreed with him but extracted a promise that they'd leave some of their own there to watch over these people until it was determined that the trafficking had stopped and the perpetrators were either dead or incarcerated.

Getting Luis secured away was first on their list. Gillian called Aleksei from her cell phone, not wanting to tire either of them with long mental communication. Explaining what had happened, she asked him to contact Dionysus for help. Aleksei responded that the Greek Lord was ready and able to help Luis and to ship him to Greece as cargo, just as a precaution.

Next was deciding how the Team was going to be divided up. They'd fulfilled their obligation to Major Aristophenes to the best of their abilities. Most of the kids had been recovered and were safe. With a little effort from the local authorities, the missing thirty or so would be accounted for, hopefully alive and hungry, though everyone secretly doubted it. Gill's Team believed that since the still-missing children hadn't been inquired after by anyone, they'd probably been killed along with their families and there was nothing but bodies to recover.

Strong suspicions remained about the local police. Rumors about corrupt cops were nothing new. Most law enforcement officers are just what they profess to be: honest, tireless, caring dispensers of justice. A few, however, were always on the alert for ways to make a quick buck, beyond the boundaries of their paycheck. If there were no crooked cops, there would be no need for Internal Affairs divisions in police departments.

With Gillian's empathy, Trocar's truth spells and Daed's and Pavel's abilities to scent fear, they did a final service for the village and relief workers. Delaying their return by a mere two days so they could blaze through the various agencies working on the rescue effort, the Team managed to ferret out five more individuals who had been involved in the child trafficking operation. DNA evidence confirmed their findings. Two Shifters and three Humans, four males and one female, stood at bazooka and flamethrower point before a hastily convened tribunal, who heard the charges and evidence brought against them.

Daedelus was a little nervous. He hated the bastards as much as Gillian did but he was much more cognizant of the fact that they still had a camera crew with them. Gillian plainly didn't give a shit when she suggested that, given the area was under martial law, they simply execute the perpetrators right there. Daed blanched and hastily covered for his Captain, saying that it had not been decided what would be done with the perpetrators other than holding them until the local authorities decided their fate.

Pavel winked at Gillian then translated both her suggestion and Daed's to the locals crowding the tent where they were holding the tribunal. There was at once a great hue and cry to do exactly as Gillian suggested and exterminate the vermin who had preyed on their children. The regular Russian Army and Daed were hard pressed to contain the bloodthirsty local populace from carrying the guilty outside and summarily dismembering them. Daed glared at Gillian, who saluted, smiled and sauntered out into the compound, followed by the rest of her Team.

Trocar strode up to walk beside her, caught her arm and pulled her close, whispering conspiratorially into her hair for the benefit of anyone watching too directly. He made the gesture one of a lover, but Gillian caught on. Trocar was only obvious for someone else's benefit. Cooperating, she beamed a smile up at him and slid her arm around his slender waist.

"No matter what the ultimate judgment of the Tribunal," Trocar said quietly in his beautiful, musical voice, "I promise you that none of those responsible will leave the area alive."

In answer, she hugged him tightly as they walked, then by mutual agreement, they released each other and kept walking toward their tent. Gillian wasn't about to tell him no. The Dark Elf was a edict unto himself, harsh, lawful and wholly without remorse. If there were a snafu in the proceedings, he would see to it that the guilty were truly punished.

Pedophiles. World's lowest life-form as far as she was concerned. Trocar could do as he wished. No one on their Team would rat him out nor raise a hand to stop him. Bastards deserved whatever he dealt. The kids were safe but people were going to pay.

Kimber surprised everyone by volunteering to stay to oversee the operation in the villages. Astonishingly, so did Daedelus. First thing Daed did upon arriving back was commandeer a shortwave radio and order a backup platoon of handpicked Marines to police the area and keep everyone honest. Gillian busied herself by speaking to Helmut Gerhardt and ordering a number of therapists qualified in sexual abuse and post-traumatic stress disorder to attend to the children. Some of the kids were orphans of Shifters, one even had a Vampire father. Having Paramortal specialists there would help. After several days for everything to be coordinated, it took only a few hours after their return for the reporters they'd left behind to organize interviews and photo ops.

The film-crew promoter tangled with Gillian over

televising the rescued children. Daed wound up interceding when Gillian almost broke the man's nose . . . accidentally on purpose, when she knocked a boom mic into his face. Releases giving permission to photograph the area, a few willing officials and several reunited families were agreed upon. Only then did Gillian back off. The broadcast journalists got their story, and no one was going to sue anyone else.

Major Daedelus Aristophenes, M.D., Ph.D., United States Marine Corps, and his crack squad headed up by Captain Gillian Key, Ph.D., Lieutenant Kimber Whitecloud, Lieutenant Jenna Blake, Captain Luis Clemente, Lieutenant Trocar Blackthorne, the Brownies and their civilian translator-guide, Pavel Miroslav, were all the darlings of the media. Everyone received commendations, even Ignacious and the Brownie Queen, Sanovia.

There was significant air time about the heroism of the Lycanthropes, the Fey, the Elf and the Vampire helping the cause of endangered Human children. After the ceremonies and the cameras were turned off, the Brownies hurried off to help the new therapists with the children. It took some getting used to but the little people really were magic, helping to remove some of the worst of the children's memories and bring laughter back into their young lives again.

"Good job, pumpkin." Daed grinned solicitously at Gillian when they had a quiet moment away from the others and she was organizing her belongings. They were in the Team's tent, alone for the first time in years. Daed couldn't let the opportunity pass by now that he had her all to himself.

"Fuck off, Aristophenes." Gillian smiled. "I told you I would shoot you if you called me that."

Laughing, he went to her and hugged her. "I know we're not really friends, but I'd like to pretend that we are every once in a while."

"Fraternization, Major?" Gill cocked an eyebrow at him but she didn't immediately step away.

"Certainly not!" He laughed again, then grew serious, looking down at her. "Thank you, Gillian, for everything." The powerful arms that were only lightly around her tightened a little and his black eyes grew more liquid, warming with obvious attraction.

Embarrassed, she pulled away, turning back to her packing to avoid the look in his eyes. "I just came along for the ride, Daed. And thank you, by the way, for saving my ass back there. That Bear was a nasty customer."

He came up behind her, sliding his hands onto her shoulders and pushing a lock of hair back into her untidy braid. "I didn't mind."

It got very quiet and an uncomfortable silence ensued. She stiffened beneath his hands, shoulder muscles tightening.

"Gillian," he began, hesitantly, wanting to salvage something out of the moment.

Turning, she looked up at him. He was handsome, brave, intelligent, dedicated. He'd saved her life, but he still irritated the hell out of her.

"Look, Daed," she started to make it easy on both of them.

Daed could read the look in her eyes and scent her pheromones turning cold. It was a clear rejection, but he misinterpreted the reason.

"It's because I let you see that I am a Minotaur, a monster by anyone's standards. I thought you of all people would understand and be able to handle it." He was hurt and let her see it.

"Oh, for fuck's sake, no! When the hell have you ever known me to be prejudiced?" Gillian was exasperated.

She didn't want any part of a romance with him but she really didn't want to hurt him either. Even if there hadn't been Aleksei to consider, she and Daed were like nitroglycerine and gasoline. Nothing good could come out of a physical fling between them. They'd tried that once. It didn't work then; it wouldn't work now.

"You are a decent man, Daed. Regardless if I think you're an asshole most of the time, you're still decent. You are certainly less of a monster than those folks we dealt with out there. Those are the real monsters: people who prey on other people of any variety, especially children. Not men and women like you who can't help what they morph into."

She caught his hand and opened up to him so he could feel her sincerity. "I've always known you were a Shifter; you just never told me what kind. That's why it was a bit of a shock seeing a real Minotaur out there, but that doesn't matter to me. I don't care what you turn into in the 'were' sense. What matters is that we drive each other crazy. You know it, and I know it. I don't mind doing a victory dance with you, just not one in a horizontal position involving sheets and a mattress."

His dark eyes searched her face. He could feel her sincerity, believe in her words. "Can't blame a guy for trying." His smile was weak but she laughed anyway.

"No, I guess I can't. I am, however, still pissed at you for recalling me."

"Why? You were the best man for the job." He joked then ducked as she swung at him.

Gillian's glare backed him up a few steps, and his lapse into his native Virginia accent belied his nervousness.

"Whoa there, darlin', no need to get all riled up. We got what we both wanted, the kids are free and safe, and you get to go back to Romania if that's what you want, as a civilian."

"Or?" She stepped toward him and he backed up farther.

"Or you could agree to be on call for me during this Turf War until we get things straightened out a bit more."

"No."

"It would mean that you could call on us too, Gillian, if you need help. I'll send a platoon to wherever you are, make sure it's a Paramortal group, whatever you need. We'll give you special dispensation from the USMC and IPPA. I'll release you from active duty, if that's your preference. You can remain as a civilian contractor if you like. I can arrange the paperwork tonight."

Dammit, he did have the most gorgeous dark eyes and he was a charming Southern gentleman. Shit, she was going to hate herself for this, but . . .

"Okay."

"What?" He wasn't sure he'd heard her correctly.

"I said 'Okay' to the civilian contractor as long as it doesn't interfere with my contract with IPPA or piss off the Corps, and doesn't consist of you in the bargain as a bonus prize." Her eyes were cold as emeralds and she crossed her arms, waiting for his reaction.

Daed laughed, infectious and friendly. Her face inadvertently cracked into a smile, despite her intention not to let him get to her. She couldn't help but join him. Daed was a shit, but he was an endearing shit. After a moment he ruffled her hair and replied, "All right, pumpkin, have it your way. I'm not part of the deal, but I will be true to my word."

He took her with him when he made his calls to the Pentagon and to IPPA, getting Dr. Gerhardt involved so that

Gillian knew everything was on the up and up. Satisfied, and with an official document proclaiming her an independent civilian contractor on call, Gillian gathered everyone together to say good-bye to those who were remaining behind.

Trocar had explained that he wanted to help wrap up everything there, and since it was closer to the Doorway in Finland, he'd complete his obligation then return to his own world. He had a score to settle there and wanted to get back and see to it.

Daed gave the Elf a recon device. He could leave it outside the Doorway, and if ever there was need, he could activate it and it would send a signal to Daed or Gillian over a private channel to their own cell phones and computers. His farewell embrace was warm and tight, but that was an Elf thing. They weren't ordinarily touchy-feely people, but when they liked you, they liked you and demonstrated it, no matter who was watching.

He kissed her forehead and stepped back. "Good-bye, Gillyflower. I shall miss you until we meet again."

"Bye, Trocar. Thank you for everything you did."

Kimber had found she rather liked the area and the job they'd done so she agreed to remain temporarily active. Daed gave her a field promotion to Captain and put her in charge of the platoon he was bringing in. She and Pavel had to say their good-byes but promised to stay in touch. She had e-mail, and Pavel was given a laptop as thanks for his assistance. Gillian promised to show him how to use it.

"Bye, Kemo Sabe." Kimber saluted and Gillian returned it. "I'm going to miss all the trouble we could have gotten into under better circumstances."

"Me too, Kimmy." Gillian hugged her friend. "You be careful or I'll kick your ass."

"Ditto." Kimber's grin lit up the night.

Pavel and Jenna would accompany her back to Romania via helicopter, courtesy of the USMC. Neither Jenna nor Luis had any interest in reactivating anything but their retirement. The Vampire was given an honorable discharge in the field and safely locked away in a regulation casket then spelled asleep for his shipment to Dionysus in Greece aboard another C-130 transport plane.

There was no way of knowing how much damage Dracula's goons had done to him and Daed was worried about leaving him on active duty. Luis had agreed, fearing that he had some sort of ticking bomb in his psyche. He didn't want to risk his friends. After a brief conference with Gillian, he decided to leave the service and let the Greek Lord help him if he could. He'd rejoin Gillian in Romania as soon as he was safe to do so.

Communication from Romania and Aleksei had been a bit vague during their most recent phone call. He had kept his mental communication to a minimum, knowing that it would make Gillian uncomfortable to overuse it. She hoped everything was hanging tough at the Rachlav residence and that she had the nerve to continue the conversation she'd started with Aleksei in the darkened alleyway outside the pub. Part of her was longing for it, the other part was scratching madly at the "Get the Hell Out While You Can" emotional exit door.

Green eyes surveyed the twilight sky and she sighed in resignation. There was no point in not going back. Aleksei wouldn't be so gauche as to come after her again, of that she was positive, but she really didn't want to hurt him by not going back. The part of her that rationalized it as being just a physical attraction between them understood her motives just fine.

Aleksei was fantabulous, erotic, wonderful, caring, and

beyond *hot*. It didn't take a genius to figure that out. In her darker, hidden thoughts, she knew that if she ran away, disappeared from this, Aleksei would be hurt. She would always, always wonder what might have happened between them, though secretly she dreaded him ever asking her for a commitment. The truth of the matter, she realized, was that to leave now after she'd essentially given him her word would simply be dishonorable and that she could not abide.

Walking with Pavel and Jenna out to a waiting USMC helicopter, which would take them to Helsinki for the flight back to Romania, Gillian allowed herself to be drawn into their happy chatter. When then reached the aircraft, Daed thanked her again, kissing her cheek conspiratorially in front of the reporters who'd gathered like vultures to watch them leave—effectively preventing Gillian from decking him with all the cameras buzzing away. Bad PR.

The last she saw of Daed, Kimber and Trocar was on the road by the village as the chopper lifted off. She'd miss Kimber and the Elf, damn him. Daedelus she wouldn't miss, but it had been a rewarding experience.

All was going well until the pilot turned to yell back into the aircraft, "We are being diverted to Moscow, Captain Key!"

"Why?" she bellowed back over the noise of the rotors.

"Problem at the Helsinki base!" the pilot shouted across the small space.

"Divert to Reykjavik!" Gillian ordered him, thinking the Icelandic base would be the logical alternative.

"Too far! This isn't a long-range craft, Captain!"

"I am aware of what a UH-1E Slick's range and combat capabilities are, Captain," she yelled back, unimpressed by the pilot's nod of acknowledgment and irritated by the disbelief in his eyes.

He was surprised she knew that a UH-1E referred to the Corps's equivalent of the Army's famous Huey Helicopters and that a "Slick" was a chopper that had been stripped of its exterior guns. Maybe she'd been away too long. They were flying her in a craft usually reserved for Recon missions or VIPs.

"You can pick up a cargo transport in Moscow!" he informed her.

"Shit." Gillian sat back against her seat.

"We'll get back," Jenna tried to assure her, "and he'll be there, still waiting for you."

"That's not what I'm worried about, Jen." Gillian glared out of the chopper's small window into the black of night.

"Like hell it isn't," Jenna smirked, then put on her innocent face as Gill's glare turned to her.

"What is that supposed to mean?"

The brunette grinned at her commander and friend. "Aleksei isn't going anywhere, Gillian. He'll be elegantly pissed off at the delay but he'll be there for you."

"Who the fuck said anything about Aleksei?" Gillian demanded.

"You didn't have to."

"Do not start this with me right now," Gillian warned her.

"I'm not starting anything, Captain. I'm just making conversation."

"Bullshit."

"Okay, have it your way. Have you seen that new Harrison Ford movie?" Jenna's chocolate eyes were wide and guileless.

"And how are you going to start things up with Tanis when we get back? Straight to the slab for some bite and tickle?" The small blonde's dander was up. Anyone with any sense would have dropped it. Jenna wasn't that bright and burst into hysterical laughter.

"Oh my Goddess, if you could see your face! You're just being bitchy because you didn't give that poor Vampire a chance to really express himself with you." She dissolved into giggles, completely unimpressed by the fury in her commander's eyes.

"Go fuck yourself, Blaise, and I mean it," Gillian bit off. "I don't appreciate you taking information I told you confidentially in a weak moment and rubbing it in. That is beyond low, even for you."

Seeing that she'd struck a nerve, Jenna took her friend's hand. "Jeez, Gillian, I was just teasing you. Aleksei doesn't seem like the type to kiss and run. I think it'll be all right."

"I would like to believe that but I just can't yet." Gillian looked down at their hands, hers so much smaller than even Jenna's, and thought about Aleksei's strong, elegant hands over hers.

Jenna tucked an errant strand of golden hair back into Gillian's braid. "You know, not everyone betrays feelings and confidences like your parents have, or makes you work for every scrap of acceptance."

When Gillian wouldn't look at her, she went on, "Gill, I know it's not the Vampire thing. You're afraid of locking yourself into any person despite the obvious fact that professionally you made what you thought was a lifetime, significant commitment to the Corps."

"Look who's talking. You haven't had a meaningful relationship since your mother gave up breast-feeding. Besides, the Corps gives back what you put in. If I'm loyal, they're loyal. And the USMC isn't a person, it's an organization."

"An organization that can get you very dead and keep you very alone," Jenna remarked quietly.

"Some things are worse than death or being alone, like being trapped in a circular relationship, for instance." Gillian whispered, "Plus I don't think Aleksei is out to convert me or kill me."

"So now it's a choice? A relationship versus what you do for a living?" her friend countered.

Gillian's response was unavoidably delayed as the chopper landed at the Moscow airfield. They hustled off and caught a transport on a bomber bound for London. They'd catch a flight from there and be back to Romania by the next night. Pavel wisely stayed out of the entire exchange and dutifully followed the two women to their connecting flight.

On the seven-hour flight to London, Jenna and Pavel decided to catch a few Z's and stretched out on the floor, wrapped in a heavy coat, snuggled close to one another for warmth. Watching her friends rest with their heads pillowed on a duffle bag, Gillian thought briefly about the wisdom of grabbing some sleep while she could but her mind was in turmoil.

With the unexpected London stop then the return flight to Romania, it would be another fourteen to twenty hours before she would be reunited with Aleksei. Reunited. Gill blanched at just the word. It made for a realization that she wasn't sure she was ready for—that she and Aleksei might be headed for being a couple or might already be considered a couple. Aleksei seemed to think so, as did Jenna and Tanis, apparently. She deliberately kept her shielding up. With Aleksei's new mental power tools, she didn't want him accidentally eavesdropping on her few panicky moments, despite them being self-inflicted.

He hadn't offered her anything except transitioning their relationship to the next level. It wasn't exactly a proposal or even a suggestion of a long-term relationship. Hell, they could find out that they were absolutely not sexually compatible at all. Yeah, right. Gillian snorted derisively at her own thoughts on that issue. They were compatible all right. Any more compatible and they would have set the alleyway on fire during their last good-bye.

Maybe she was getting ahead of herself. Aleksei wasn't a rabid fucknut. He'd been nothing but honorable and nice. Okay and a little bossy . . . chauvinistic . . . opinionated, where she and women in general were concerned. She still didn't want to hurt him by running like hell, as her Self-Esteem Demon was demanding her to do. Sighing, she realized that she did care what he thought and, after a brief mental struggle with her inner emotional claustrophobic, accepted the fact that the tall, dark and scrumptious Vampire held a great deal of interest for her and it wasn't purely physical.

So deep in her thoughts was she that she nearly slit the throat of the copilot, who laid a gentle hand on her slender shoulder.

"Hephaestus's Hells!" she gasped, her Buck knife manifesting from her calf sheath into her hand and placed against the throat of whoever had touched her.

"Captain Key?" squeaked the copilot, a bit taken aback to find six inches of steel against his windpipe.

"Don't ever do that again!" Gill ordered, hastily resheathing the knife. "What is it?"

"London HQ would like you to assist with an ongoing investigation if you can spare the time. It seems they need an empath of your caliber," the pilot responded.

He resisted the urge to wipe his brow and straightened

his shoulders as he unbent himself into a standing position again. One thing was for sure, he wouldn't lean over her again for any reason.

"I really need to get back to Romania," she heard herself saying to her astonishment and dismay.

"I explained that in anticipation of your answer, but they were most insistent that they speak to you first before you turned them down."

"All right, fine. Tell them they've got exactly thirty minutes, then I'm bound for hom— fangland." Gillian turned away to look out the window again, hugging herself as she bit her tongue as punishment for almost saying "home."

The copilot vanished and left her to her thoughts. She opened her mind a little and reached for Aleksei. *"We've been diverted to London. There's something they want me to investigate, but I'll be back as soon as I can."*

Brief. Succinct. Completely to the point. His response wasn't. *"Thank you, bellissima, for caring that I might worry."*

Shit. Did he have to sound so fan-fucking-tabulous? That voice was like chocolate-covered sin. Deep, melodic, laced with sensuality, power and raw desire. There was an undertone of a promise in his words. He would be there, waiting, but when she arrived, their waiting would be over. *Oh joy, oh goodie, oh shit.*

"Don't let it go to your head. I just wanted you to know I am coming back," she bit back.

"I have faith in you, Gillian," Aleksei's magical murmurings told her. *"Be safe and return to me."*

Cronus on a cracker. He cut the connection first. Lovely. For some reason she felt unreasonably annoyed. Must be the anticipation of what she would find upon her arrival to London. Yup. That was it. Like hell it was.

CHAPTER
5

"Son of a bitch," Gillian breathed, her entire posture stiffening.

Pavel reacted instantly, flanking her on the left as Jenna moved up to the right. Both waited for Gillian to explain what was making her tense.

"Now what?" Jenna hissed, watching Gill's reaction.

"Inspector Wanker and his Shifter sidekick," the petite blonde informed her.

Jenna shifted her gaze to where Gillian was looking with undisguised displeasure. A handsome blond man in a suit, accompanied by a very slender leggy woman with blond-frosted hair, were walking toward them. The female Shifter looked friendly, the man looked pissed.

"Dr. Key." Inspector Brant McNeill's voice dripped with proper British tones. "How nice of you to return, just as you promised."

"Fuck," Gill swore under her breath but managed what she hoped passed for a polite smile.

Inspector Claire Jardin was less caustic, "Gillian, how good it is to see you. I reminded Brant just this morning that you were an honorable woman and would make good on your promise."

Jenna choked back a laugh, covering it with a sudden coughing fit as Gill's teeth audibly ground together. They were screwed. There was no way Inspectors McNeill and Jardin were going to let them out of the Country until they answered a few questions and helped out with whatever the issue was.

"Hey, Claire." Gillian stuck her hand out for the obligatory shake. "Hi, Brant, how's it hanging?"

The handsome blond man blushed profusely, his eyes hardening at Gillian's comment. He chose to ignore it and remain professional. The handshake he delivered was brief and firm, and conveyed his nervousness with the sweat on his palm. "Please come with us, Dr. Key. We have a car waiting."

It wasn't lost on him that Gillian had ignored his title. She'd ignored Claire's too; but Brant wasn't a fool. He knew she didn't like him and took it as a slight. In that aspect, his perception was right on the money.

Gillian didn't like him. She could feel his enjoyment of his temporary power over her and Jenna. At present all he was to her was a police officer who focused on his authority rather than what he represented. Nope, it was official. Brant McNeill was an ass, in her opinion, Fey blooded or not.

Claire was different. Gillian's empathy was "on" all the time so she picked up subtleties from those around her. She had known the woman was a Shifter from the first encounter but not what variety. Studying her classic profile from the backseat of the limousine, Gillian was still perplexed as to "what" she was.

On cue, Claire turned toward her. "This will not take long," she said in her French-accented English. "Just a few questions about your friend's kidnapping and the murdered prostitutes you witnessed, then we would appreciate it if you would help oversee a Field Operation being carried out by your Dr. Gerhardt."

"Helmut is here?" Gillian was surprised.

"Yes, he arrived yesterday. When he learned that you would be diverted back through London, he asked if we would detain you long enough for you to assist him."

"Fabulous," Gill muttered, ignoring Claire's shy smile and Brant's not so shy smirk.

"Remind me to put a tarantula in Helmut's shower."

"Oh, Gill, that's mean," Jenna admonished but she giggled anyway.

"Naw, that's lethal," Gillian whispered. "Helmut is a notorious arachnophobe. It'll be just as hilarious as me standing amid a group of his graduate students doing Goddess knows what and answering questions at a purported haunted site at fucking three A.M."

"Gillian Diana Key!" Jenna gasped, laughing and holding her sides.

Pavel had the temerity to chuckle. It succeeded in drawing a twisted smile from their fearless leader, who was stalking behind Inspectors McNeill and Jardin like a small, predatory beast: beautiful and deadlier than the two Scotland Yard pros could imagine.

The drive back to the Yard was fairly brief. Gillian patiently and succinctly answered every question put to her by Inspector McNeill. Only Jenna and Pavel noticed that she used a tone of voice usually reserved only for people she thought were too stupid to get it if she used words with more than two syllables. With Inspector Jardin, she was much more polite, but then Claire hadn't pissed her off at every turn. Brant seemed to be determined to have a power struggle with the little blonde over every issue. One day, he would push too hard and Gillian would kick his ass, cop or no cop.

Since it finally was apparent that Gillian really didn't know shit about Tanis's captors, the ongoing prostitute murders, exactly where she and Kimber had been taken or who was orchestrating the slaughter, just as she'd said, Brant called a halt after Claire coughed and surreptitiously pointed at her watch. He took the hint and closed the folder. From the description of the house, and the general vicinity, they'd probably be able to find it without her direct help. It irked him that this annoying woman couldn't give them more information but he was at least satisfied that it wasn't because she wouldn't. She really didn't know.

It was all Gillian could do to keep from smiling triumphantly at the arrogant detective. She didn't like him and made no bones about it. Intellectually she knew that as a cop, he had to assume that she knew more than she was letting on. Empathically he pissed her off with his stupid authority trump card. If he hadn't been such an ass in the beginning, she'd have been much more cooperative.

Truth was, she had a fair inkling of where they'd been taken. Pavel would certainly have been able to backtrack at least to the area, but pointing that out right now didn't seem like the best idea, especially to someone like Brant McNeill. He tolerated Claire Jardin as a partner, but Gill could sense he had some deep-seated unease over her being a Shifter. Hell, he didn't even like himself. She was betting it was because of his Fey background that he tried so hard to cover up. She'd given them as much as she was able.

The police were stepping up Paramortal patrol Teams in the seedier districts of town, including the area Gillian had described, trying to prevent the murder of any more streetwalkers, and the Yard was going full out to find the estate. Their further assistance wouldn't be needed in this matter. Since Gill had no proof that Dracula was directly involved with their abduction other than the word of Jack the Ripper, it wasn't a credible enough lead to pass along.

Mentioning Jack to the detectives didn't seem like a wise move either since Kimber wasn't there to corroborate her story. Plus, Gillian could no more remember a viable description of him than she could of her third-grade teacher. She figured Brant wouldn't believe her explanation anyway. Partial amnesia due to Pixie venom probably wasn't high on his list of excuses.

Claire followed her to the ladies' room with Jenna after they concluded the interview. It had been a long evening with too many cups of coffee. As they washed their hands, Gillian took a shot at satisfying her own curiosity about the slender French woman.

"How did you get to be employed by Scotland Yard?" she ventured as Claire reached for a paper towel.

"I had worked as an Inspector in Gascony for several years," Claire replied, completely unruffled. "I met an English gentleman who worked with Interpol and he brought me back to London. It was simple enough to transfer my credentials and license here and Scotland Yard seemed all too happy to have me."

"That's amazing," Gillian replied. "You must be very skilled to have impressed the Yard."

The lovely woman smiled. "I simply use my intuition."

It was Gillian's turn to smile. "I bet you use more than

that. You're a Shifter, correct? You can read people's body language and scent far better than a Human can and much better than a cross-bred Fey like Brant."

"Oh, *chérie*, do not let him know that you suspect his heritage," Claire warned her. "He does not acknowledge it himself, but I have always suspected him to be part Fey."

She paused a moment, then met Gillian's eyes. "You are correct, I am a Shifter. Most people who are familiar with us notice. I am an inherited Shifter. I was not attacked or bitten. My family is Cheetah. Some may regard it as a Curse. To us, it is simply a family experience. A family totem, if you are familiar with shamanism."

When Claire said "Cheetah," Gillian's eyes widened. She'd never known a Shifter variety outside the usually thought of varieties: Wolf, Leopard, Jaguar, Tiger, Bear, Lion, Hyena and, of course, Daed's Minotaur. The fact that Claire had described her Shifter inheritance as a family totem rather than a Curse was interesting. The only other inherited Shifter that Gillian knew was Daedelus. His Minotaur Line traced back to ancient Crete.

"That's fascinating," Gill responded. "I know only one other inherited Shifter, but I've never known or heard of a Cheetah."

"We are indigenous to Africa. My family had immigrated there long ago. There is still a Cheetah preserve that my relatives manage. My great-grandmother left there about eighty years ago and returned to France. We have always been this way. It is something to be spoken of with acceptance, not annoyance."

There was no trace of bitterness in her voice, Gill noticed. She appeared well adjusted, the way Cezar's pack and Daed appeared to be. Still, Claire did the slight glance away that most Shifters seemed to do when they first met someone and were unsure of any inherent prejudices. Gill's empathy picked up the ripple of her emotions simultaneously: confident, proud . . . but insecure—would this person accept me?

"Thank you for sharing that with me," Gillian said kindly. "I don't normally ask such a personal question, but I like you and wanted to get to know you better."

Her feelings and intentions were genuine. She did like Claire and she had been curious about her origins. Unbidden, her own pheromones shifted, her empathy flared just a little and Claire could feel and scent her sincerity.

"My God, you really are a natural empath!" Claire exclaimed.

"Powerful too," Jenna put in, making both of them jump. She'd been so uncharacteristically quiet that Gillian had forgotten she was there.

"Apparently." The Frenchwoman laughed.

"Let's get out of here, I'm not big on powder room discussions." Gillian grinned back.

"No, you just don't like anything so girlie as a bathroom chat," Jenna snorked at her friend.

"What about you?" Gill groused on her way out of the door. "The Missouri tomboy who traded her Barbie dolls for Tonka trucks and Tommy guns."

"Hey, at least I met more guys that way," Jenna protested. "You try getting any males interested in you while you're changing the curtains in your Barbie Dream House."

They argued all the way out to the limousine, Pavel trailing behind them, Brant and Claire bringing up the rear. Claire was giggling her ass off at their obvious friendship and camaraderie. Brant was scowling, stiff and completely formal—a blond disapproving presence as they piled into the limousine that would take them to their next destination. Gillian sat facing forward, Jenna across from her and Pavel on her right. Claire settled in next to Jenna, leaving the seat next to Pavel for Brant, who looked decidedly uncomfortable squeezing in next to the big Werewolf and the door.

He would escort Dr. Key to where she needed to go. He would protect her if necessary because that was his job. He would even take a bullet for her if the situation demanded it. Brant McNeill was honorable; he was professional; he was reliable. He was a good cop but he didn't have to enjoy each and every assignment. He definitely didn't enjoy Dr. Key.

The two former Marines kept up their light banter as they drove through the darkened, misty streets of London. Claire kicked Brant in the shin in an effort to get him to lighten up and enjoy the company. He wasn't having it and remained pressed against the side of the car's door as far away from Pavel as he could get without being overly obvious. A slight frown rested on his handsome features.

Gillian popped a cigarette into her mouth and lit it. Jenna rolled down the window a bit and joined her in her nicotine bliss by lighting one of her own.

"You cannot smoke in here," Brant admonished them.

"Arrest me then, because I'm having a cigarette." Gillian spoke matter-of-factly and blew a stream of blue-gray smoke out the window.

Brant shifted in his seat and looked away, his face darkening a little. It was noticeable even in the gloom of the car. Claire reached over and patted his knee. He rewarded her with a blistering glare and she subsided, turning her attention back to the women.

"This is Piccadilly Circus." She indicated the brightly lit neon lights of the area they turned into.

Gillian glanced up at the street signs, enjoying the cheerful atmosphere of London's well-known area. The Ritz-Carlton Hotel loomed into view and another street sign became visible.

"Berkeley . . ." Gill whispered to herself, thinking.

"What?" Jenna blew a smoke ring and looked at her friend.

Gillian blanched suddenly and whirled in her seat to look at Brant and Claire. "Where are we going? Exactly?"

"Number Fifty, Berkeley Square," Brant responded, his brow furrowing even more. "Why?"

"Shit! And you didn't think to warn me before?" Gillian snapped at the detective.

"Why in hell would I warn you before, Dr. Key?" Brant snapped back.

"Because she's an inherent empath, Brant," Claire told him, clicking onto Gillian's reference. Her partner's eyes widened slightly.

"I . . . I am sorry, Dr. Key. I didn't think . . ." Brant stammered.

"Have you even read my file, Inspector McNeill? I am assuming you have a file . . . Or do you only know what you hear on the news?" Her tone was scathing and he flushed deeper red.

"Dr. Key, I have read your file. I simply did not focus in on that particular detail," he tried explaining.

She waved him off and turned her attention back to the direction they were going. Jenna poked her knee.

"What's Fifty Berkeley Square?"

"The most haunted house in London," Claire said softly.

"Oh shit," Jenna breathed.

"Exactly," Gillian said.

When they pulled up, she could pick Helmut out of the

crowd of students easily. Dr. Helmut Gerhardt was six feet three inches of sandy-haired, blue-eyed, Austrian masculinity. He was dressed in his usual way, tweed sweater, jeans and expensive leather shoes. His sandy hair was unruly and rumpled. He had been her professor, her advisor, her mentor and her friend. Now he was also her boss at the IPPA, but she could live with it.

As far as Gillian knew, Helmut wasn't married, didn't have a girlfriend, wasn't gay. He'd never been anything but appropriate with her—almost bordering on fatherly in his demeanor and concern for her while she was under his tutelage.

She respected his intellect, admired his insight, abilities and talent; truly loved him as a friend now that they were professional colleagues. He was both brilliant and gifted in psychic abilities—limited telepathy, some rudimentary telekinesis and empathy that was as strong as hers but more limited in scope since he could only "read" living Humans and Human crossbreeds. In her mind, though, she was ever the student and he was ever her teacher. That was something Helmut might have changed if he could, but he'd rather be her lifelong friend than her short-term lover.

He turned and his familiar blue eyes crinkled in welcome as they piled out of the car. Gillian walked in as dignified a way as possible toward him, Jenna, Pavel and the two Inspectors following her.

Helmut met her halfway and enfolded her in a warm hug. "How nice of you to come, *Schatzi*," he whispered teasingly to her in his Austrian-accented English, using his pet name for her.

"How nice of you to invite me, *Scheisskopf*," Gillian kidded back, affectionately calling him a "shithead" while standing on her toes to kiss his cheek and grin.

"One day, someone will not be flummoxed by your charms, my dear, and you will find yourself on the receiving end of a long overdue reprimand." Helmut chuckled, shaking his finger under her nose as he scolded her kindly.

His sharp eyes scanned her face and form quickly, no trace of sexual interest, only fond concern in his look, which settled back on her own very green orbs. She looked tired. Tired and . . . something else. He frowned slightly and she ducked her head, blushing a little in her embarrassment of being scrutinized by her teacher. No time now to find out what was bothering her, but he knew she'd just come off a rather arduous assignment; he was the one who had sent her on it. There would be time later to fathom the shadows in her eyes. She had also dropped her defenses in his presence, the reflexive gesture of trust— one empath to another. That was something she could not afford to do. Not now.

"Keep your shields up, Gillian," he ordered her softly, before taking her hand as he turned to greet her accompaniment.

Gillian introduced her group to Helmut. He, in turn, introduced her to his graduate students and the little coven of Spiritualist practitioners who were all huddled in coats and robes in front of the infamous house on Berkeley Square.

The name plate beside the door read, MAGGS ANTIQUARIAN BOOKSELLERS, an innocuous name for such an inherently dangerous place. Fifty Berkeley Square was only one of several haunted houses on that segment of street. House numbers Fifty-three and Forty-four were also haunted but to a lesser degree.

Gillian had allowed Helmut to take her hand as he led her to the front of the group and he made his introductions of his former student. "Dr. Key's empathic talent differs from mine in that she is not limited in her sensitivity to Humans or even the living. Her range encompasses both the living and the long dead, which is why I asked her here tonight."

Helmut paused and looked over the crowd. Intense interest from his students and the Inspectors. Her friends, Jenna and the Shifter Pavel looked unimpressed. They'd seen the show before. What worried him a bit was the Spiritualists, who didn't seem impressed or concerned about where they were or what benefit Gillian could be to them tonight.

"I know most of you think you know why you're here. For those who do not know the history of this place, allow me to enlighten you with a brief rundown. It may give you insight as to how you want to proceed, and what you can expect once we enter this place."

Helmut had a marvelous speaking voice for a Human. His accent was the softer German of his Austrian heritage rather than the harsher sounding syllables of Germany. He'd learned English from a British teacher so his tone held traces of aristocratic Brit. Smooth, melodic, soft-spoken generally, the outstanding lecturer and teacher had his little audience in the palm of his hand in moments. Even Gillian enjoyed hearing him again and, though she knew the story, was intrigued by his telling of the tale.

The houses on this particular row had been built over an ancient plague pit. During the years the Black Plague had ravaged Britain, beginning in 1348, death had been so rampant that entire families, even smaller villages, were completely wiped out of Human life, sometimes within a single day.

London was a burgeoning city even then. When the Black Death descended and killed off a full third of the population, there were few who were brave enough to tend to the sick and dying. Fewer still who would prepare and transport the bodies for individual burial. Huge, deep pits were dug in the spongy turf, away from the main populated areas of town. The dead were brought, stacked like cordwood on carts and unceremoniously dumped into the gaping maw of the earth, taking their pestilence with them.

Unfortunately for some, there were no modern medical procedures to ensure that all who went into the pits were truly deceased. Some were so catatonic with the illness that they gave the appearance of death to the fourteenth-century peasant eye. Assuming the lifelessness of the victims and wanting the bodies cleared out quickly before they began to rot or the rats to feed, the still living were occasionally and accidentally mingled with the dead. The unfortunate person awoke then, sick, weak, confused, in the mud, blood, festering wounds and stench, surrounded by the bodies of their friends, families and townsfolk. Too weak or sick to crawl out of their living grave, with no one who would respond to their pitiful cries for help, they were left to the horror of death amid the decaying bodies of the plague victims.

Ghosts generally begin as the result of extreme trauma or extreme emotion at the time of death. Every now and then there is a Curse involved or invoked, but generally Ghosts are the product of the deepest, most primitive emotional responses in a Human being at the moment of death. Since there were so many victims buried in the immediate area, Ghosts were plentiful and thought to be the spiritual impetus which caused the hauntings along Berkeley Square.

There was the eighteenth-century nobleman, Lord Clermont, in Number Forty-four, the older gentleman waiting eternally for his daughter's return in Number Fifty-three and the odd plague Ghost that would rise and scare the shit out of the occasional tenant from time to time. Quiet, mournful Ghosts, all of them.

Number Fifty was a little different. Its legend began along with the rest, after the row was built in the 1700s. What started as a family home quickly became a nightmare. No one knew how the first Ghost came about, but a girl of three or four had been seen weeping and wringing her hands in the upper levels. The story was, she had been frightened to death in the nursery.

A young woman named Adeline fell to her death from one of the upper-story windows, fleeing the incestuous advances of her uncle, a formerly gentle, kind person who suddenly seemed like a man possessed. Perhaps he was. Adeline's Ghost often hung from the window ledge, screaming in horror, replicating her fall, night after night.

One man kept his insane brother locked in the uppermost room at the top of the house. The man eventually died in that room, his jaws open in a soundless scream, his face white as a sheet.

A chambermaid and a knighted gentleman both died after spending the night in that room. The woman, after being pulled from it, shrieking; her mind shattered, she died days later in a mental institution. The knight died in the room, firing his pistol at some unknown horror. A sailor dashed downstairs, throwing himself out of a window to impale himself on the wrought-iron fence in his terror-stricken state to get away from whatever it was that inhabited the upper stories of Number Fifty Berkeley Square. All of them were now eternal residents of the Dickens-style location.

The current tenants, Maggs Brothers, were used-book dealers. They had obtained the lease and the house over fifty years ago. Their employee contract had a paragraph not found in any other agreement between employer and employee. It stated that the employee must agree to never, under any circumstances, even during the bright light of day, be alone in the building and to never, ever, attempt to open the door to the uppermost room, enter it or use it even for storage. Sign it after your interview and you could work there. Refuse and Maggs Brothers would just as soon you found employment elsewhere.

Gillian's hand tightened slightly on Helmut's as he swiftly told the tale of Number Fifty. She was claustrophobic and hated thinking of anyone being buried alive in a plague pit. Likewise, she didn't like so many innocent people being victimized by what appeared to be a malignant, intelligent presence. Ghosts couldn't directly cause physical harm to anyone, but scaring the life out of a person was definitely in their repertoire.

Reading her tension easily, Helmut turned and looked down at her. "Now you all understand why we asked the esteemed Dr. Key to join us. Gillian? Will you walk with the Spiritualists? They wish to assist the known spirits into the next transition of their lives. We have the permission of the owners to be here and to attempt this. They would like their building to be cleansed if it is possible to do so."

She looked hard at him, understanding what he wanted from her. Yes, it was a dangerous request but he had faith in her. No, he wasn't overstepping their friendship. Helmut wanted everyone safe. If the Spiritualists were determined to do this and had asked for his help, it was a prime opportunity for his graduate class to come along, observe and see what they were getting into with their own careers. He knew if anyone could pinpoint the moment anything nasty came after them out of that upper-level room, it was her.

"Sure. Love to. Let me just disarm myself . . ." The sarcasm in her voice was apparent only to Helmut and Jenna.

Inspectors McNeill and Jardin took her gun, her knife, and her garrote, wordlessly and wide-eyed. They hadn't even known she was still armed. Pavel smirked to himself. He had. He could smell the gun oil and the silver.

"You coming?" Gillian turned back to Helmut with a wry smile.

"Of course, I would never ask anyone to do what I am not willing to do." He winked at her then swept his arm in front to indicate that she should lead.

"Listen up," Gill barked in her Marine Captain voice, making the Spiritualists and students jump from the whip crack of command in her tone. "My . . . friends . . . er . . . staff"—she chose her words carefully so they would follow her directions to the letter—"will follow directly behind me."

At least she hoped they would. A nod from Jenna and Pavel confirmed her request. "Do not, for any reason, touch me or distract me. I have to focus on what I'm doing in there. With all the paranormal activity in this vicinity, I have to pay very close attention or I could misread something and put us all in danger because I didn't notice the 'right' something. Is that clear?"

Patiently she waited, looking over the group, meeting eyes with as many as she could and seeing them all nodding in agreement. "Do exactly what Helmut tells you, what my staff tells you, and if I begin to speak, yell or issue an order, do exactly what I tell you. If you see me run, *run*. Do not ask questions at that point, do not linger. If there is something in there that can scare me and my crew, you do not want to find out what it is."

Without waiting for further confirmation, Gillian turned and ran into a tall Human man in a Mack. "Cronus's balls! Do *not* ever do that again!"

The man looked sheepish but extended his hand, which held a key. "I'm from the bookseller, miss. I'm supposed to let you in then lock up when you leave."

"You are not going inside, is that understood?" Gillian said bluntly.

"But I must—" the poor man tried to continue.

"*No*. No civilians, no nonpractitioners, no one goes in that house who does not have some element of training in the Paramortal or supernatural. Not at night, not tonight, not now."

He nodded blankly but turned and proceeded up the walkway to the door. The lock clicked open and Gillian waved him back. She stood on the threshold, focusing her empathy and preventing anyone from going around her into the house. When she felt she was ready, she walked in. The rest of them could only follow. Hopefully it would be a mission of mercy for the trapped spirits and not an expedition into a portal of the Abyss.

CHAPTER

6

T HE first thing she did was flick on the light in the foyer. Gods above, it was practically reeking of metaphysical energy inside. Power skated over her empathy and raised the hair on her neck and arms. What the hell had Helmut gotten them into?

"Why did you do that?" one of the Spiritualists wanted to know.

"What?"

"Turn on the light. Isn't it supposed to be dark? Ghosts like the dark, don't they?"

"You've been watching too many horror movies," Gillian told him. "Ghosts don't require darkness to scare the shit out of you."

"Oh." The Spiritualist blanched a little and fell back with the others.

"Are you going to be all right?" Jenna was at her elbow.

"I hope so. Helmut probably assumed that Inspector Dickhead would tell me where we were going so I'd have time to prepare for this better." Gillian was looking around the foyer, up toward the stairs, into the rooms off to the sides.

"Tell him, sweetie," Jenna urged her. "They can reschedule this for another night or later, when you've had time."

"I can't feel anything really nasty at the moment, while there is a lot of activity. There haven't been any big incidents in years. Maybe whatever the thing was, went dormant."

She ignored Jenna's well-intended suggestion. She hadn't told the absolute truth. There was something nasty in this vicinity all right. It was there. Just on the edge of her empathy. They weren't on its radar yet. Gill hoped they would stay out of its attention range.

"We'd like to start with the Ghost of the little girl, Dr. Key," the male Spiritualist who'd spoken earlier informed her.

"What's your name?"

"Richard."

"Well, Richard, we will start where the Ghosts want you to start. Unless, that is, you've got a brazier, willow oil and incense under your robes somewhere and you know the little girl's true name. Otherwise you will risk calling the Big Bad Thing that apparently runs this ectoplasmic enclosure."

She started up the stairs without waiting for his response, noticing as she got to the first landing that Helmut was right behind her, followed by Jenna and Pavel. The rest of them filed slowly up, some of them following her lead and flicking on lights in the rooms adjoining the foyer and the stairwell.

The sound of crying started before she felt anything. At

the back of the line trooping up the stairs, one of the Spiritualist women gave a happy squeak.

"That's her! She's waiting for us to help her into the light, finally!"

"Hey!" Gillian hissed down toward her, and was completely ignored.

Helmut saw the look on her face and the vigorous shake of her head and stepped in. "Miss? Er . . . Nutmeg?"

The girl looked up toward him. "Yes, Professor Gerhardt?"

"Gillian is advising against calling out suddenly and loudly, my dear. Remember, she cannot afford to be distracted if we attract any unwanted attention from the yet-unseen occupants," Helmut said, not unkindly but firmly.

"Nutmeg?" Jenna, Gillian and Pavel chorused together in a not so quiet stage whisper.

It drew a sharp gesture to stop from Helmut, who glared at them and moved farther up the stairs toward Gillian. "It is her chosen name in her group," he whispered.

"Nutmeg?" they chorused again, more quietly but also more incredulously.

"Just. Go. On," Helmut bit out in his most polite voice.

"For Hell's sake, Helmut, coven names?" Gillian was now officially annoyed. "What is this? Amateur Hour at the Abyss?"

She poked him in the shoulder, speaking in what might be interpreted as a conspiratorial voice. "Make no mistake, there is something very unpleasant, very close by. I do not want to be trying to lug body bags out of here if they wake it up by being poser dorks!"

"I thought you said you couldn't feel anything nasty!" Jenna grabbed her arm.

Gill shook her off, focusing on Helmut for the moment. He interrupted her next sentence.

"You did not feel anything and now you do?" His deep blue eyes bored into her.

"Actually I felt something when we pulled up. Sorry, Jenna, I didn't want to scare you," she admitted to her friend then turned back to Helmut, who was still below her on the stairs.

"This whole area is an ectoplasmic, spirit-ridden plague pit, for the love of Hathor! And you're bringing those devoutly dumb do-gooders in here? We should have a coven all right, a coven of *real* experienced Wiccans and Spiritualists, probably even a Voudoun or two with a protective circle around the whole block!"

"Now, *Schatzi*, there are several of them who are 'real,' as you call them in their group," Helmut admonished her. "We are only supposed to be observing, after all. They are not my responsibility, nor yours. And please lower your voice, it does carry so."

"Helmut." Gillian sighed, speaking more quietly so as not to alarm the rest of the gang, "They may be here of their own free will, have signed waivers in their hands in case of Death by Booing, plus twenty percent off coupons for dry cleaning when they shit themselves in fright if what Goes Bump in the Night comes after us, but right now, as the Empath you asked to oversee this, they are very much my responsibility. I don't want anyone killed!"

Whatever Helmut might have answered was obliterated by excited squeeing and pointing from the Spiritualist group, gasps from the graduate students and an "Oh shit" from Inspector McNeill. Watching everyone's eyes widen made Gillian turn to see the diminutive form of a tiny girl on the landing behind her. The child was fully formed in

Technicolor but transparent, wringing her hands, with tears rolling freely down her cheeks.

Frowning, Gill watched her closely. Her empathy should have spiked with the Ghost's arrival, especially so close to her. Something wasn't right. This was less like a Ghost and more like a shade—the impression or imprint of a spirit rather than the emotional energy a Ghost gave off.

Warning bells were going off in Gill's head. Something should be obvious to her but wasn't. Shit, she was tired, aggravated, she missed Aleksei . . . *No* . . . She was *not* going to go *there*.

Frowning, she focused her scattering thoughts. They were in an unknown dangerous situation that she suspected Helmut, with all his academic genius, had vastly underrated. All these people. Her eyes glanced back, at the line moving up the stairs, following her blindly. Responsible for them was what she was, no matter what her former teacher said.

Unconsciously she straightened her shoulders a little. Responsible. Accountable. In Charge. Fuck. This was a bad idea to begin with and it was getting worse by the moment. She could feel the aura of every single person, Human or not, who followed her. She could feel the presence of regional Ghosts looming at the edge of her empathy; she could feel something really, really nasty, lurking, waiting, anticipating . . . poised and ready to pounce. An involuntary shiver went down her spine. She hoped no one noticed. No one did.

She was halfway up to the second landing, Helmut, Jenna, Pavel, right behind her. The Spiritualists and grad students trailed down the stairs but Brant and Claire were about two thirds of the way up to the first landing, pushing their way through to where she and Helmut were. Typical cops. They run in when everyone else runs out. Gillian couldn't fault their bravery but now wasn't the time for heroics. Taking a quick head count, she realized there were missing people. Where the hell were those two Spiritualists? Richard and what was the girl's name? Cinnamon? No, Nutmeg . . . Where was Nutmeg?

Why couldn't she feel the child's spirit? What wasn't she remembering? A Ghost . . . with no feeling of spirit, no emotional overflow . . . blank, like a slate, empty like a mannequin . . . a shell . . . a decoy. Decoy. A decoy was a lure. A lure was . . . *Bait*.

Oh. Shit.

"Son of a bitch!" Gillian went pale as she tried to think, yell orders, move and act all at once.

"Gillian?" Jenna's eyes were wide and puzzled.

"Get out of here! It's a trap!" Gillian snapped, spinning Jenna around and into Pavel, who kept his feet only by virtue of Lycanthrope reflexes.

"Helmut, get them out of here, *now*! That little girl Ghost is nothing more than bait, and we are the fish!"

He didn't ask how she knew. Gillian's horrified look, and the fact that she was leaning over the upper railing shouting at the others, gave him a clue that this was not a good time for a chat.

"Everyone, please proceed quickly down the stairs and back to the street, do not panic . . ." Helmut was saying in an oh-so-rational tone.

"Get out! Get out! *Get out!*" Gill was practically screaming when no one moved at first and then didn't move fast enough to suit her.

Now she was digging for something in the big side pockets of her cargo pants while hollering at the assembled string of her charges to move it. Helmut stopped trying to insert sanity into the situation, took Jenna's arm and guided her past him, beyond Pavel's position. Gamely, he moved up to stand with Gillian, who glared at him as she dug a tissue, a vial of willow oil, a cigarette and a lighter out of her pants.

"Goddammit, *get out of here now!*" she bellowed in her best command voice.

There was an edge of panic in her voice that sent the graduate students scurrying back down the stairs and toward the door. The Pseudo-Spiritualists weren't cooperating. One or two were backing down the stairs, tripping over Brant and Claire as they held on to the railing to avoid being mowed down by Helmut's class. The rest of them were looking among themselves for the missing Richard and Nutmeg, and muttering louder and louder.

Gillian couldn't yell at them for that. Hell, she'd just screamed loud enough to wake the dead in several blocks. She lit the cigarette, shook willow oil onto the wadded Kleenex, lit that, drew in a lungful of smoke, then flicked the burning tissue into the hallway behind Helmut as she blew the tobacco smoke to mingle with the oil's scent while murmuring a flimsy prayer of protection.

"Bad idea, Helmut, bad!" Opening her arms and her empathy, she stepped past him to the edge of the hallway.

"Piccola, *are you all right?*" Aleksei's baritone voice rumbled through her psyche. He sounded worried with an edge of anger when she didn't answer immediately. "*What have you gotten yourself into,* cara mia?"

"*Not now, Aleksei. Busy.*" She cut him off, slamming her shields down on what was about to be his further protests.

On cue, there was a bloodcurdling shriek from the floor below, followed by a scream of such raw agony that everyone below the first landing bolted for the door. So much for the protection. All she'd done was aggravate it.

"Where are Richard and Nutmeg?" one of the Spiritualists wailed.

"Down that hallway," Pavel informed them, keeping Jenna behind him, just in case, much to her annoyance.

"Move it, Furboy." She tried to push past him, but he was a lot taller and a lot bulkier than she was.

"Stay back," he growled at her, his voice going to an inhuman gravelly range that bespoke imminent shifting.

"*Gill!*" Jenna roared up at her friend as she kicked Pavel in the back of the knee.

"No, Jenna! Get out," Gill ordered her.

"Bite me," her friend spat back, nimbly leaping over the Werewolf, who had crumpled on one side after her reprehensible attack on his leg.

Pavel's arm shot out and clipped her leg as she jumped over him, flipping her forward. He caught her before she planted her face on the ancient, dusty carpet runner.

"Gillian said, 'Get out,'" he told her, pressing her down with his bulk as more screams could be heard.

Abruptly the front door slammed shut hard enough to crack it down the middle. Human muscles weren't enough to open it and only about a third of them had made it outside. Panicked, the remainder of the group began banging on the door and screaming.

"No," Gillian whispered, concentrating above the din two floors down.

Helmut took her hand gently, trying to lend her his own power and shields. He felt her answering squeeze. Whether or not he could help her, she was glad he was there. Someone took his hand on the other side: Jenna. He knew without looking. Pavel took her hand, then someone took Pavel's. They were forming a circle but it needed to be closed. That meant moving farther into the hallway past where Gill was and no one was terribly keen on that idea. All shrieking, screaming, pounding and praying unexpectedly stopped as though an invisible switch had been thrown.

"Squirrel shit," Gill muttered to no one in particular, her eyes darting around, trying to visually pinpoint the source of her fear.

They all felt it then. The very air became heavy, dark and putrid, almost like liquid that has filled a grave for too long. No one needed to be gifted to know there was something nasty on the stairwell with them. Everyone looked and immediately wished they hadn't. The screams would have started again except everyone was simply too terrified to do anything but stare wide-eyed and dry mouthed at the amorphous horror coalescing over their heads.

It was a cloud yet it wasn't. A swelling, swirling morass combining with the very air around them. Ectoplasmic tendrils snaked out, ruffling hair, touching faces, while the main segment of it boiled darkness and nothingness together in an otherworldly broth. The pitch matte black of the Abyss warred with vacuous dead-fish-belly gray as it roiled and bucked.

Here and there the hint of a face, an arm, a torso—all rotting, all putrefying, not reaching but pushing. Pushing as if held within a barrier inside the thing that was, at the moment, haunting everyone in the house.

Terror. Ghost fear went from a trickle to a T3 pipe and dumped over all of them with a revolting, dizzying gloop. Eau de Corpse was next. The odor of decomposing, diseased Human flesh rolled through the already thick air.

"Where the hell did that come from?" Helmut gasped, instinctively crouching lower, away from the thing.

Alarm bells were clanging in Gillian's mind. This was *not* normal Ghost activity, if any Ghost activity could be considered normal. Experimentally, she put her hands out flat, breaking the chain with the others as she fought to keep her empathy open, shove down her fear and ignore the rest of them, who were starting to shriek and gag.

Where is it? She had an idea about what was happening but needed to tap into the energy fields of the Earth itself. Not easy with the emotional barrage of fifty or so panicked and screaming people clamoring at her shielding. Gillian's thoughts were compartmentalizing, keeping the part of her that she needed right now available, putting other parts on automatic and closing off external stimuli in others.

The interference from the mass's power was torquing her sensitivity into a realm she'd never felt before. It was as if thousands of souls were trapped in anguish rather than agony, but it was disturbing and painful. She felt vaguely nauseous but kept up her searching.

This was a plague pit, bodies were dumped in here. Some might have been alive. Fear, death, blood . . . like a massive sacrifice . . . They might have prayed . . . cursed . . . Her mind was working frantically, trying to put the pieces together so that what she instinctively felt would make sense to her consciousness.

A sudden surge of elemental energy arched against her splayed palms, staggering her as she fought to track it. The power angled both up and down away from her, into the forbidden upper room, down again through the lower hallway. It originated from the ground beneath the house, front and behind . . . to the sides too . . . The power was three-dimensional, up, down, sideways, like a cross-sectioned corridor . . .

Uh. Oh. Cold horror spiked down her spine.

"Goddammit, I hate being right all the time," she groused, reflexively wiping her hands on her pants and turning back to Helmut.

"What?" Helmut grabbed her hand again, pulling her back beside him as she grasped for the person nearest her on the other side. It happened to be Claire.

"How did you get up here?" Gillian ignored him and stared at the slender policewoman whose icy hand found her own. Brant was next to her, taking her hand and one of the Spiritualists', staring open mouthed up at the malevolent cloud.

"We thought you might need us," Claire whispered, her eyes wide with horror.

"Jesus," Brant breathed.

"Jesus saves; the rest of the party takes half damage," Gill said distractedly, looking back up into the dark cloud.

Brant glared at her. She overlooked him and spoke to Helmut. "I know what it is but you're not going to like it."

"For Crissakes, what?!" Helmut barked at her. This was out of his league and out of her league, he was sure of that. Whatever she was about to tell him, he already knew he wasn't going to like it.

"This house is directly over the exact conjunction of two ley lines." There was no way to tell him gently.

"Bloody hell, like the Michael and Mary lines in Glastonbury."

Since Helmut rarely swore, Gillian looked at him sharply, then continued, "Exactly. Only there, it's a dimensional energy Doorway on the top of a hill. When whoever it was dug *this* plague pit, they inadvertently dug in exactly the right place. With the amount of blood, the sheer number of deaths, the dying, the fear, probably a multitude of prayers and curses being flung around—"

"Gott im Himmel!" Helmut reverted to German, then caught himself. "It was like a huge ongoing sacrifice! They opened a Gate!"

"Yup." Gillian nodded. "Sucks to be us right now."

CHAPTER

7

"A Gate? To what?" Brant wanted to know. He leaned in front of Claire trying to look into Gill's eyes.

"Beats me," she admitted, "but I bet it's not anywhere you'd want to spend your vacation."

"Gate? Did you say this house is over an open Gate?" A male Spiritualist was halfway onto the landing and tugging at Helmut's jacket.

"I believe so," Gillian informed him.

"Oh shit, we've got to get out of here," he squeaked.

"Hold it." Gill's voice crackled with command. "What's your name?"

"Hemlock."

"Hemlock? What is it with your group and herbology names?" She frowned at him, then continued, "Okay, Hemlock, let me share some information with you before the fog eats your friends. If you run in panic, you will only antagonize it. Look at it."

She pointed upward, releasing Claire's hand. He looked

and turned an odd shade of green. The cloud was still roiling and shifting but much more leisurely.

"See how it's slowed down because everyone's staring at it and not running around shrieking like cracked-out field mice? It's waiting."

"Waiting?" Hemlock's squeak appeared to be a permanent vocal inflection.

"Waiting for us to cut and run. It feeds on fear, Hemlock. Tell your people not to move or provoke it. We need a Circle. I need your best, most sensitive, most gifted people up here on this landing *right now*."

Hemlock turned and whispered loudly to the string of terrified people to do as he asked. Several of them started up the stairs, eyes glued to the amorphous mass. It was a tight fit but they had fourteen, counting Gill, Helmut, Claire and Brant. Jenna and Pavel were trying to push past everyone and join them.

"No, stay there," Gill snapped.

Jenna froze and Pavel nearly ran into her. "Gill?" Jenna asked.

"Pavel is overly sensitive about Ghosts and spirits. Just stay there. If we fuck this up, there won't be anything left to save anyway. Stay there. Get out when you know it's time to get out."

"How will we know?" Pavel asked. He was rather glad they didn't have to go up closer to the thing but felt embarrassed that he was on the skittish side around Ghosts, especially after the experience with Dante.

"You'll know," Gill reaffirmed.

"Fuck, I knew you'd say that," Jenna grumbled, leaning back against Pavel's warmth reflexively.

Hands clasped together both on the stairs and in their

Circle. Some were sweaty, some icy cold, more than a few trembled. Gillian waited, until almost everyone's hands were joined, then she took Claire's hand, then Helmut's. She could feel the nearly audible slam as the Circle closed like a spiritual vault.

"Follow my lead," she whispered to all of them. "Reach out with your feelings toward me. Let me bring us together."

"I will assist you as well as I am able, piccola." Aleksei's deep-timbered voice caressed the inside of her head.

Shit, she'd forgotten he was even there. Focusing on everything else that was happening had relaxed her shielding against the Vampire. It wasn't a question of keeping him out, it was her attempt at preventing his worry and anger. Since he was offering, he obviously was aware of their predicament. If he was becoming as powerful as he believed, he just might be able to help them. Right now, she was up for any allies they could get.

Wordlessly, she gave her consent for Aleksei's assistance and immediately felt the Vampire's strength added to hers. He didn't take control, earning her immediate gratitude and respect, but waited for her to use what he could offer her. She swirled his power with her own and Helmut's. The Spiritualists seemed to be strong enough, but she'd rather gamble with their lives on known variables first, such as herself, Aleksei and Helmut.

Rather than waste energy on direct protection by shielding every person in the house, she reached out and gathered the Circle to her, making herself into a conduit for their combined energies. A bright beam of power flashed upward from the center of the Circle, encompassing the entity from the bottom, up and around its fluctuating mass. The cloud boiled. Darker colors making their way to the surface, more body parts, faces, streaks of substances showing clearer.

"Hold on." Her voice was barely audible but they all heard her through the links.

The thing wasn't verbal. It couldn't speak directly but the entire house and probably half the block felt the adamant assertion of *"No"* as the Circle focused and pressed it away from the living beings in the room. The whole house vibrated to its foundations as the cloud shook in wrath. Negative energy metamorphosed as ghostly fear washed over everything in the foyer, stronger and worse than before.

Everyone quailed and shrank back instinctively. No one wanted it to touch them as the form expanded, filling the upper half of the space with its sickly gray-black-rust-bodies-parts-faces-slimy-chunky, pulsating accumulation spread out toward the huddled group. The air was thick, pungent with the smells of death, disease, decay. Gillian was shaking in her combat boots right along with them, wondering how in hell they were going to get out of this alive. It fed on fear and had an out-and-out smorgasbord of dread at its disposal, giving it incredible levels of preeminence over all of them.

Her focal point was the hub of the cloud, dead center. She kept up the light, pushing the thing away from them, her anger building by the moment. Dammit, she hated being afraid of anything. The stinky cloud and the stinky situation were pissing her off.

She could feel it, creeping over them and into them like a miasma. A veritable orchestra of feeling was pulsing through her. The victims of the plague, the victims of the house and the amorphous creature. It was from the Gate, she was sure of it. It was nasty, it wasn't really intelligent, just determined. Determined to have the psychic equivalent of a dinner buffet.

Later, she wouldn't remember what she'd done, what specific article actually motivated her retaliation—whether it was the screams of the long unmourned plague victims, the stark terror of those in the house with her, or the memory of the empty image of the dead little girl decoy that torqued Gillian's anger into overdrive. Maybe it was just that the fucking thing was behaving like a bully, throwing its considerable psychic weight around and scaring the little people to death.

Bullying was a huge trigger for Gillian, especially when people she cared about were on the receiving end. Right now, Helmut, Jenna, Pavel, Claire and, all right, Brant too, were in mortal danger and mortal terror. Absolute rage washed through her. It was an emotional state she hadn't been in for years, never allowing herself the indulgence of freeing her temper completely. To do so was simply too irresponsible and dangerous for anyone around, particularly herself. Giving in to unadulterated rage was not the hallmark of a good soldier or a good Human being.

Being an empath, Gillian was all too aware of the effect of volatile emotions on others and tended to shield automatically. Most of who Gillian was and what Gillian felt was locked securely away for the benefit of herself and others.

Not this time. This one time, she gave in to her fury and let it swell, feeding off the creature's hatred and malevolence, knitting the fear and despair of the thing's victims, the horror of the Spiritualists and the terror of her friends into the mix.

"Let me help, piccola,*"* Aleksei intoned in her mind. *"It is too much power, you cannot control—"*

Deliberately, Gillian shoved him back, broke their fragile connection. She didn't want him to feel her like this, know her this way. It was too intimate, too intrusive; she was too ashamed of her lack of control and the level of overwhelming wrath that was burning like an aeon flux in her soul. Helmut was there instead, using his talent to support the living while Gillian warred with death. He shielded the others in the Circle from what she was about to do, helpless to do anything but watch, unable to extend that safeguard over himself, the rest of the people in the house or her.

Gill's rage spiked. Collecting all the available power to her when her fury reached its zenith, she drove the lot of it up into the entity in a tidal wave of pure force. Her aim was to hit it, push it back into the Gate and hold it there—hopefully damaging it enough in the process so it would stay put. There was no way at that particular moment for her to individually close an interdimensional Gate that had been open for the past six hundred years. Their only hope was hurting the thing badly enough so it would think twice before venturing out of whatever abyss had spawned it in the first place.

Too late she realized the shielding she'd held the thing back with was in the way. A slight miscalculation that came from being blinded by her own anger. The power surge she had gathered hit the existing shielding with alarming force and punched through. Like a metaphysical, ectoplasmic javelin, it tore apart the almost equally strong shield, widened at the apex like a mushroom; then swamped the engorged cloud, effectively causing the original shield to implode in on itself. The supernatural backblast from Gillian's mistake literally flattened every telekinetically gifted Human and non-Human in the house and on the grounds outside but the cloud was suddenly, amazingly gone.

Unfortunately for Gillian and everyone else on the landing, the rickety structure was ill equipped to handle the weight of all the beings slamming onto it, backed by the force from the power of the combined minds in the room. Ancient wood and mortar crumbled, planking snapped and everything fell twenty feet to the main floor. Fortunately, everyone on the landing was unconscious by the time they hit the ground. Boneless inertia was what saved all of them from being crushed to death by the fall.

Dust motes fluttered and settled around the fallen. At the Gate's mouth, a quivering formless mass slid into the pit from which it originated. Within its shattered collection of lumps, shining streaks of light rose as the souls that had been inadvertently freed took flight to whatever final destiny they had incurred with joyous pipings of noise, which were lost in the quiet of the wounded house. All became eerily silent.

In Romania, Aleksei's heart nearly stopped as Gillian broke their fragile connection. His mind rang with Gillian's cry of rage and the unexpected, immediate silence that followed. Frantically he cast his thoughts for her. The tiny amount of her blood taken during their kiss had afforded him some peace of mind with that tremulous bond, but Gillian had destroyed it in her fury. He couldn't hear her anymore. Worse, he couldn't feel her. Aleksei's own furious bellow brought Tanis immediately to his brother's side.

"She . . . I cannot feel her, Tanis. I cannot determine if she lives." Aleksei slumped against the thick stone wall of the Great Hall for support. The shining silvery eyes lifted to Tanis's face, turning flat as pewter with fear for Gillian's safety.

Tanis could do nothing except extend a comforting arm around his brother's shoulders. "We will find her, do not worry," he said gently, offering assurance when he had none himself. "Day is upon us. At the moment, Aleksei, we can do nothing until dusk. Rest, gather your strength. She is alive, you must believe that."

Nodding numbly, Aleksei allowed his brother to steer him down to the crypt below the castle. "You are correct, of course. Gillian would be very difficult to kill."

"She has Pavel and her other friends with her," Tanis said. "I am certain that between the Wolf, the professor and the lovely firebug, your little Captain is well looked after."

Aleksei noticed Tanis's designation of the word "your," in relation to Gillian and the notation of "lovely" in reference to Jenna. It was a small gesture but important. Tanis wanted him to know that his interests had shifted.

"I do not care much for certain aspects of her profession," Aleksei admitted.

"I understand," Tanis agreed, "but it appears that we must make a few concessions if we intend to date . . . Is that the correct term? What I mean is, these women are far stronger, more capable . . ."

"I know what you mean," Aleksei said wryly. "They are capable, strong, exceptional, but I cannot ignore my basic instinct to protect and cherish them."

"Somehow I do not think they will mind the 'cherish' part, it is being overprotected that will raise their ire more than a little."

Aleksei sighed, a very un-Vampire-like sound. "I know, I will try not to be a domineering ass."

"You will have to do more than try, as I have done." Tanis chuckled as he opened the secret chamber behind the marble sarcophagi containing the bodies of their parents, and the empty ones for himself and Aleksei.

The brothers ducked to enter the chamber. It was essentially a duplicate tomb dug deeply into the rich Romanian soil, which had been walled and carved with limestone imported from Italy by Aleksei's father. Crypts, the real crypts for himself and Tanis, were hidden here, away from any potential disturbance by the curious, stupid or incalculably brave. Tanis waved a hand and opened the sepulchers for them both.

"Rest well, brother, we will need our strength," Tanis said softly as he settled for the day.

"Thank you, Tanis," came Aleksei's voice, almost as an afterthought.

"Think nothing of it."

Tanis's last thought before he let the torpor take him was a silently muttered curse for Gillian. Wherever she was, she'd better damn well have a valid reason for being unable to contact Aleksei or he'd never forgive her for causing his elegant noble brother this level of emotional pain.

"Mother fucking son of a bitch," Gillian groaned, realizing that everything except her left pinky toe hurt like hell.

Where was she anyway? Tentatively, she opened her eyes a slit. Stark, sterile, white room with low-level lighting . . . Okay, it looked like a hospital. Her nose wrinkled. It smelled like a hospital: antiseptic, overly cleansed. There was a faint scent of blood in the air. Was she injured? She turned her head a little and immediately wished she hadn't. The room spun briefly before her vision righted itself again. Yup, the bed had slats up on either side so she wouldn't roll out.

Ha! she thought, wincing at even the smallest movement. *Like that's going to happen.* Hell, she couldn't even move without about a zillion nerve endings firing and telling her that was a bad idea.

"I see you are awake," a masculine voice said from her left side. "Tell me what you remember, if you can."

Gillian tried to turn her head toward the voice but a bolt of pain shot up through her neck. "The stairs, the whole landing gave way . . . We fell."

"Good. Very good," said the voice, "You are extremely lucky to be alive, young lady."

"I'm not so sure," Gillian grumbled, thinking the voice was vaguely familiar. "Do you have any morphine on you, Doctor?"

"I will send a nurse with some additional medication for you, but we want to go easy with too many strong narcotics for the time being. You are muddled from the anesthesia at the moment and, of course, have been given pain medication. The morphine will have to wait, for now." The voice hadn't moved position but Gillian felt him lift her arm gently, feeling her pulse.

"So I have a head injury?" she asked, closing her eyes against even the soft lighting in the room and swearing silently. If she had a concussion, they'd withhold narcotics from her until they were sure she wouldn't succumb to a coma.

"It looks that way," the doctor said. "Of course, we also do not want to pollute your blood."

Gillian's eyes flew open suddenly. The way he worded that gave her a very uneasy, creepy feeling between her shoulder blades. "Where's Helmut, Jenna and Pavel? And those two Inspectors . . . Brandt and Claire . . . ?"

She managed to turn her head and saw the doctor, in full

surgical scrubs, gloves, plus the mask, holding her wrist delicately, checking his watch as he counted her heartbeats. His eyes flicked up to meet her own and she frowned. Odd-colored eyes: not quite brown, not quite . . . rust. Rusty brown . . . cinnamon colored . . . Where had she seen eyes like that?

That voice too . . . familiar, but . . . Something was wrong. The voice was beautiful but there was something else there, something thick, heavy, palpable in the tones and inflection. A sense of dread began to form at the edges of her mind as her empathy clicked on like a switch.

Dammit, she didn't want to think just now. Her head hurt but she felt incredibly muddled. It was almost like the aftereffects of the Pixie venom she'd experienced the last time she was in London. Why would she feel so disconnected after a fall? Pain, yes, but not the vaguely disorienting feeling.

"Your friends are recovering as well," he assured her, lowering her arm back to the bed. "I am certain they will be along shortly to check you out and take you home."

"What exactly happened to me?" Gillian asked, still trying to piece together what was bothering her about this doctor.

"You wound up with a segment of the staircase impaled horizontally through the front of your abdomen. Fortunately, it was largely a superficial wound and I was able to save your female organs." The doctor's eyes seemed to glow for a moment.

"Female organs?" Gillian shook off her languor. *Who used euphemisms like that anymore?*

"I had surgery?"

Tentatively she felt her stomach, then lower. There were two tender places, one on her right hip and one about four inches above her left hip. The shard must have cut through mostly the top layers of skin and muscle, not penetrating anything very deeply. In between the two areas, it was tender but not as much as at the entry and exit points.

"Yes, your wound was not very deep. At first we feared that it had gone through your ovary, but once we took an X-ray, we were able to determine that everything was as it should be. You are quite intact, with the exception of your virginity, of course." Now the eyes above the mask hardened, reddened. The voice was taking on a distasteful quality. He chuckled maliciously, which annoyed the hell out of her and felt like broken glass inside her skull. Vampire. Goddammit. Now what?

"What the fuck business is that of yours?" Gill snapped, her mind suddenly unpleasantly clearing. "What kind of doctor are you anyway and what the hell was that remark about 'polluting my blood'?"

"I am a gynecologist, Dr. Key"—he raised his hand to the back of his head and the ties on the surgical mask— "and you should know by now that Vampires do not like tainted blood."

The mask slipped down and Gillian went rigid with terror. It was a face she'd seen only once before, and then only briefly, through the fog of Pixie venom aftereffects. Exact recollection of his features was impossible owing to his ability to shift and blur his appearance like a chameleon. But those eyes . . . she remembered those rusty cinnamon-colored eyes now as they were blended with the face. It all clicked into harsh, horrible reality.

Jack the Ripper, in all his twisted glory, was at her bedside. He had performed surgery on her, only hours before. Jack the Ripper. Scalpel. Operation. And herself under anesthesia. Gillian suddenly felt nauseous.

•

"I see you remember me, Dr. Key." Jack's face melted into the dark beauty of a Vampire as he smiled at her. Too bad it was absolutely chilling; it spoiled the beguiling effect.

"Get the hell away from me!" Gill hissed. She was scared to death, drugged, weaponless, and less than two feet away from one of the most demented serial killers ever known.

The Vampire grinned down at her, letting her see the fangs slowly elongating, enjoying her reaction as she shrank back as far as possible against the opposite side of the bed. A flick of his left wrist brought a gleaming scalpel to his hand.

Jack killed by exsanguination, but not through a bite. He killed and then did bad things to the body afterward. Showing her the knife was just part of his style. Intimidation. Fear. Jack fed off it as surely as he fed off blood, only this time he wasn't stalking his prey; his prey was lying helplessly in front of him in a hospital bed.

When the thought of being helpless crossed her mind, Gill grabbed it like a tiger on a horsemeat roast. Her reflexes were way off owing to the drugs in her system, but she managed to clamp her fingers on Jack's wrist before he could pull away. As she fought to hold his hand away from her, their eyes met. Jack was smiling, the otherworldly lure characteristic of the Reborn gracing his face. Only his eyes remained chillingly cold, detached. There was no seduction in them, no sensual need to be close for feeding or sex. There was only death. Specifically hers.

She had no hope to match him in strength, no intention of screaming or crying out. Giving the bastard the satisfaction of her terror wasn't something she was willing to compromise. Jack would know by her scent, elevated heartbeat and blood pressure that she was scared to death. Vocalizing that fear for his jollies wasn't on the agenda.

Almost lazily he twisted his wrist free of her grip. "Not bad for a Human, Dr. Key, not bad at all."

Gill wanted to knock the smirk off his face along with his fangs. "Gee, thanks. Nice to know I can impress a creature like you."

He flinched almost imperceptibly at the word "creature." "You have no idea what variety of 'creature' I am, Dr. Key."

"Au contraire," Gillian rasped, her voice husky as her throat was still dry from the anesthesia tubing, "I know exactly what kind you are."

"I can sense your fear, Dr. Key . . . smell it . . . why not scream?" His smile was sepulchral. "I am almost certain someone will hear you. Whether they will hear you in time is quite another matter."

Her blood seemed to freeze in her veins. "Because I won't give you the satisfaction, you sick bastard. You have gotten enough from me already."

Jack's eyes went from cinnamon to blood colored. "Not nearly enough, my little soldier. But that will change soon enough when we dance our final dance."

"Doctor?" A male nurse poked his head in, just as Gillian was about to opt for falling out of the bed and somehow scrambling away from her tormentor.

"It's time to change her dressing, unless, of course, you would rather do it yourself," the nurse continued, completely oblivious to the drama in the room.

"No, you go right ahead. Dr. Key and I have completed our discussion for now." Jack smiled and patted her shoulder, squeezing it with just enough pressure that Gill knew she'd have a bruise later. He jerked his head in a brief nod, flashed his fangs again then turned and left, giving the nurse a light pat on the back as he passed.

"You were lucky, miss," the nurse informed her. "If that shard had penetrated even a bit more, it might have severed your abdominal artery or one of your ovaries."

As he drew back the covers and opened her standard hospital gown, Gillian squeezed her eyes shut tightly. "Yeah, lucky," she whispered, more to herself than to the nurse, who was gently changing her bandages.

Lucky, hell. Right now she wanted to dive straight into a mound of paperwork at the IPPA headquarters and never come out again. That alone pissed her off. She hated desk jobs, paperwork, politics and all the highfalutin bullshit that went with them. She was a field operative, a trained commander and psychologist. Why this one Vampire rattled her cage like no other being ever had bothered her immensely.

Thinking back on the romance novels her college roommate had mooned over, Gillian had a brief, disturbing thought that if she weren't quite so much the badass, and a bit more of a femme fatale, she could run and tattletale to Aleksei and Tanis about Jack. Then it would be their problem and not hers. Regrettably, it would also probably get the two of them killed.

Newfound powers or not, noble, ethical, trusting Aleksei was, in her opinion, nowhere near Jack's caliber in clout, deception or abilities, and the serial killer won hands down in the sick twist category. Tanis was just like his brother: honest and straightforward. They'd be dead before they ever uncovered what Jack was really up to. No, she couldn't draw the two of them into this immediate nightmare.

Shit. Aleksei. She had to call him, or at least get word to

him that she was all right since she'd demolished the connection they'd shared. No doubt he was frantic with worry about her and she definitely didn't need him showing up here, in London, and accidentally running into Saucy Jack. That was a disaster waiting to happen. If Jack had an inkling that she was becoming involved with the Romanian Count, most assuredly he would make both of their lives hell. As Dracula's First Lieutenant, The Ripper would have a host of Vampires and various Paramortals at his command. They'd use her as the bargaining chip to bring Aleksei to heel. That sucked.

She had to get out of there, and fast. Gill waited until the nurse finished, refusing the morphine patch he offered to let her head clear. After a brief argument, she agreed to a Demerol injection, just to take the edge off the discomfort. As the door closed behind the nurse, she tried sitting up. Her head spun, whether from the Demerol or from her injured state, she couldn't tell, so she lay flat and used the electronic control for the bed to raise her torso into a sitting position. Any movement she made seemed to involve her abdominal muscles, which screamed and protested her attempts at premature activity.

She was nearly crying in frustration when the door cracked open and a cultured voice with a light Austrian accent inquired, "Gillian? *Schatzi*, are you awake?"

"Helmut!" Gill had never been so glad to see anyone.

As her former teacher and mentor crossed the room to her, she took a quick inventory of his injuries. He had a bandage on his forehead and the skin around the edges of the dressing were bluish purple; left arm in a sling and pulled tightly against his chest. He still managed to give her a clumsy hug.

"God, I thought I had lost you," Helmut said unsteadily,

then gave her a gentle shake from his arm around her shoulders.

"If you weren't so ill, *liebling*, I would take a stick to your bum for frightening us all to death."

Gillian blushed under her mentor's gentle reprimand. "I'm really sorry, Helmut, I lost my temper. I haven't done that in years, but that thing just pissed me off. It was like a giant bully cloud and I got mad."

"Yeah, well, next time, try not blowing the shit out of the structure the rest of us are standing on," Jenna said dryly from the doorway.

She leaned against the door frame, favoring a splinted foot and crutches, frowning. Then her face split into its familiar generous grin and her mahogany eyes sparkled. Pavel stepped around her, looking slightly shamefaced.

"Cujo here thinks he did a bad thing by not catching you and me as we fell. I told him even superawesome magical Werewolf foo is no match for Gravity. It's the Law."

Everyone moaned at her quip. At least they were all right too, and Gill allowed herself a moment's respite from her guilt then she had to ask.

"What about the others? Did everyone get out all right?" There was trepidation in her voice. She wanted to know but yet she didn't.

Helmut predictably glanced away for a second then met her eyes squarely. "We lost two, Nutmeg and Richard. It was . . . Well, it wasn't pretty. The entity essentially sucked them dry like an amorphous spider."

"Ugh," Gillian grimaced. "I'm sorry, Helmut. I know you relied on me to keep everyone safe and I fucked up."

"No, you didn't," Helmut said sharply. "We went in there with too little information. I should have researched everything much more thoroughly. I was hoping to impress my class and the observers with my former protégée. This is my fault. I should have handled it differently. It will plague me for the rest of my life."

"Professor, did you not ask Gillian to help because she was the best at what the two of you do?" Pavel asked quietly.

"Yes, but I should have planned better," Helmut responded.

"I understand that, but if you had not brought her in, and the rest of you had tried to handle this on your own, would it not have been much worse for everyone? If the entity had behaved the way it did with us . . . Would not more have died?"

Helmut met the Lycanthrope's eyes and saw that Pavel wasn't trying to rescue his feelings; he was legitimately trying to be logical about the situation.

"I supposed you're correct, Pavel. But it doesn't make me feel any better that anyone lost their life."

"No one thought it would, Professor, I simply wanted to point that out to you." The blond Wolf turned away to stand by Jenna.

"And nobody is going to have a massive pity party over this. Those people knew what the risks were before they went in there," Jenna said flatly. "They knew there were risks and had signed waivers against death or bodily harm, so you two are not going to go into mournful mode and that's final or I will kick your asses, respectfully, of course, Captain."

Jenna glared at all of them. She was a soldier, like Gillian. She was well aware of risks, potential problems and consequences in everyday decisions, as well as unique and dangerous situations. Bemoaning what had happened was not like Gillian; Helmut she didn't know, but she knew her Captain. There was something else going on here because the short blonde was teetering dangerously on vulnerable. A mopey Captain was an ineffective leader, and they couldn't afford that.

"So, tell me what's really bothering you." She smirked at Gill, intending to draw a response. She wasn't prepared for the one she got.

"Jack was here," Gillian said out of the blue.

"What!?" Jenna nearly shrieked then quickly lowered her voice, unconsciously twitching her fingers in anticipation of grabbing a weapon.

"Right here, at my bedside. He informed me that he'd performed the surgery on me to remove the shaft of wood that went through me." Gillian's voice was just a trifle bit tighter than normal. No one else but Jenna heard it.

"We're getting out of here. Professor, go sign whatever discharge papers you need to. Pavel, go with him. I'll get Gill out of here."

"Who is—" Helmut started but Jenna cut him off.

"Now, Helmut. Go. Now. Talk later." She shoved him toward the door, where Pavel grabbed his arm and hustled him down to the nurse's station.

Jenna disappeared out the door for a few moments, then hobbled back in wearing a white lab coat with a radiology badge on it, pushing a wheelchair. Gillian didn't want to ask where the hell she'd gotten everything on the spur of the moment. Jenna was always resourceful, just like a good Marine.

Reaching into her pocket, she produced a roll of gauze and some first aid tape. Within minutes she had Gillian's entire head swathed in the white material. Unceremoniously she dropped the head of the bed flat.

"Ow!" Gillian grumbled, regretting her hasty decision about the milder painkillers.

"Shut up, I'm getting you out of here," Jenna hissed, helping her friend into the wheelchair and disconnecting Gill's IV. She piled Gillian's overnight bag, along with hers and Pavel's, onto the patient but, seeing the discomfiture it caused, helped Gillian up and stuck all the bags back into the chair, with Gillian shakily perched on top, a hospital blanket tucked around her.

A quick look out the door showed her that Helmut and Pavel were still arguing with the charge nurse at the desk. Jenna didn't waste time, wheeling Gillian out into the hall and into the nearby stairwell.

"Stairs? Are you nuts?" Gillian gasped, momentarily dizzy from trying to turn her head back to look at Jenna.

"You wanna meet Jack shut up in an elevator?"

"No."

"Then shut the fuck up and let me do this."

Jenna positioned herself behind the wheelchair, lowering Gill stair to stair, as quickly as she dared. Every bump and bounce sent searing agony through Gillian's battered body but she gritted her teeth and kept it to herself. There was no way in hell she was getting out of that hospital alive, with Jack in charge of her care. At least not through the front doors. Exiting horizontally through the morgue was not on her list of things to do so she suffered through Jenna's hastily devised escape plan.

Thankfully, they were only on the third floor so she had barely two flights of stairs to contend with. It didn't keep her from a shaky release of breath when they finally reached the bottom. Jenna checked the hallway, then shoved Gillian's wheelchair out into view.

"Where is everyone?" Gillian asked. "There's nobody in the halls." The whole place looked like a deserted *Dr. Kildare* set.

"It's three A.M., that's why. All the good little patients have taken their comatose medications and are sleeping. We, however, are lurking in corridors trying to avoid your favorite serial killer."

Without further ado, Jenna limped for it, pushing Gillian in front of her, toward the nearest exit doors. Closing her eyes, Gill just sat back and hoped that her career wasn't going to be cut dramatically short by Jenna dashing her brains out against a door frame or smashing her face into a cinder block wall.

CHAPTER

8

THEIR happiness in escaping was short-lived as Jenna barreled around the corner of the building, pushing Gillian like a chariot driver in the Coliseum except hopping on her one good leg. Inspectors McNeill and Jardin appeared in their pathway. Both bore evidence of their involvement with Fifty Berkley Square. Brant had a bandage on his forehead and across the side of his throat. Claire looked disheveled and her clothes were torn, but being a Shifter, she had no permanent injuries.

Brant moved to halt the careening wheelchair, staggering briefly as Jenna tried to keep moving through him. "Bloody hell!" the detective exclaimed. "Just where do you think you're going?"

"Jack the Ripper is a surgeon in this hospital, and you're standing here quizzing us? Real bright, Sherlock," Jenna snapped, shoving against Brant's restraining hands.

"Now get the fuck out of the way!"

"Jenna! Jenna, wait!" Helmut appeared behind Brant

and the surprised Claire, flanked by Pavel, whose blue, blue eyes were wide.

Brant wasn't a Scotland Yard detective for nothing; he assessed and made a determination based on what he was seeing. None of it added up or made sense, but he'd go with it . . . for now.

"Claire, get the car," he snapped, tossing a set of keys to the Werecheetah, then bundling up Gillian and hurrying after the slender Lycanthrope.

"Get that wheelchair collapsed and into the boot when she brings it round," he ordered the other three.

Obediently they all scurried after, stopping as Claire power-slid the car close to the side of the building then leaped out to help. In short order they had the wheelchair in the boot of the vehicle and Gillian in the backseat with Helmut, Jenna, Pavel and their bags. Brant motioned to Claire, who liquidly moved around the car to the passenger side as he glided into the driver's seat.

"Where to now?" Brant asked curtly, wanting this disorganized, irrational, unbelievable situation over and done with.

"France," Gillian muttered. "We can't risk public transportation. He's got informants and spies everywhere, even in immigration."

"Who?" Brant demanded. "Who has spies everywhere? There is no political body nor terrorist group currently operating with the ability to have that complex a network."

"Shows what you know, my Fey friend." Gillian's words were slurred from exhaustion and from the drugs she'd been on. She didn't remember that Claire had warned her not to mention the likelihood of Brant's Fey heritage. Nor did she see him turn crimson then pale.

"We are in a war," she continued, oblivious to the

detective's discomfort and her verbal diarrhea. "Jack the Ripper is just one of Dracula's lieutenants. There are spies, there are informants. That's how our friend, Tanis— you remember him? Well, that's how he wound up a prisoner here. It's not your fault. None of the local or international law enforcement agencies suspect, no matter how integrated they are with Paras. It's too insidious, too bold."

"Too stupid," Brant spat. "You expect me to believe that one of the worst serial killers in history is alive and well and working in a London hospital?"

"Forgive me for insinuating my opinion," Helmut interjected smoothly while placing his hand gently over Gillian's mouth in anticipation of a colorful outburst, "but why would these ladies make something like that up?"

That made Brant pause. What made him step on the gas and get the hell out of the parking lot was the appearance of the alleged Ripper, with a large constituent of hospital staff running behind him out of the building and canvassing the parking lot. Well, that and Jenna shrieking behind his left ear.

"That's him! That's the asshole!"

"Sit back and do be silent!" he ordered her.

"Roll down the window, I'm going to shoot the son of a bitch!" Jenna growled, trying to fumble under Gillian to get into her bag.

"No—" Brant started to yell, but Claire interrupted him.

"Please, Jenna, just sit back and let Inspector McNeill get us out of here. We will have our chance to track him down, but first we must get away."

"Why France?" Brant wanted to know.

"Not a lot of Vampires," Gillian mumbled around Helmut's hand.

"I thought there were a lot of them that were my Countrymen," Claire chimed in.

"Hollywood myth in action," Helmut informed them, "Most are Eastern European, British, East Indian, Greek, Egyptian and South American. French Vampires are no more elegant, cultured nor powerful than any of the others. They simply get better press."

Gillian started to giggle at Helmut's sarcasm and winced. Pavel, who hadn't taken his eyes or nose off her, noticed immediately.

"She is bleeding and in pain."

"Well, give her something for the bloody pain, patch up the bleeding and keep her still!" Brant was in no mood for another crisis at the moment. "We need to get out of London, find a nonobvious road to Dover, traverse the Chunnel, and locate a hideout in Calais. If she needs medical attention, I have no clue as to where we are going to locate a doctor if your alleged Vampire Army has spies stationed in major medical facilities."

Jenna and Gillian exchanged a look. They'd been in worse battlefield and covert mission conditions than this: wounded, without supplies or backup, no ammo and their adversaries hot on their heels. What was he freaking out over?

"You haven't done this before, have you?" Gill mused from the backseat. She tried, but couldn't quite keep the smirk out of her tone. Brant caught it.

"Done what? Helped former U.S. military personnel escape from a hospital? Evade and avoid fanged menaces who may or may not be a serial killer from eighteen eighty-eight? Or have a conversation with a recent surgical patient who by all accounts should still be unconscious or at least malleable due to the painkillers she ought to be taking?"

Brant paused for a breath, "No, Dr. Key, I have not done any of those things before. I don't expect that you would have training programs for any of it, have you?"

He'd meant his remarks to be snarky and cutting, but to his surprise, Gillian and Jenna applauded. Jenna, a little more enthusiastically than Gillian, who discovered that any additional bouncing hurt.

"Very good, Brant," Gill quipped. "Spoken like an honest-to-Goddess smart-ass. We'll make one out of you yet."

"Lovely," he bit off, realizing that he still wasn't winning any victories.

"Trouble ahead," Claire purred softly.

Pavel echoed her statement. "Turn off, Detective . . . Take another road. I can scent them, as can Claire. There are several waiting in ambush to attack the car."

"Hijack," Jenna said slowly to Pavel. "If you are going to hang with us, you should know the right terms."

"Why are you greeting Jack when he is not here?" Pavel looked confused.

"Why am I . . . I'm not saying 'Hi' to Jack, nimrod. I am saying 'hijack.' It's a term used to describe ambushing a vehicle," Jenna said impatiently.

"Language barrier. He is Russian, you know," Gill said helpfully.

"Shut up, you're supposed to be resting."

Brant jerked the wheel and they skidded around a corner on two tires. He punched the gas, shifted like a rally driver, and they hauled ass. All the time he was alternatively praying and swearing. How had Gillian guessed his darkest secret? An empath was what Dr. Gerhardt had said. She couldn't read minds, so it must be something inherently "different" about him. His stomach twisted.

He had suspected he was a changeling but had it confirmed by blood work several years before. Brant didn't want to be different. He wanted to be a normal policeman, with normal abilities. Everyone had hopped on the Paramortals Are Brilliant bandwagon, and he did not like attention that did not come from his duties and abilities as an Inspector. No one in the department talked about it or brought it up, knowing that he was sensitive about his looks.

Male Fey had a problem with Humans assuming they were all gay due to their incredible, almost feminine beauty. Brant was straight and a bit of a homophobe. It pissed him off to no end to have someone question his orientation. He kept his hair cut short, trying to play down his looks, but you couldn't hide those winged dark eyebrows against the platinum, shimmering hair or the starlight in his blue eyes.

Maybe he should talk to Gillian if they had a moment when they weren't being hunted. Give her a chance, let her try to help him figure himself out.

"Look out!!" Jenna yelled.

"Verdammen Sie es!" Helmut threw his arm across Jenna and Gillian as a dark shape landed on the car hood.

Brant braked and it tumbled off only to bounce back to its feet and make a quick gesture with its hands. The car engine abruptly died. The two Scotland Yard Inspectors had guns out and were moving out of the vehicle when a silky familiar voice called out.

"Gillyflower? Are you well?"

"Trocar!!" Gillian squeaked from a dry throat, "Don't shoot, guys, he's on our side, remember?"

Visibly sagging in relief, Brant nodded, holstering his

gun. "I thought you guys didn't carry," Gillian remarked, struggling to sit up more.

"This is a special circumstance, Dr. Key," Brant retorted.

"Aw, you're special!" Jenna quipped, earning an icy look from the Fey Inspector.

"He rode the little bus to Inspector school," Gill giggled. It was either laugh or cry from the pain that was seeping through her best blocking efforts.

"Do shut up, Petal, and allow me to assess your wounds." Trocar practically took the car door off its hinges in his haste to get to Gillian. The tall Dark Elf knelt and, with uncharacteristic tenderness, placed a hand on Gillian's forehead and one on her abdomen.

As incongruous as the rest of their culture, Grael Elves had as much ability to heal as to harm. All you had to do was befriend one of them and you had a friend for life. A trained healer could do amazing things and Trocar had paid attention in his studies. Wizard, assassin, healer, warrior; he was well versed in many skills after three thousand years.

Trocar had many friends over the ages and had made as many enemies. Gillian had earned his respect and loyalty long ago. The Blood Pact they shared would have kept him loyal even if he disliked her, but since he held her in high esteem, with as much affection as one of his kind could hold for a Human, he would cross any obstacle to aid her.

"Thanks, Trocar," Gillian whispered and visibly relaxed under the Elf's touch.

"My pleasure, Petal, now hush."

Gillian felt the warmth immediately. It was almost painful as he forced healing into her tired and bruised body, but she endured it. Trocar, Jenna and Kimber were three people she literally trusted with her life. The women had gone through all aspects of the military with her and remained her stalwart friends despite her being their commanding officer.

The Elf had become their friend and companion and remained so, evoking some jealousy among the Special Ops unit they worked in. It was sort of a political coup to have an Elf in your command and Gillian had two. Mirrin, the High Elf Prince, had been reliable and friendly but he had only gravitated toward Gillian and Trocar.

Trocar had surprised himself by giving both the Humans and the High Elf a chance. Friendship, real friendship, didn't come easy to his kind but he tried it and found out he got back everything he invested and more. Gillian was his friend, and he had come to help her. Aleksei had contacted Kimber Whitecloud when he didn't hear from Gillian. Kimber was still in Russia, overseeing the platoon assigned to the cleanup of the damaged area. She had known the best man for the job of finding her former Captain was an Elf and had gotten in touch with Trocar before he vanished into the Doorway in Finland.

He'd left at once, opening a Portal and stepping through to London. Gillian had been fairly easy for him to locate. Hospital privacy policies were no match for a stealthy Grael who was computer literate with his own brand of ethics. Randomly choosing, he'd visited several searching for her, then narrowed the choices down to one of three. He had literally gotten lucky when he saw the car with Gillian in it tear out of the parking lot of his latest selection. He'd run diagonally across the lot to catch up to the speeding car before it rounded another corner and got away from him.

"Did you Portal here?" Gillian asked quietly.

"Yes. Feeling better?"

"A lot, thank you."

"Do not move, Captain. My healing is warring with the Human medication in your system. You may feel disoriented or even ill."

"Portal?" Brant asked.

"Elves have the ability to straddle time, distance and dimension, Inspector," Trocar informed him. "We can travel to any 'when' or 'where' we wish but it is not done often so that we do not interfere with any natural order."

Crystalline eyes locked with Brant's starry blue ones. "You do not know much about any of the Fey, do you?"

"No," Brant blushed, embarrassed.

"Gillian can help you and I will teach you, if you wish," Trocar offered.

"Maybe another time," Brant acknowledged.

"Can we go now?" Jenna asked.

Everyone piled into the car again. It was a tight fit so Trocar sat in front with Brant, with Claire on his lap. He released the spell holding the car, Brant fired the engine and they took off.

They made good time getting out of London and headed for Dover. The Chunnel was probably the least obvious way for them to get into France. In Calais, Gillian was thinking, they could ditch the car, rent a new one and start the long drive to Romania and hopefully safety.

After Trocar's healing, Gillian was able to squirm around and get some clothing on. Anything was better than that stupid hospital gown. Jenna had thoughtfully packed a soft velour jog suit and helped Gill wriggle into it in the cramped backseat of the car. Unfortunately it was in Jenna's size and Gillian was swimming in it. At least it was loose and comfortable over her abdomen.

Ahead of them loomed the Chunnel, the underwater passageway through the English Channel, which separated

England from the mainland and France. Brant was wary, the Lycanthropes were edgy, Jenna and Helmut were sweaty and tense. Gillian was coming out of her drug-induced agreeable state and was beginning to get on everyone's nerves. Trocar sighed. It was going to be quite a journey.

"We should probably ditch the car," Gillian stated abruptly.

"Whatever for, Gillian?" Helmut asked.

"Ambush," she said, as if that explained everything.

"Do you not think, Captain, that if they are indeed waiting in ambush in a long underwater tunnel, it would be wiser to remain in a vehicle which is actually a metal shell, rather than trying to amble through, given your current condition?"

Trocar's dry tone let her know that she was not command ready yet and it irked her. "Thank you, Lieutenant, I was actually gravitating toward you, Claire, Brant and Pavel being able to hear them without the car's noise as a distraction . . . Oh wait."

"I am just saying," Trocar shot back, hiding a grin as Gill realized there were going to be plenty of other cars, motor coaches, trucks and buses inside.

Gillian reddened. She really needed to shut up until she was better. She shifted to a better position on Pavel's lap and allowed Helmet to cradle her upper body and head. Insulting Jack the Ripper more than once and living to talk about it was nothing short of a miracle. There was every chance that he would come after her or be assigned to her "care" once again if they were captured. The thought made her stomach hurt.

"Why didn't I become an archaeologist?" she muttered to herself.

"Because, my dear, the Paramortal world would have

missed your brilliant mind and devotion to your profession." Helmut grinned down at her.

"Gill, go to sleep," Jenna said under her breath.

"Fine."

"Gillyflower . . ."

"I said fine."

"Gott im Himmel," Helmut whispered, wondering why he'd ever had the idea about Fifty Berkeley Square in the first place.

Jenna giggled. Everyone jumped at the unexpected noise. "I was just thinking we're all like a bunch of circus clowns piled into one of those miniature cars."

"I hate clowns," Gillian announced then closed her eyes.

"We are making a stop in Rouen," Brant notified them. "We need petrol."

"A bio break would be great," Jenna said. "I could use a coffee and something to read."

It was early so the streets of Rouen were rather deserted as the overloaded car chugged to an exhausted halt at a petrol station near a sidewalk café. Everyone bailed out except Gillian, who took the opportunity to stretch out across the empty backseat. Dawn was making a tentative appearance in the Eastern sky as her eyes closed and she drifted off.

Trocar took a moment to phone Aleksei in Romania and let him know that Gillian was safely with himself and armed Inspectors. The Vampire was happy to learn that she was safe but was furious as his suspicions were confirmed that something had happened to the petite blonde. It took the Elf several minutes and careful diplomatic phrasing to convince Aleksei that Gillian was safer where she was at the moment, rather than being transported back to Romania immediately.

Fumbling with change in her pocket and balancing on

her crutches, Jenna's mind was not on her surroundings for once. There was an English copy of *Paramortal Twilight* magazine on a newsstand in a tiny sidewalk café with Gillian's and Helmut's pictures on the cover and she wanted to buy it for her friend. No one was there yet but there was an open courtesy payment box attached to the wall. She didn't see the Vampire as it materialized into solid form behind her but she felt the iron grip as it closed its hand over her windpipe.

Claire, Helmut and Brant were all making use of the facilities, Pavel was scouting outside, Trocar was on the phone across the street from her and Gill was crashed in the backseat. She was on her own. Jenna was used to Vampires so one thing she was damn sure of, if one slipped up behind you and snatched at your breathing apparatus, it was a good bet it was up to no good.

Struggling was a bad idea. It would only take the slightest increase in pressure from the Vamp's fingers to crush her windpipe beyond immediate repair. She shuddered as fingers ran through her hair then tightened to deftly tip her head back. Hot breath on her throat was her only warning before fangs sank deep and she was jerked back against a hard male form. Mercifully the strange blood drinker clouded her mind at that moment, erasing her memories of the attack. He took but a little of her blood, laved a tongue over the pinprick wounds, closing them and healing them instantly before melting into mist and vanishing.

Jenna shook her head to clear it, bracing a hand on the wall next to her. She stared at the magazine in her hand then at the payment box. Damn, she must be really tired. She felt dead on her feet. Since she couldn't recall if she'd paid for the magazine or not and Trocar was calling to her, she tossed it on a nearby table and scooted for the car as fast as she could on her crutches.

No one from the car saw a tall, darkly cloaked figure emerge from the even deeper gloom of a nearby alleyway, pick up the discarded magazine and sit down at one of the shadowy tables. Only the waiter who came to inquire if his mysterious regular customer wanted his usual order saw the elegant, black-gloved hand skim the cover, stopping to touch a leather-clad fingertip over the photo of Gillian's delicate face.

"Soon, *chérie*," whispered a voice that was roughly hewn yet hauntingly beautiful all at once, "we will discover whether or not you can truly help a monster like me."

"Pardon?" the waiter asked.

"Forgive me," the cloaked figure intoned. "Only coffee."

"Oui, Monsieur Garnier."

CHAPTER
9

THEY sped out of Rouen with a full tank of petrol, coffee and pastries for everyone. Gillian happily swigged down nearly half a pint of light coffee before she realized she'd forgotten to put sugar in it and gagged.

"Hathor's hells, I forgot to modify it," she grimaced.

"You're on drugs," Jenna smirked, swirling a stirring stick through her own beverage.

"Not enough apparently. I can still see and hear you," Gillian smirked back, finally locating the sugar packets and correcting her oversight.

They'd talked her into some of Trocar's magical Elven medication after she refused the field-pack morphine injection that Jenna located in their combat first aid kit. It took the edge off the pain in her abdomen and allowed her to sit more comfortably in the cramped quarters of the car.

Claire's cell phone rang abruptly and everyone jumped. The slim Shifter answered in English, then switched to rapid-fire French. No one interrupted; Gill's group was smart enough to know she'd tell them if they needed to know and Brant knew that, as her partner, he was already involved.

Snapping the phone shut, Claire's sweet face was rather grim as she looked at her partner. "That was the Yard. They have been in contact with Interpol and insist that since they have two agents and part of Gillian's Team in France, we are to investigate something which may have to do with what she has described to us."

"What does *that* mean?" Gillian wanted to know.

"There have been a chain of murders South of us," Claire provided. "Very brutal, very random. What is not known is who or what is behind them, but since your information has come to light, there is speculation that this may have to do with the Turf War that you have described."

"While Gillian is a competent officer and field agent, she is in no shape to involve herself in any special operations at this time," Trocar fairly growled at Claire. The problem was, in his irritation, his voice came out silkier and sultrier than ever. Claire was suddenly staring into his eyes, completely mesmerized.

"Oh Goddess, he's bespelled her." Gill sighed.

"Not intentionally, I assure you." Trocar sounded miffed.

"Well, fix it, she can't stay like that," Jenna snapped.

"Now what the hell is wrong?" Brant sounded exasperated.

"Elfstruck," Helmut said helpfully. "It's a Paramortal psychology term. He's accidentally made her fall in love with him."

"Good God, is there no end to the havoc you people wreak on others?" Brant was definitely exasperated.

"It. Was. An. Accident," Trocar growled again.

"Goddess, you are beautiful," Jenna breathed heavily as she stared at the back of Trocar's head with undisguised lust.

"Oh shit," Gill said.

"Oh no," Helmut agreed.

"Her too?" Pavel was incredulous.

"I cannot believe this," Trocar stated flatly, shifting in his seat a little to stare into Jenna's sparkling brown eyes.

"Psych," Jenna quipped, grinning. "Had you going there for a second." She poked the Dark Elf in the arm. Trocar swore eloquently at her in half a dozen archaic languages before turning back to the legitimately bespelled Claire.

"What?" Jenna's eyes were wide and innocent.

Gillian doubled a fist and slugged her friend in the shoulder, "That's not funny."

"Ow!" Jenna rubbed her abused arm. "I thought it was funny."

"Will you just *fix it*!" Brant bellowed.

"As long as they don't have sex, it will wear off," Gillian said helpfully.

"What?!" Brant was horrified.

"Inspector, I do not know if I should be offended by your clearly apparent prejudice between Human and Elf pairings or if it merely has something to do with me on a personal level." Trocar's voice was perfectly level but Gillian knew he was jerking the stuffy detective's chain.

"I am not prejudiced!"

"Indeed you should not be with your Fey heritage," Trocar added.

Brant yanked the steering wheel so hard to the left that they nearly careened into a fence. "Did she tell you that? Did Dr. Key tell you that?"

"Of course not, Gillian would never break a patient's confidence."

"I am not her patient!"

"But you seem so agitated, perhaps you should speak with her privately . . ."

Brant felt like crying for the first time in his long life. Was there no end to this insanity? No matter what he said, it would only make things worse. He abruptly pulled the car over, parked it and got out. They all watched as he stormed down the road a few yards then came back to the driver's side. Fists clenched, he waited until Helmut rolled down the back window.

Everyone braced for a barrage of shouting but Brant's voice was level, "My agitation stems from wanting to understand all of this, from trying to make sure Gillian stays alive, and now from being informed that we are to investigate a potential serial killer while I have a wounded woman and an Elfstruck partner in my car.

"I am frightened for Gillian, I am worried about the success of this mission, I am sickened by the thought of the plight of the victims which have brought us here. I am trying to do my job. Please stop making it more difficult than it is already."

With that, he climbed back in, released the brake and shifted into first. "Can we continue now, please?"

It was silent in the tightly packed confines of the vehicle for the space of a heartbeat, then Claire's breathy voice shattered the quiet. "I must have you, Trocar. I will die without your touch."

Jenna and Gillian giggled, Helmut chuckled and even Pavel snickered at the lovely Shifter's blatant comment. She was still staring into Trocar's jeweled eyes, completely oblivious to the rest of them in the car. Trocar was trying to remove her arms from around his neck gently and turn her so that she wasn't straddling him.

Brant gave up and drove. There was no point in trying to sort through this with all them in the car. They were all crazy, he was sure of it. Just focus on the road, look at the scenery, let the kilometers eat away at his agitation and frustration. France had a spectacular countryside, even in the Autumn. He needed to just focus on the beauty around him and not on the psychopaths in his car.

Time went by swiftly as he tuned all of them out and just focused on his driving and letting his thoughts run where they would. They drove into the former Gauvodon Region of France. Pastoral, postcard pretty; it looked like an area where the Tourist Administration took all of their publicity photos. He pulled over to consult his Global Positioning System and determine where they needed to be exactly.

One thing was certain: If he wanted to remain sane, he needed to learn to let things roll off his back more. Maybe Trocar and Helmut were right; maybe he should talk to Gillian on a professional level. He had been under a lot of stress lately. It would make sense that it was getting to—

An unearthly, unholy howl-bellow-roar broke the calm of the predawn and of his thoughts. All of them were up and out of the car in an eyeblink. Even Claire was up, gun drawn, but she was clinging to Trocar's left hand like he was the dessert bar on a cruise liner.

"I am stopping myself from asking the obvious question," Gillian said quietly, trying not to look obvious as she cradled her aching abdomen, abused from her sudden leap from the car.

"Aye," Pavel agreed, "but you know Shifters are not bound by daylight. We just prefer the night to hunt and to change."

"How do you know it's a Shifter?"

"The scent is not a natural one," Pavel offered, "but neither is how it looks."

Gillian felt an icy bolt slam down her spine and into her stomach. "How do you know what it looks like?" Her voice held the ghost of a quiver.

Pavel simply pointed. All eyes followed the line of his arm and finger to a hillside nearly a quarter mile away. Mouths collectively fell open and everyone backed up and into the car in one jumbled motion. An immense dark shape was traversing the side of the hill. Even from where they were, the thing was clearly enormous. The massive quadruped was stalking the hillside then paused to scent the air and give another horrific howl.

"What the hell is that?" Brant whispered in a shaky voice.

"Loup-Garou," Helmut informed them. "It's a type of Shifter commonly confused with a Werewolf. I've never seen one, in the flesh, however. I thought they were only legend in this century."

"Me too," Gillian agreed. "I thought the last few had died out in the early eighteen hundreds."

"Well, it clearly didn't read the same history books you did," Brant hissed.

"We are downwind of it," Trocar mentioned almost casually.

"Shit," Jenna moaned softly.

"Brant, back up the car slowly," Gill instructed him unnecessarily. "We need to get out of this immediate area."

"Thank you, Dr. Key, for that observation." Brant wasn't pleased, but he shifted into reverse and slowly began backing up.

Everyone's eyes were glued to the creature, who paused at the sound of the transmission changing gears. The huge head swiveled and pointed directly toward them. It disturbed everyone that they could clearly make out the muzzle lifting, as the creature scented the air again. Moonlight flashed white around the mouth. Teeth. Lots and lots of very big teeth.

When it moved, it was a blur. One moment it was stationary on the hillside, the next it was halfway to the retreating vehicle, stopping once again to scent the air. Unfortunately it also provided the car's occupants with a good look at it as it stood in the fading headlight beams.

Roughly the size of a North American bison, the Loup-Garou stood nearly six feet high at the shoulder. Massively built, it looked like a cross between a tiger, a Tyrannosaurus rex and a timber wolf. Its body was covered in what appeared to be short, coarse hair that ranged from nearly black to a rusty brown. There were horizontal stripes on its legs and belly, like an eland might have or a Tasmanian wolf. Its head was three feet long and nearly two feet wide, the short, thick neck disappearing into immense shoulders—no doubt to support the weight of those huge jaws and teeth.

"It looks like . . . Goddess, what is the genus?" Gillian turned to Helmut.

"A Creodant."

"That's it!" Gillian whispered excitedly. "This is an amazing find for us in the parapsychology world and for paleontologists!"

"I believe the more immediate problem is getting away from your amazing find so we can live to tell people about it," Jenna said, her eyes never leaving the hulking horror, which was now moving toward them with its head lowered and tail flat out in an aggressive, stalking manner.

"Mon Dieu!" Claire squeaked, throwing her arms around

Trocar's neck. "I cannot die before I have you; I must have you!"

Trocar sighed and gently held Claire off while he removed a small packet from a hidden pouch in his cape. He waved it under her nose and she collapsed against his shoulder with a happy smile on her face: out cold.

"If you have harmed her . . ." Brant took his eyes off the approaching Loup-Garou to glare at Trocar.

"She will sleep, have pleasant dreams and wake in a few hours, none the wiser."

"Shit! Look out!" Gillian yelled, pointing in front of them.

Brant slammed on the brakes out of reflex just as the Loup-Garou leaped at the car. Its momentum and power carried it over the vehicle instead of into the windshield. Everyone automatically ducked down as the beast sailed over. There was a heavy thud as it landed on the road behind them.

Gillian's *"Go! Go! Go!!"* was completely unnecessary as Brant sat up, shifted and nearly drove his foot through the floorboards, trying to get them out of there. The car jerking and the sound of metal ripping let them know that he still hadn't been fast enough. He shifted gears anyway and ground the transmission as the car catapulted forward. They narrowly missed a tree as Brant fought the wheel to bring them back onto the road.

A glance in the rearview mirror showed the gigantic prehistoric-looking Wolf dropping what was left of the rear bumper and starting after them. It was chilling, the way the thing picked up speed. Massive shoulder muscles bunched and elongated with each bounding leap—like having a freight train suddenly come to life and decide it didn't want you on its tracks.

Twenty kilometers per hour, twenty-five, then forty, fifty; the damn thing was keeping pace with them. The entire car had a collective sick feeling in their various stomachs as they watched the slavering beast bounding along. Gillian blanched when she watched the speedometer tick to sixty, then realized that she was looking at kilometers per hour, not miles. Still damn impressive for a mutated Wolf running on asphalt.

Brant gunned it, sparing a quick look in the side mirror to see the thing finally dropping back and disappearing from view as they screeched around a hairpin curve. Maybe they'd find a populated area where they'd be safe. No, that was a bad idea. Too many civilians might get injured or killed if that thing followed them into a village or one of the little farms that dotted the area. Great, now what to do?

"We can't go into any village," Gillian stated, echoing his thoughts.

"I am aware of that, Dr. Key," Brant said, more calmly than he felt.

"Do you think it's still following us?" Jenna asked. She had turned as far as she could in the cramped backseat and was staring out the rear window.

"Absolutely," Pavel confirmed. "It has our scent and it was already hunting. It will most assuredly follow us."

"Dammit, I knew you were going to say that," Jenna pouted.

"What's that, up ahead?" Helmut pointed to a large gated estate silhouetted on the crest of a distant hillside over Brant's shoulder.

"An old fortress of some kind."

"It looks like it's inhabited from the lights on the walls and in the upper windows," Helmut noted.

"Oh right." Brant realized that Helmut was suggesting it as a temporary shelter. The ancient stone walls of the enclosure appeared to be about fifteen feet in height. The gates were heavy, wrought iron, flush with the ground and locked from the look of things as he skidded the car into the gravel drive.

Frantically pressing the horn, Brant felt panic rising as the unearthly howl-bellow-roar shattered the early morning quiet of the French countryside once more. Everyone collectively turned and looked back down the road. They were situated sideways on the hilly ridge and able to see most of the valley.

With unerring determination the creature was coming. It was closing fast on the vehicle, and no help from the estate was immediately apparent. Powerful legs propelled its huge bulk down the road. It could have easily veered off and come straight up the hillside but it seemed focused on their former path. Whether that was a display of intellect or sheer instinct remained to be seen.

"Get out of the vehicle," Trocar commanded them.

When no one moved, he opened the door, cradling the unconscious Claire in his arms, and yelled, "Get out!"

Tossing Claire over his shoulder, the tall Elf sprinted to the juncture between wall and gate. A booted foot found enough purchase on the stones while he lifted himself up to the spikes at the top of the iron gate. Catlike, he climbed quickly to the top of the stone wall, lifting Claire off his shoulder and lowering her as close to the ground of the enclosure as he could before letting go. She fell in an untidy heap but was on the inside of the fence.

"Gillyflower, come to me; the rest of you, climb if you want to live."

They didn't need a second invitation. His sharp command

had them moving already. Pavel picked Gillian up, ignoring her protests, and passed her up to Trocar. The Elf stood her up on the thick wall next to him and reached down as Jenna hobbled to the wall. Pavel practically tossed Helmut up on the opposite side of the massive gate.

Helmut scrabbled for purchase against the stones, his injured arm hampering his effort. A quick boost from Pavel and he was up, on top of the wall. He glanced around; Jenna was safely next to Gillian and Trocar, the women bracing each other as Jenna's crutches were still in the car. Brant had his gun drawn and was standing in front of the gate. His hands were visibly shaking but he was trying to protect all of them. Too bad he was going to die for his effort.

"Inspector, get up on the wall," Pavel literally growled at Brant.

"Get on the gate, Pavel." Brant ignored him and focused on the nightmare loping toward them.

Pavel didn't give him another chance to argue; he grabbed Brant by the belt and collar and literally tossed him over the spiked gate. The detective landed heavily on the other side, rolling to avoid breaking his ankle. He popped up, gun in hand and furious. Furious until he saw what was occurring just a few feet from him.

There's a reason Werewolves in the movies are shown with little to no clothing on. It is because when they shift, they will literally rip through the seams of any garment owing to the rapid expansion of body mass. Pavel shifted before their eyes, his clothes falling from him like tattered multicolored leaves.

"Pavel, no!" Gillian yelled too late.

Pavel was six feet three inches tall in Human form. As a shifted blond Wolf, he was Welsh pony–sized and several hundred pounds. The charging Loup-Garou's bulk was even more pronounced as it hurtled up the long driveway, straight for the Russian Lycanthrope. Nearly a ton of muscle, bone and teeth hit Pavel in the chest at ramming speed.

The impact slammed him into the gates, shattering the lock and swinging one side of them open. Pavel rolled to diffuse the force of the blow, paws scrabbling for purchase, neck straining away from the colossal jaws snapping near his throat. His claws ripped bleeding furrows in the great beast's neck and shoulders and his own teeth closed on the slavering muzzle, biting deep and crushing bone.

It screamed in fury as Pavel regained his feet, wrenching itself out of his jaws and slamming into him with its shoulder. Pavel staggered and went down again as the huge head whipped around and the thing's teeth ripped through his shoulder. His roar of pain was drowned out by the creature's own bellowing howl.

Trocar had leaped off the gate onto the Loup-Garou's back. Gillian caught the flash of silver in his hand as he drew some kind of Elven stiletto. She was powerless to do anything but watch two of her friends risking their lives. Brant was trying to find a target to fire at, but the fast-moving mass of Loup-Garou, Russian Shifter and Dark Elf gave him no clear target to aim at.

Pavel was limping on three legs, barely keeping his throat and abdomen clear of the clashing jaws. Trocar couldn't let go long enough to stab at it. He was in serious danger of being crushed as the Loup-Garou bucked and rolled in an attempt to dislodge the obstructive presence on its back. The Elf leaped clear as the beast threw itself backward—a lithe, elegant, black-clad form, landing on his feet like a cat. The Loup-Garou scrabbled to right itself as a bleeding and injured Pavel closed in and Trocar charged back into the fray to help.

Brant gave up trying to target anything and fired several shots into the air, hoping to attract the notice of the estate's occupants. All he succeeded in doing was getting the Loup-Garou's attention. He watched in horror as the great head rotated from Pavel to himself. The beast apparently objected to sudden, loud explosive noises as it oriented on the source of them: one terrified Scotland Yard detective. It barreled toward him with a speed that literally took everyone's breath away.

"Gott im Himmel." Helmut managed a small prayer as the creature crossed the distance to the detective in two titanic bounds.

"Shit." Gillian was much less elegant but no less heartfelt. This was very, very bad and nothing anyone did would stop Brant from being shredded by the Shifter dialed up to Vegematic.

"Charles!" a female voice suddenly shrieked in a register that only dogs, Lycanthropes and apparently scared-shitless people could hear. Everyone flinched at the noise except the Loup-Garou.

The powerful muscles that had been propelling it forward toward its meal became its worst enemy as it tried to turn in midair. Almost two thousand pounds of snorting, snarling death actually froze midbound for a split second. It managed to perform a twisting maneuver in-flight that was astonishing in execution and speed. There was an audible crack as the creature's spine literally snapped from the force involved in halting its leap of toothy death toward the Fey detective. The ground trembled as its bulk slammed into the gravel and the Loup-Garou lay still.

The feminine shriek was repeated as a lithe form dressed in lilac silk bolted past everyone to cradle the massive head. It was disconcerting watching the delicate-looking woman with the Jaws of the Abyss propped in her lap.

"Charles, no! You must change!" the dark-haired woman cried in a distinctly accented voice.

The huge form seemed to ripple and shift before their eyes. It wasn't so much that a male form appeared as it was that the beast literally seemed to melt away from the man's form. He was apparently Human, dark haired as the woman, and quite naked.

"Well, that's intriguing," Jenna observed.

"The fact that he is naked, alive or fully Human?" Gillian wasn't really asking Jenna, she was making observations of her own as Trocar lifted her off the wall.

What was before her was a Human male. The woman had Fey blood, of that she was certain: the female's aura was brushing Gillian's empathy with the peculiar sparkly feeling that only the Fey had. It reminded her of how Trocar, Mirrin and Brant felt. The interesting thing for her was that the man held none of a Shifter's feel. Pavel and the rest of Cezar's pack back in Romania, Claire and every other Shifter she'd ever encountered had a particular "feel." Each species did. Even among the Reborn, every variant had its own touch on her empathy. That this man, who had so recently been a gigantic, bizarre, extinct species of Wolf, now lay before her, completely and wholly Human, was nothing short of phenomenal.

"Pavel," Gillian said softly, kneeling gingerly by her own injured Lycanthrope, "he doesn't feel like you or any other Shifter I've met."

Pavel shifted as well, becoming Human with a non-ravaged shoulder as his magic did its work. He was still pale and exhausted from the encounter but was now intact. Trocar stepped up to hand him a travel bag, which the Elf had retrieved from the car.

"Aye, his abilities are the result of a Curse rather than of a virus, as the rest you have met have most likely been," Pavel told her.

"That would make sense then." Gillian became thoughtful. "It's straight magic, rather than a magically oriented virus."

Helmut came over to sit beside Gillian and Pavel, who was trying surreptitiously to dress in front of them. "The Loup-Garou Curse has been thought to be only legendary . . . until now.

"There have been rumors of Werewolf activity in France for generations, beginning in the late seventeen hundreds, and in Louisiana, but I have never seen any confirmed information on the subject."

"Perhaps we should ask him, when he regains consciousness," Trocar suggested, kneeling by the fallen man and his slender companion.

"I have a lot of things I wish to ask him," Brant groused, dusting himself off and picking up Claire from her crumpled heap on the ground.

"I can answer your questions since you already know my husband's secret." The woman spoke in softly dulcet tones.

"Please do," Gill prompted her to continue.

"Charles . . . my husband, has been victimized by this Curse for several years." The woman lifted her face to look at Gillian, displaying the astonishing beauty of the Fey. Her hair was blue-black, her skin pearlescent and her eyes a wide lavender, framed by a midnight fringe of thick lashes. Only the deep-grooved bleeding claw marks marring the line of her jaw detracted from her beauty.

"Let me attend to this." Trocar spoke in his own magical voice as he reached for her face.

She turned stardust-filled lavender eyes to him and nodded, but her hands never stopped stroking her husband's hair and face. Charles was still out cold but his spine had straightened out with his shift, causing him to turn just enough that his genitals were exposed. Trocar thoughtfully removed a garment of some kind from a fold of his cape and covered the man as best he could before attending to the woman.

After cleaning her wounds and healing them as well as he was able, Trocar scooped the man up in his arms as if he weighed nothing and rose. "Lead on, Fair One, I will follow."

The delicate-looking woman rose, her gown now stained with saliva and blood, beckoning them to accompany her. "My name is Dahlia . . . Dahlia Chastel."

Introductions went around as the walking wounded entered the French estate. It was elegant, provincial, a combination of modern convenience and old-world ethnicity. Behind the ornate front doors were a second set of four-inch-thick, reinforced steel doors with a rod and grooves locking mechanism that would keep out a small army or one maddened Loup-Garou. Hidden from the outside, they were visible as the party entered. Gillian was betting they had similar reinforcements at the windows. The small castle was a cleverly disguised bunker to keep its occupants safe.

The room where she instructed Trocar to bring Charles was immense. Ceilings high and covered with intricate paintings of the Elven Courts, golden vermeil was splashed over everything. The walls were painted a clear turquoise and the furniture was ornate and contained shades of coral in the fabrics and patterns. Trocar laid Charles on an large ornate antique couch. Dahlia scooted in and laid her husband's head on her lap again.

Jenna limped over and sprawled on a chaise longue; Brant followed and deposited Claire on another then took a seat in a high-backed chair nearby. Gillian, Helmut and Pavel arranged themselves on a floral-patterned divan then shuffled over to make room for Trocar, who dragged Gillian under his arm and held her against him. She glared up at him for his audacity.

"I can help heal you further, Petal, if you will merely sit still and let me hold you."

"Right."

Crystalline eyebrows rose and Trocar managed such an impossibly innocent expression for a Dark Elf that Gillian had to grin at him. Fine. She'd let him and his magic soothe her aching muscles, just this once.

Dahlia reached for a buzzer installed on a nearby end table. Shortly thereafter an honest-to-Goddess butler appeared. She ordered food and refreshments for all of them in that sweetly magical voice all Fey have then turned back to her unexpected guests.

"I must apologize for my husband's indiscretion in attacking you. I assure you that he has no control over this Curse and cannot remember anything about the events that occur during his change."

CHAPTER
10

THEY listened as Dahlia told them about Charles's family Curse over a French country breakfast. His family was descended from the original Beast of Gavaudon. A distant relative, a former ship's Captain, was involved in the African slave trade, and he made a colossal mistake by kidnapping the grandson of a very powerful woman. The woman was the Shaman of a tribe whose name had been lost in obscurity.

The slavers butchered half the village, then in full view of the old woman chained the rest to sell into servitude. The Shaman tried to intervene when they clapped irons on her grandson. Charles's ancestor brutally stabbed her for her trouble. Using her own heart's blood as a reagent, the dying woman placed a Curse upon the slaver Captain. He would become outwardly what he was inwardly: an un-speakable Beast who would stalk the darkness when the moon shone full. The old woman's blood gleamed black in the silvery moonlight as she uttered the Curse, her breath misting with her own blood and her eyes upon the moon as she called down the judgment with her final breath.

The Curse would descend upon the man's ancestors, appearing through the male line once every second generation, from grandfather to grandson; it was unbreakable, uncleansable, unremovable unless the wrong done to the Shaman, her grandson and her people could be righted again.

"Wow," Gillian remarked, "there really is no way to undo this, is there?"

"No." Dahlia shook her head, sparkling teardrops falling onto the rich silk of her nightgown. "We have researched, tried to find answers. This started when Charles turned thirty. That was three of your years ago. It has become a nightmare for all of us. We moved to this area in the hope that there was enough open countryside and enough livestock to sate the beast."

"So, he knows what he is," Helmut asked gently.

"Yes, he does. He has contemplated suicide more than once over it. I have managed to talk him out of it, but I fear for my husband's life in more ways than death by his own hand." Dahlia sounded completely defeated.

Gillian glanced over at Brant, who was listening intently. The British detective exchanged a surprising look of complete understanding with her. While society in general had improved dramatically for both Human and Paramortals, both groups still retained harsh punishments for murder and heinous acts. Britain did not have the death penalty, but France did. Most Shifter factions also retained their own rather gruesome version of capital punishment.

The problem was, Charles Chastel was not a virus-infected Shifter. Since his affliction was the result of a Familial Curse, there was no clear jurisdiction as to who would make the rules about any punishment forthcoming. It was situations like this that made Brant wonder why in hell he hadn't just taken up painting as a profession instead of dealing with the complexities of modern police work.

Gillian's exhausted mind was whirling. She knew Brant was struggling with this and why. It disturbed her slightly to know she and Brant understood each other so obviously, but she'd let that go. Charles's future was more important than her agreeing with someone she mildly despised. Claire was still asleep so they'd have to wait for her input. Gill thought there ought to be a way out of the situation for Charles but was certain that he and his wife had truly tried every avenue to fix it.

Since Charles was suicidal, she could try to help him with his depression. A lot of Shifters, and Vampires for that matter, went through a depressed state at some point after their transformation: Vampires and their fangxiety, Shifters and their conversion disorders. She'd speak with him when he came to and see how bad it was. If he was actively suicidal and wouldn't verbally contract not to take his life, she could have him involuntarily committed for seventy-two hours to a locked psychiatric facility for observation. It probably wouldn't help but it would buy them some time.

Goddess, she felt like hell. Her incisions were throbbing, she had a headache and felt like she wanted to sleep for a week. Aleksei was still going to be pissed off; in fact, the whole Vampire group waiting for them in Romania was probably rather displeased with her at the moment. Now she had a suicidal Lycanthrope with a nearly hysterical Fey spouse on her hands and Jack the Ripper on her tail, and she was too tired, too injured and recently had too many chemicals in her system to think straight. For the first time in years, Gillian felt like curling up in a corner and crying.

It would be so nice to be able to hand off responsibility for a while, even a day, even a minute—not have everyone depending on her decision-making skills, limited as they were at the moment. Life was simpler when she was a soldier. She'd been just a cog in a very large wheel. Being in command of her unit was fine. Even though she made the immediate decisions on assignment, the big choices were made by someone else.

As a therapist, she helped the client make decisions, followed the rules of her ethical principles. It was a bitch being at the top end of the proverbial food chain. She outranked Brant, even as a civilian; her affiliation with Interpol and the Marine Corps trumped Scotland Yard's jurisdiction. The buck stopped with her. Shit and double shit.

Aleksei Rachlav and his large, comforting presence crept into her thoughts. She immediately shoved them back down into the nether regions of her mental basement. No, no and *hell* no. Thinking about being curled up against that expanse of muscled chest instead of Trocar's lean form; those powerful arms around her, the long elegant fingers stroking her hair; his deep, resonant, magical voice murmuring in his odd combination of Italian and Romanian to trust him . . . that it would be all right . . .

"Gillian?"

"What?" She raised Nile green eyes to Jenna, who was staring at her oddly.

"Are you all right? You seemed to phase out there for a moment."

"Yeah, I'm fabulous."

"You are exhausted, Captain," Trocar reprimanded her.

"Not any more than anyone else, thank you," Gill barked back, miffed that anyone noticed her mind wandering.

Trocar raised a crystalline brow, and she shoved away

from him to sit more upright on the divan. He didn't move, just crooked a finger at her and beckoned her back to her former semireclining position against him. Her answering glare told him she wasn't in the mood for any more comforting.

"Please forgive me," Dahlia chirped, suddenly flustered. "You are all tired and injured, and I am speaking of things that can wait until you are rested."

Gillian snorted, "No, it's fine. This is important and we can rest later. Tonight is another full moon and Charles will be out ravaging the countryside if we don't figure something out."

"We have a room, below the wine cellar, where he normally waits out the Curse."

"Why was he not in it last night?" Brant beat Gillian to the question.

Dahlia blushed prettily. "We had a quarrel. He left to go riding for a while and was caught outside at twilight. His horse came back without him, uninjured, thank the Old Ones, and I secured myself in a safe room that we have upstairs.

"I was watching the monitors around the property and saw your vehicle drive up. I did not want to risk going outside and hoped that you would drive on . . . Then I saw Charles after you all." Her eyes welled up and spilled over again. She cuddled her husband's head against her breast and sobbed.

"It was very brave of you to come out of the house," Gillian assured her, shifting her tone and her empathy to a comforting zone for the despondent woman's benefit.

"I could do not less. I would like to believe that Charles would retain enough of himself not to harm me, but he has never allowed me to take that chance."

"Smart man, your Charles," Helmut interjected. "It would be foolish to risk yourself in that manner. He cannot possibly remember his deeds while he is in his transformed state. Those affected by a Curse are different from those affected by a true Lycanthrope virus."

Everyone fell silent except for Dahlia's quiet sobbing and the clink of a gilded spoon on fine bone china as Jenna poured another cup of coffee. One could almost hear the noise from all the mental wheels turning as the group tried to think their way out of this mess. They didn't know Charles Chastel; they only knew what he turned into and what the consequences of that conversion were. Despite his bad timing of tonight and the murders which had occurred over the past year, none of this really was his fault . . . except . . .

"Wait a minute. You said you found out about Charles's . . . er . . . problem several years ago." Gillian had a thought suddenly, and it wasn't a good one.

"Yes, that is correct," Dahlia agreed.

"Brant, when did the Yard say that the murders in this region began?"

He looked confused for a moment, trying to remember exactly what Claire had told them in the car, then visibly straightened to look Gillian directly in the eyes. "She said over the last few months, I believe, Dr. Key."

A very cold, sick feeling suddenly exploded in her stomach. Charles was suicidal; that was already established. He had exhausted all known methods of solving his problem. There was no cure, no hope. Gillian knew of a phenomenon recognized in American colloquial speech as "death by cop." Someone who had nothing to live for but who didn't want to actually take their own life occasionally went ballistic and intentionally set up a circumstance where they would be killed by law enforcement. Death by cop had been practiced for a long time; it had just taken modern psychology a while to catch on to it.

Gillian turned to Dahlia. "If you both knew what he was, and you say that tonight's activities were a fluke, how do you explain the vicious murders which have occurred in the past few months? The reports say that the victims were literally torn apart. It would be very difficult to do that if you have him barricaded in a safe room, now wouldn't it?"

Dahlia began crying again, rocking Charles against her and shaking her head. This was going to be very bad, Gillian could tell already.

"He wants to die," Dahlia blubbered. The Fey woman managed to look positively ravishing even with tears and mucous smeared on her face.

"Shit," Gillian said under her breath.

"Indeed," Helmut added.

"Death by cop?" Brant interjected. When Gillian and Helmut looked at him, surprise on their faces, he supplemented, "I do try to keep abreast of things, you know. It *is* my job."

"Dahlia," Gillian said as gently as she could, focusing a peaceful, calm aura toward the woman, "we have to figure this out together. If you are helping him in any manner, you are an accessory to those murders. I can't help Charles and I can't help you if you don't tell me the truth."

It took some coaxing but Dahlia explained as best as she could. She hadn't figured it out herself until recently what Charles was doing. Every month since the discovery of his affliction, on the afternoon of the full moon, she would lock Charles in their safe room, returning for him after a full forty-eight-hour period to make sure he had shifted back to Human form. This had gone on for over two years, a mourned and hated routine to keep her husband and the populace safe.

Lady Chastel was as pragmatic as she was lovely. She had fallen in love with a Human, married him, and had resolved herself to outliving him, but she'd be damned if she would be robbed of one moment of time for them to be together. Both of them spent time researching Charles's condition through various avenues. Charles was the curator of a small museum in Rouen, giving him time and professional resources to investigate his ancestor and the Loup-Garou Curse. Dahlia had connections with the Fey, whose network of knowledge was immense indeed.

They had managed to track down several other families who had been afflicted by the Curse. None, however, had been to Africa during the height of the slave trade and none knew anything about a particular tribe with a Shaman who knew Blood Rites well enough to place a generational Curse on anyone. For reasons unknown, the Loup-Garou Curse was unique to France or French-held territories. Further study showed that each of the families affected was of purely Western European lineage; no influx of different heritage was shown.

Charles seemed to be the only one consigned to the gigantic horror that he had become. Most of the Cursed were normal Shifter sized—about that of a Welsh or Shetland pony and resembling an extremely large, traditionally thought of wolf. His shifted form was the only anomaly from the pattern.

The Twilight Court of which Dahlia was a minor noble had looked into it for their fallen sister. She wasn't well thought of, marrying a Human, but they considered it a minor issue that would be resolved when Charles died after a Human lifespan and Dahlia came back into the fold. They had no more luck than the Human researchers. All of the Loup-Garous were innocent victims of ancestral Curses. Sometimes the Curse was generational, sometimes it was gender based and occasionally, as in Charles's case, it was both generational and gender-specific—grandfather to grandson. Most of the families opted for letting the Curse die with them at some point in their lineage.

Charles and Dahlia had decided not to have children at all, rather than resort to abortion of a male fetus if she were to become pregnant. He didn't want to run any risks of a descendant of his having to deal with the lack of information his own family had provided. No one had talked about his grandfather except in hushed tones. There were no family reunions, no birthday or Christmas cards.

The Chastel family had been as tightly locked down as Buckingham Palace for information. Charles hadn't known he had a paternal grandfather until, at eighteen, he was taken to a lonely, overgrown cemetery near a tiny village in the region and shown a simple iron cross with the name "Chastel" on it. Under the name "François Chastel" was "Burdened of the Beast." His father explained that his grandfather had suffered from delusions and became very violent monthly. Since Paramortal disorders weren't fully comprehended at the time, Grandfather had been branded a "lunatic" and buried away from the village, outside of Holy Ground, owing to the likelihood of evil possession and possible contagion from mental illness.

It had been a nice, neat, tidy explanation package that Charles had wholly bought into . . . at least until he turned thirty and found out just how real Grandfather's problem was. By that time, his own parents were dead, killed in a light plane crash three years prior. There were no known family members to contact, no loose notes or secret panels containing wall safes that could tell him about his heritage. When he met Dahlia at an antiquities auction several months after his parents' death, he fell in love with her and the idea of a normal, stable family.

Apparently she felt the same because, Fey or not, she consented to marry him within a month. The couple settled into a quiet comfortable life in Rouen. Charles was curator of the family museum, while Dahlia kept herself involved in the intricate politics of the Twilight Court and with organizing beautification projects for the lovely hamlet. All was rosy until he stayed late in the museum the night after his thirtieth birthday. He had no memory of leaving the office, only of opening the exterior door and stepping into the glowing light of a full moon.

He woke the next morning, naked in a field—no car, no clothes, but with a bad taste in his mouth, and his feet and hands nearly in ribbons from cuts, gashes and gouges. There was a tiny home in the distance so Charles limped there, found a terrified couple who ushered him in, gave him something to wear and warned him about the Beast of Gauvodan who had risen again and was stalking the land. They gave him a ride back to the museum. His car was there, his keys still in the door, which was wide open.

Charles called the police immediately. They investigated, determined that he had been the victim of an attempted kidnapping owing to the defensive wounds on his hands and the damage done to his feet and sent him home. Dahlia was waiting for him, frantic and loving. Both of them missed the headline in the paper about the murdered family, nearly a province away.

They hired extra security for the museum and installed a

safe room in their house, complete with steel bars at the windows and extra locks on the doors. Life went on as usual until a month later. Dahlia was gone to a Twilight Court function and Charles was alone, securely locked in their home. He awoke the next evening to a completely ravaged and decimated home.

Again, he was naked, and again, the police were called. They could find no forced entry, no damage to the outside of the home at all. With shifty eyes and patient explanations, they suggested that Charles might "get some help" for his obvious trauma over his recent kidnapping. Charles knew he was being shuffled off, so he waited until they left before viewing the security tape from the various cameras around the home.

What he viewed both horrified and sickened him. Watching his own transformation into an unspeakable Beast threw him into a complete mental breakdown. Dahlia returned to find him gone, no note, no explanation. After weeks of searching, she found him in one of the numerous cave systems of France, naked, shivering, and quite out of his mind. Loving care, decent food, and her unswerving devotion healed him to the point where he could communicate what had occurred and show her the tape.

Instead of packing her things and returning to Fey-ville, Dahlia showed extraordinary character. It was a bad situation—in fact, it sucked—but she took her vows to Charles seriously. For better, for worse, she was staying, even after Charles pointed out that there were no words pertaining to "for when your husband turns into a monster once a month" in their wedding vows.

When it became apparent that no hope was available or in sight, Charles's depression took a turn for the worse. He decided that if he couldn't cure it, he would end it. Dahlia was to lock him in as she had done for years, but Charles would have a way out. He refused to tell her where the key was or where the opening to the outside lay. To him, it was now in the hands of fate. If he died, it was justice. If he lived, he became vengeance. She was at her wit's end to convince him otherwise.

Gillian and the others listened intently to the story. All of them were looking for holes in the explanation, any glossing over of the facts, but Dahlia was straightforward and Gill could feel that she wasn't lying. What to do? What to do . . . ?

Gill unconsciously tapped her front teeth with her finger. Jenna handed her a cigarette to supplement her oral fixation. She took it, ignoring Trocar's raised eyebrow.

"We'll wait until he comes to, then I need to talk to him alone."

"All right," Dahlia agreed. "But first rest, please. Charles will likely be asleep until the evening."

They declined her offer of separate rooms and dozed where they sat. Brant moved over to hold Claire so she didn't roll off the divan and break her delicate nose. Peace fell over the household except for the quiet bustling of the servants as they went about their daily tasks.

CHAPTER
11

GILLIAN awoke to the sound of crying. It took her a moment to realize that it was herself and that Trocar was patting her shoulder comfortingly as she leaned trustingly against him. Abruptly she shoved away and glared up at the spectacular beauty of the Dark Elf.

"I'm fine."

"Forgive me, Petal. But you do not appear to be fine."

"Stop calling me that."

"As you wish, Gillyflower."

Exasperated, she jumped up and was rewarded with a wave of dizziness. Trocar thoughtfully caught her before she could face-plant into the richly woven area rug.

"I suggest you remain seated or reclining, Captain, until you are fully healed."

"Fine."

"Gillian—"

"I said, fine."

Trocar sighed and arranged his former commanding

officer on the couch, then went off to locate sustenance for them. Jenna, Helmut, Brant, Pavel and Claire were all still sleeping. Dahlia and Charles were nowhere to be seen. He easily located the kitchen from the distant sounds of onions being chopped. The staff was more than accommodating and promised to send a meal out to them directly.

His inherent ability as an Elf and as an accomplished assassin allowed him to transverse the entire interior of the estate without detection in search of their hosts. When he had established that Charles and Dahlia were not within the house, he moved his exploration outside. The car was where they had left it, at the gate. The gate itself was still broken and hanging by a single hinge on one side. Two men were working to stabilize the heavy iron and reattach it to the stone wall.

In the distance to the back of the property, he could see a pair of horses and their riders. The field from the house to a distant tree line was clear. The riders were nearly against the picturesque forest, far enough away that he could not hear any snippet of conversation. Since he was in full view, he remained where he was, on a flagstone veranda, and watched them. When they turned his direction, he waved and was rewarded with them cantering his way.

Charles dismounted first, handing the reins of his horse to a groomsman, who suddenly appeared at Trocar's elbow. Dahlia leaped lightly down from her steed, then took her husband's hand. Trocar looked them over. She was as lovely as any Fey had a right to be. Charles was a handsome man for a Human, not quite six feet tall, lean with wiry muscles. His dark wavy brown hair was now whirled and tumbled over his forehead and collar. He looked handsome and fit, despite having healed a broken spine the night before. The rust-colored angora sweater he wore complemented his coloring. Black riding jodhpurs rode over slim hips; tan-leather-topped black riding boots graced his lower legs. Intelligent dark brown eyes regarded the taller Elf as Trocar greeted his wife.

"Lady Dahlia . . . And you must be Charles. I am Trocar." He kept his introduction brief and respectful.

"Good morning," Charles said in lightly accented English. "I apologize for everything that happened last night. My wife has filled me in on the situation."

"No apology is necessary, it is hardly your fault."

Anguish ghosted across Charles's face as an empty look replaced the intelligence in his eyes. This was truly a shattered man, devoid of hope, certain that he had no life, no future.

"Thank you, Trocar. I understand that all of you wish to help me but I am afraid the kindest thing you could do for me is to slip one of your daggers into my heart while I sleep."

"*Charles!*" Dahlia cried out, tears welling up in her lavender eyes. With a sob, she clapped her hand over her mouth and fled.

"Daggers?" Trocar's bemused expression reflected his surprise, but he didn't interfere.

"You are a Grael, correct? My wife has told me much about all the denizens of the Fey. I assumed that you would have a remarkable collection of daggers. If I am mistaken, I am sorry."

Trocar smiled one of his rare smiles. "I am indeed Grael. And you are correct about the daggers. It is impressive that you took the time to learn about Fey society."

"I love her; I could do no less." Charles's expression hardened. "Let us go in. I understand that the authorities are here. I would prefer to end this charade."

By the time they got back into the main sitting room, everyone was up and eating, even Claire. Her eyes were clear again and she greeted Trocar with a friendly smile instead of an impassioned pounce. Brant grinned gratefully at the tall Elf, assured that his partner was back in working order again.

Gillian was a little worse for wear. She refused any further painkillers, preferring Trocar's healing methods to keep her mind clear and her empathy functioning correctly. Everything ached from her hair to her toenails but she could focus. After the meal she shooed everyone out, including Dahlia, so she could speak to Charles alone.

Brant and Claire had instructions to focus the full resources of Scotland Yard and Interpol on tracking down any descendants of the African tribe that Charles's ancestor had so wronged. Helmut was online, hunting for information from the International Paramortal Psychology Association's massive database about Lycanthropes, Curses and Loup-Garou Curses in particular—their pathology, any treatment recommendations, removal methods and proclivities toward suicidal tendencies. Jenna and Pavel were combing the immediate area around the estate to see if they could figure out how Charles was leaving the sealed room.

Charles was cooperating with Gillian as best he could. He reiterated freely his desire to end his life and, therefore, the Curse. Gillian honestly couldn't fault him. The situation definitely sucked, but she wasn't one to give up on anything or on anyone. She conducted a brief but thorough intake procedure, had Charles sign all the necessary documents to make him her patient and assure confidentiality.

The benefits of having a client who had nothing to lose was his complete and total honesty about himself, his desires and his intent. Charles simply didn't give a shit. If they locked him up, he'd break out of any conventional institution on the next full moon. If they left him loose, he'd do what he could to be killed. Gillian was trying to find something for him to hold on to, something for him to remain connected with to rekindle even the smallest spark of hope within this tormented man. She wanted his anger, his despair, his frustration; that she could work with. All he was giving back was his apathy. Apathy was the enemy. Apathy had to be banished.

"What is the one thing that you care about?" Gillian asked him, after a long silence.

"Dahlia," Charles answered her without hesitation.

"Dahlia wants you to live." Better to just be blunt at this point.

"I know."

Gillian watched as the love for his wife faded from his eyes and a resolute, empty look replaced it. "Do you know what can happen to a Fey when they lose their mate? Their chosen one?"

"She will go on, Dr. Key. She is a strong woman, she has plenty of support, she will survive. Dahlia is a survivor."

"The Fey have an ability which allows them to cease to exist if they experience a great loss, such as the death of a loved one," Gillian continued, ignoring Charles's statement.

"What do you mean?" Intelligence was back in the sharp brown eyes as Charles peered at her intently.

"If they love, truly love, as Dahlia seems to love you, they can will themselves into death. Some can even literally fade into nothingness, destroying themselves in the process, never to return."

Pain sparkled in Charles's eyes now. "No! She has to live. I do not want her to suffer because of me!"

"She is suffering now. She watches you, sees your desire to leave her."

"I do not want to leave her! I just want to end this!"

"Death is final. She could win you back from a rival but she can't reclaim you from death."

"I cannot continue to live like this." Charles's voice was despondent but Gill took hope from the amount of pain in his eyes.

"Do you know, Doctor, that I was even considering having myself turned into a Vampire? I thought perhaps that might break this goddamned Curse." He met her eyes fully, a man without hope but wracked with anguish over his wife dying because of him.

"I'm afraid it wouldn't have worked," Gillian said gently.

"I know. I realized that if I went mad . . . from the Curse, that is, and changed into . . . what I become, but still maintained Vampire abilities, no one would truly be safe, not even Dahlia."

"Nothing would be able to hold you. You'd have intellect in your Beast form as well as the power and true ruthlessness."

Gillian breathed an internal sigh of relief that Charles Chastel was, at heart, an honorable man in every way. A hybrid like that, she would not have wanted to face under any circumstances. She was pushing him way too fast, not giving him time to process and recover, but there was no help for it.

"Let's talk again in a little while. I want to know what the others have found out." He needed a break and she needed time to think.

"Very well, but you will not change my mind, Dr. Key," Charles said in a flat voice.

"I'm not trying to, Charles." Gill managed a genuine smile in his direction. "I'm trying to help you change your own mind."

She limped off in search of Trocar for a quick healing jolt. The pain was lessened, but she was stiff and sore from all the escape activities since her fall, injury and surgery. Right now she wanted a huge, soft bed and crisp linen sheets to wrap herself up in so she could forget about everyone else's issues.

What she had to do was consult with Brant and Interpol— better to get Helmut involved as well. There was still the problem of the people Charles had eaten recently. He knew there was a possibility that he might mangle a person rather than just livestock by letting himself out of his cage; that made him liable for the killings in the area but she wasn't sure about the murders prior to his discovery of what he was. Gillian wasn't so egocentric that she would make a judgment call on something this complex all by herself. Gathering up Brant, they arranged a conference call on his cell phone with the Yard and Interpol, inviting Helmut in as a consultant.

They explained to the best of their collective ability what the situation was with the Chastels and asked for advice on how to handle it. Caucusing like that always made Gillian's stomach hurt. She hated politics with a passion; she hated having to reexplain a situation to people who were removed from it, safely sitting behind desks instead of being chased by slavering horrors through the Gallic night while in a postoperative chemically enhanced state.

The discussion dragged on throughout the day. Jenna remembered Gill's laptop being in her belongings, so they were able to set up a video conference call, saving Brant's cell battery. Gillian smiled weakly at the discovery.

Knowing someone else had to remember things for her proved just how wiped out she was. She wasn't in any kind of shape to deal with this. Her stomach hurt from tension, her abdomen hurt from the surgery, her entire body felt like it had been run over by a herd of starving wildebeest. Falling into her bed at Castle Rachlav and sleeping for a week sounded like a tremendously good idea.

Aleksei. Shit. She really ought to call him, let him hear her voice and that she was all right, from her own mouth. Unfortunately that would also mean that she had to hear his voice and that would suck right now. Gillian wasn't sure how she would respond to the warm, magical tones of the Vampire and the modicum of security he represented. Frowning, she realized she did know. Listening to Aleksei and his black velvet voice would trigger an unconscionable response. He would be reassuring, probably a little chastising, and more than a little concerned. It might just make her believe in him even more than she did, or worse . . . cry. That *so* wasn't happening right now.

"Gillian?"

"What?" Cronus on a cracker, she'd let her thoughts drift and hadn't been paying attention. She stared at Brant, trying to psychically divine what the hell he had just said.

"Your thoughts?"

Great. No help there. The British detective was staring back at her expectantly.

Helmut thoughtfully provided her with the information she needed. "Do you think we should take Charles into custody immediately or should we let the Interpol agents handle everything when they arrive?"

Her exhausted brain rallied. "Let them do it. Saves us from having to deal with the paperwork."

Brant unexpectedly smiled. "All right. Good thinking, Dr. Key."

She waved her hand glibly and collapsed back into the couch cushions. "Hey, I try."

He turned back to the computer screen to talk to the Interpol agent again. Helmut moved closer to her on the couch and leaned in, whispering.

"*Schatzi*, you are exhausted. You really should go lie down where it is quiet and you can really rest. The agents are coming from Paris. It will be a while before they get here."

Gillian ignored his observation. "Helmut, there just isn't a right way to solve this one, is there? I can't help Charles, not with the time frame I have. I understand he has to be held accountable for his actions but none of this really is his fault at all. Sometimes this job really sucks."

She'd caught bits and pieces of the ongoing conversation. Charles Chastel was to be apprehended and tried for the murders of six people in the area, including the original family, victims of his first change. Now someone had to tell Charles and Dahlia what had transpired. *Thanks for your hospitality . . . "You have the right to remain silent . . . Anything you say can and will be used against you . . ."*

"Gillian, go lie down," Helmut insisted, interrupting the imagined Mirandizing of Charles Chastel. "There are plenty of spare rooms in this chateau where it is a great deal quieter and you can rest."

"Do you watch horror movies, Helmut?" She grinned, trying to rally.

"No, I don't . . . Why?"

"Separating the characters in the movie is a sure sign the person off by themselves is going to get butchered by the axe-wielding maniac. Are you trying to get rid of me?"

Helmut laughed. "Not in a million years, *Schatzi*."

"Then I'm staying right here."

Brant took care of informing Charles and Dahlia what had happened. Charles was characteristically stoic when he was told the situation. Dahlia just as typically cried and clung to Charles's arm. Brant sighed. Gillian was right. Sometimes the job just sucked. It wasn't Charles's fault that he was a Loup-Garou. It *was* Charles's fault that he had disregarded the safety and well-being of others and had murdered people when he could have prevented it. Still, it would never have happened if the original ancestor . . .

There was a honk outside, indicating the arrival of someone, hopefully the Interpol agents. Brant went to the door, followed by Charles, who was only too willing to give himself over to the authorities and end his long-standing nightmare. Dahlia remained at his side, determined to see her husband through his ordeal to the end.

Claire walked in to flank all of them. She'd awoken during the ages-long discussion, and Brant had quickly filled her in. No worse for wear over her temporary crush on Trocar, she stood behind Dahlia, a slender, strong presence just doing her job. Pavel was inside the house somewhere, either taking a shower or walking guard. Gill wasn't sure.

Four male agents were at the door. Gillian watched them from her vantage point on the couch. Automatically, her empathy registered: two were Human, one was a Shifter and one was a Vampire. She could see through the open doorway that the sun had set. They had come in either a van or a shielded limousine of some kind to have the Vampire along.

"Good evening," the Vampire said, eliciting rolled eyes from Gillian and Jenna.

Why did they do that? It was so stereotypical, Gill thought to herself, watching the procession file into the house. She could feel Charles's confusion when they didn't immediately clap handcuffs on him. He was flustered and very uptight; not that it was news. He was about to go to jail for a very long time, if he was found guilty in a Court of Law. The only thing to be decided was which Court.

Dahlia had argued that as a standing member of the Twilight Court, Charles had rights as her spouse, and could be relegated to their authority. Brant had argued right back that Charles had been killing Humans and was inherently Human; therefore, he needed to be judged through the Human judicial system.

The Shifter agent, an Egyptian named Tariq, accompanied Charles to his room to gather his personal effects. The Vampire agent, a Kenyan named Zuberi, was explaining to Dahlia in rapid-fire French what would transpire. The two Humans, Philippe and Ernst, remained by the open door, waiting for their comrades and soon-to-be prisoner.

Dahlia was crying to Gill's right, shifting the former Marine's attention from the front doorway and the two agents. She staggered painfully to her feet and moved haltingly toward the woman, intending to give her some measure of consolation before they whisked her husband off to jail.

"Is Dr. Key in?" a chillingly familiar voice with a very clipped, upper-crust British accent asked.

Goddammit, she felt like shit. She was imagining things, but that voice sounded just like . . .

"Come in, please," Dahlia blubbered through her tears. "Dr. Key is right over there . . . Monsieur . . . ?"

"Please, madam, call me Jack."

Sweet Mother Isis, it couldn't be. Not here. Not now. *Stalker! Gah!*

Gillian's head jerked toward the voice. She watched in horror as Jack the Ripper stepped across the threshold of Chastel Manor, invited in by the lady of the house.

Trocar was suddenly beside her. "Run, Captain," he hissed into her ear then shoved her toward Jenna, Dahlia and Helmut, who was standing by the Fey, thinking to comfort the woman.

"Run. *Now*." Trocar's voice wasn't loud, but the alarm in it was evident. Jenna and Helmut snagged Gillian and Dahlia respectively and tried to do what he said. Helmut and Dahlia were making much better time than she and Jenna were, since both she and the firebug were wounded in ways that made walking to the kitchen for a sandwich an ordeal. Blade drawn, Trocar faced the legendary Vampire alone. A tall, stylish black-garbed lethal presence between Gillian and a very ugly fatal encounter.

Gillian heard the gurgle of blood from a sliced windpipe before she smelled corpuscles spilling. She turned back, hand going to a nonexistent pocket with a nonexistent gun. Shit. Damn. Hell . . . and fuckadoodle doo. She was still wearing Jenna's jogging pants. No pockets and definitely no gun.

Agent number one, she thought it was Ernst, crumpled at the doorway, a red waterfall pouring from his neck. Philippe, the other Human, never got a chance to fire the gun he spun around with before he too went down, clutching at a severed throat. Jack casually wiped the scalpel in his left hand with a white handkerchief, leaving a scarlet blossom on the snowy linen. His eyes narrowed as he regarded Trocar. The Dark Elf moved almost too fast for the Human's eyes to follow but Jack noticed. Trocar sailed through the air and fetched up against the ornate fireplace after the Vampire casually backhanded him across the jaw. Momentarily stunned, the Grael shakily regained his feet, determined to die if necessary rather than permit Jack access to any of the women.

"Oh fuck," Jenna breathed as she tried to yank Gillian after her, causing both of them to stumble, Gillian teetering against Jenna's wounded leg and Jenna bouncing against the corner of the wall. Both of them hit the ground rather hard, jarring Gillian's battered insides and Jenna's leg.

Brant, ever the observant cop, began firing at the dark shape that stood inside the doorway. Claire's gun joined his in making a lot of noise as a tall brunette woman ran in past Jack, directly into the line of fire, with a large buck knife in hand yelling, "Come in, all of you, you are invited." She was either a Human thrall or a Shifter paving the way for Jack's retinue of Vampires. Sometimes Vampire protocol sucked.

The gunfire spun the woman around, but didn't stop her as she recovered and went straight for Claire. Scotland Yard apparently needed silver-tipped ammo as standard issue for the Paramortal Vice Squad. Trocar got there first; fortunately his blade was sterling silver. The stiletto flashed as he delivered several lethal blows to the woman's midsection. She folded like a lawn chair and he dropped the corpse at his feet, turning back to meet several Vampires who swept in with preternatural speed.

"Trocar!" Gillian yelled, helpless to prevent what was about to happen. She agonizingly rose from her position on top of Jenna, jerking away from one friend in her haste to get to another who was about to die. Tariq and Charles barreled around the corner—evidently they'd heard the commotion—knocking her flat again. Zuberi had Dahlia and Helmut on the floor, covering them as much as possible with his own body.

Dahlia was screaming bloody murder since this was an occasion that called for it. Two dead agents and a dead woman were lying in a red lake two inches from her delicate nose. Zuberi was suddenly on his feet, meeting the charge of two newly arrived Vampires, while Helmut and Dahlia were crawling away with record speed toward Gillian and Jenna.

Trocar was locked in mortal combat with one of their attackers. The Vampire was shorter but much stronger than the Elf. From where Gillian was lying, it looked like Trocar was about to be torn to pieces as he fought to keep the creature's fangs from his throat. Tariq shifted abruptly into an enormous Barbary Lion, pieces of his clothing fluttering away like butterflies and body slammed the Vampire away from the Dark Elf. Pavel appeared out of nowhere already in Wolf form, knocking another enemy Vampire off Zuberi.

"Dr. Key, how terribly rude of you to leave before we had a chance to chat."

Jack's voice was closer than it had been, Gill realized as she struggled to her feet, her face draining of color as she looked toward his voice. Her nemesis was standing rather close to her, away from the actual fray. This was very, very bad.

Jack was dressed in black again, no doctor togs this time. He was at once familiar yet not, his ability to shift and blur his visage like a chameleon keeping her from forming a clear picture of him in her mind, but his eyes were the same. Rust brown, an eerie cinnamon color—they were sickeningly familiar.

"Jenna, get out of here," she ordered her friend.

"Come on, run! We can make it!" Jenna yanked on her arm, trying to pull her away.

"No," Gillian said flatly. "No, we can't."

There was nowhere to go. Trocar, Pavel, Tariq and Zuberi were now all fighting for their lives, Helmut was pulling Dahlia back toward them; Brant and Claire had emptied their clips, reloaded and were still firing ineffective bullets at the Vampires while Charles was plastered up against the wall, watching the entire scene in abject horror.

"You are quite right, my dear." Jack smiled and moved suddenly so that he was around the fighters and much closer to Gillian. "I am afraid that you have been terribly naughty, escaping from the hospital as you did. You must be punished."

"Real brave of you, Jack, coming after me when I'm less than forty-eight hours post-op. Must be a real kick to feel superior to a wounded Human." Gillian was scared out of her mind but she wasn't about to let him see that she was about to throw up or faint.

He tsk'd at her. "Now, my dear girl, you really should learn not to bait your betters. I do not have any reason to fear you, healthy or injured. I do have reason to want to see you suffer."

Gill really thought she might barf then. Jack was way too close to her and his diseased psyche was leaking all over her empathy. Fighting down nausea, she backed up, trying to put more furniture in between them, like that might actually help. She heard a body hit the floor but couldn't take the time to turn her head to see who it was. Panic was fluttering at the edge of her mind. If saving her friends meant surrendering to Jack . . . she just didn't know if she could do it.

Rust-colored eyes locked with her green ones. Jack

wanted her. She could guess why, knowing the quality and length of her life would be shot to hell after he got hold of her. Still, if she went with him, her friends would be safe. Injured and sick as she was, she couldn't stand the thought of Jenna, Dahlia or Claire being butchered by the sexual sadist. Gill was a lot of things but a coward wasn't one of them. Yeah, she could do it. She wouldn't like it but she could do it.

"Let them all go and—" She didn't get to finish the sentence as an unearthly bellowing howl split the air. Everyone turned toward the sound, even Jack, whose own face paled at the sight of Charles Chastel shifting into his blighted form. Curse or not, Charles was reacting as any Shifter would when under great duress. Strong emotions could trigger a change and there were few stronger emotions than stark terror.

Dahlia shrieked and nearly climbed up Helmut like a tree, trying to get away from the sight of her husband becoming a Loup-Garou before her eyes. Helmut seemed to agree with her assessment of the situation and tried to climb the wall closest to him. Both of them collided with Claire and Brant, who suddenly developed survival skills of their own and were backpedaling away from the gargantuan beast suddenly in their midst.

The Loup-Garou rushed forward, sinking its formidable teeth into the nearest pelvis, which happened to belong to one of Jack's Vampire friends. The fanged one screamed as the beast wrenched its head, tearing away one leg like confetti from a piñata. Zuberi threw himself as far from the beast as he could, watching with the rest of them as it began shredding the Vampire into mincemeat.

Tariq and Pavel, both massive beasts in their own right, still backed away from the prehistoric Wolf as it rounded on Zuberi and the remaining Vampire that Jack had brought with him. Its sheer body mass dwarfed both the Wolf and the Lion.

Trocar frantically signaled Pavel as their friend moved parallel to Jack. The Werewolf saw what the Elf wanted and lunged, his body weight shoving Jack away from Gillian's immediate vicinity. Leverage, surprise and Pavel's heavy lupine shoulder sent the serial killer skidding toward the snarling Loup-Garou. Being a Master Vampire besides a sick twist, Jack managed to keep his feet, twisting to right himself then backing away from the creature as Pavel ran like hell toward his grouped friends.

Helmut, Gillian, Jenna and Dahlia were collectively moving backward toward the kitchen followed by Claire, Brant, Trocar and lastly Pavel. The Loup-Garou had Zuberi, Jack and the other Vampire cornered. It was stalking them almost leisurely.

Gillian had a unique flash of satisfaction as she saw the Ripper's eyes widen in fear as the Loup-Garou approached, jaws dripping saliva and blood. It was momentous watching the infamous serial killer looking literally into the jaws of death. The other Vampire was too frightened to do anything but scream as the beast pounced then tore into its midsection.

Zuberi took the opportunity to yell at them all to "get the hell out of there," as he blurred toward them, but he wasn't fast enough. The Loup-Garou plucked him out of the air like a parakeet and bit down. Jack closed his eyes, not daring to move with the Loup-Garou so close, splashing Zuberi's blood on his polished shoes. It was as if he were communing with something. As he opened them, there was a flash of triumph in their rusty depths and a glint of white as he smiled. He was calling for help. She could feel it.

"Run! He's calling for reinforcements!" Gillian yelled at anyone who would listen.

On cue, more Vampires and Shifters poured into the house through the front door and went straight for the feeding Loup-Garou. No one wanted to see how everything turned out so they all dashed out the back door, as best as they could. Trocar plunked Gillian on Tariq and Jenna on Pavel's back, picked Dahlia up in his arms and ran for the tree line, the Werewolf and Werelion passing him easily in their mad rush for safety.

Helmut, Claire and Brant were close on their heels. Nobody needed to glance behind to know they were being followed. One of the newly arrived Shifters howled ferociously as Jack's troops poured from the door, sprinting toward them. There was the possibility the new Vampires and Shifters were only fleeing from Charles . . . Nah.

The group made it to the trees, where Dahlia pointed to a large oak several meters away; Trocar obediently carried her there. The Fey tapped on the trunk of the majestic tree. There was a creaking, grinding sound and the tree's bark peeled back swiftly, revealing a dark hole. Nobody was crazy about the idea of trying to cram inside a tree but Trocar melted into the darkness so they followed anyway.

The dark entry was forbidding but no worse than the scene they'd just left inside the manor house. As she stepped inside after slithering off Pavel's back, Gill could feel the wall of wood surrounding her and a step downward. She hobbled down, grasping Jenna's hand instinctively and following Dahlia wherever she would lead them. The howls and snarls of their pursuers were coming ever closer.

CHAPTER
12

ONCE they were all inside, the bark closed behind them, sealing off the approaching hunters, who clawed and beat ineffectively at the seamless tree trunk. Inside, the hewn steps curved down and around, opening into a chamber that glowed softly with some type of luminescent lighting. Gillian couldn't tell what it was but the various lantern-like globes hovering around the room gave off a warm rosy glow.

Everything in the chamber was crafted from the living wood of the tree. Furniture, floor, walls, ceiling were all permanently placed and part of the tree itself. Fairy magic had crafted the dwelling; form and function harmonized with nature's purity. It would have been more impressive if they'd had time or inclination to appreciate it but they had an unknown number of Vampires and Shifters after them. While the Vampires would be forced to leave close to sunrise or shortly afterward, depending on their respective ages, the Shifters would be an issue to contend with as they were not bound by daylight. Jack also might have allies in the Fairy sector, who could conceivably open tree trunks. Gillian wasn't sure anyone wanted to contemplate that particular issue at that particular time so she kept her mouth shut.

"We're trapped." Gillian was close to hyperventilating and very pissed off at herself. She was a trifle claustrophobic on a good day. Besides, being wounded, rattled, shaky, hurt and perplexed by her own professional conduct on a scale of once or twice a minute instead of once or twice an hour made her cranky. Logically, she knew she had an excuse. Idealistically, she knew she could have handled everything better if she'd been able to rest quietly in a hospital bed without the threat of a serial killer stalking her across Western Europe. Realistically, she wanted to have five minutes in a locked room with Dracula, Jack and a handheld thermonuclear device.

"Non," Dahlia whispered in her breathy voice. "The tree is spelled from within. Only one of my people can open it."

"What if he has one of your people up there?" Gillian understandably wanted to know.

"That's not funny," Jenna gasped as she sagged against the wall and slid down, rubbing her injured leg.

Trocar moved back toward the entry area. "No, it is not, but it is a possibility. We do not know who or what is allied with Dracula's forces. The very fact that Jack stalked Gillian to a remote area of France suggests that he has a sophisticated network of operatives or spies."

"Who the bloody hell have you pissed off, Doctor?" Brant was pale as he reloaded his pistol.

"Lord Dracula," Gill said tiredly. "But I didn't actually piss him off. I'm allied with some folks who did, so he's after me as a bargaining chip along with a host of other Paramortal affiliates. The nutcase up there"—she pointed up toward the surface—"is an unfortunate acquaintance from London and the one who is ultimately responsible for your prostitute murders; both the recent ones and the ones back in eighteen eighty-eight. I was under the effects of Pixie venom when last we met and sort of insulted him."

"You insulted a sexual sadist Vampire serial killer and you didn't think that was an important detail to share with Scotland Yard?" Brant was clearly not happy.

"Hey, it's not like you would have believed her," Jenna defended her friend.

"It wasn't my fault!" Gillian insisted.

"Can we please focus on our immediate situation?" Helmut suggested.

"The situation where we've just run inside of a tree because a variety of Paramortal persons of interest are clamoring outside to rip our faces off, kidnap Gillian and in general make our lives interesting . . . in the ancient Chinese curse sense of the word 'interesting'? That situation? Sure." Jenna was being snarky. Gill chalked it up to the pressures of the moment. Everyone else glared at her.

Tariq evidently had his own opinions as he shifted back from Lion form. "I understand that you could not have known that this killer was on your trail, Dr. Key; however, I have three dead or dying colleagues in that house and that is a fact."

Dahlia wordlessly handed him a wrap to cover himself with. He was as naked as the re-Human Pavel, who also gratefully took a gauzy-looking coverlet and secured it around his waist for modesty.

"I know, Tariq. And I am sorry. If I had any idea Jack

was stalking me, I would have warned your Team." Gill was biting her lip and very pale.

"I am sure of that, but I need to let Interpol know." Tariq asked for Brant's BlackBerry and quickly sent an e-mail to his superiors. Gillian followed his example with a hastily worded report to the IPPA and Daedelus Aristophenes. After a moment's hesitation, she e-mailed Aleksei, telling him only that she, Jenna and Helmut had been injured in London but would return as soon as possible. Claire and Brant collectively sent word to Scotland Yard. Within a few hours the area would be crawling with agents of varying organizations. Hopefully they would manage a dragnet to snare Jack and a few of his followers.

They were able to track the time with Brant's cell phone and Helmut's watch so they settled down to get what rest they could. Gillian was looking decidedly improved when they all woke several hours later. Trocar had been able to use his healing skills on Helmut, Jenna and herself. While the Grael's therapeutic abilities were extraordinary, he needed time, reagents and his subjects in a healing trance to effect a true restoration to health.

Cautiously they ascended the internal stairs, allowing Dahlia room to open the tree again. They were met by twenty-some agents, male and female, both Human and Paramortal. Everyone had gotten the message. There was even a platoon of Black Watch soldiers intermixed with the Interpol and Scotland Yard personnel. The area around the estate was secure as was the manor itself, which was taped off with miles of yellow crime-scene tape. A tent with sort of a mobile command center had been erected near the edge of the woods where Gillian and company had been ensconced.

Debriefing everyone took most of the day and a good

portion of the evening. There were at least eleven recorded enemy deaths, including the female Shifter who had initially invited Jack into the house and the ones the Loup-Garou had chewed up. One of the French Interpol agents came down from Chastel Manor to inform them that other than the three agents, two of the Chastels' staff, and Zuberi, Charles was also among the deceased.

After sorting through the official report, adding their group's analysis to the chain of events, it was determined that after he had survived the initial invasion of his home, managing to hold Jack at bay long enough for the others to get away, he had followed the attackers into the field where their group had fled. When the troops showed up, the Loup-Garou had been indiscriminately vivisecting anything living in the field.

Seeing a prehistoric, bison-sized Wolf mangling everyone within reach of its massive jaws had resulted in a hail of silver-tipped gunfire. Charles had been killed on the grounds of his estate, his body reverting back to its Human form in death. Since none of the agents and officers had seen a Loup-Garou before, the body had been removed for autopsy quickly, to make certain he had attained true death.

Dahlia was inconsolable at first. Gillian sat with her, talking softly, offering what comfort she could. Grief counseling was just part and parcel of her training. A lot of her clients had issues with loss and angst, particularly those who had trouble with their newly reborn or evolved state. She stayed with the Fey woman all evening, waving off Trocar and Helmut, who were perched over them, in favor of allowing Dahlia privacy in which to grieve for her husband. Charles had gotten what he wanted: death by cop, but on a grander scale than he could have imagined.

A Fey representative from Scotland Yard came to visit with Dahlia so Gillian excused herself and went to find her little group. Helmut and Jenna were happily eating croissants and drinking coffee at a small table in another part of the large tent. Trocar, Brant and Claire were chatting with a knot of personnel at another table. Pavel was being examined by a medic to make certain he hadn't been seriously injured in his scuffle with the Vampires and the Loup-Garou.

Gill got herself some coffee and a beignet, grateful that she was able to perform even that small task for herself without someone hovering over her. She staggered off, exhausted, beverage and pastry in hand, for a quick bite and a cigarette; then, finding a cot, she flopped down on it to get a few hours of sleep in safety. Another night on the grounds ensued. There were a lot of loose ends to tie up before Etienne Bonaly, the senior Interpol agent in charge, was willing to let everyone go. When Gillian awoke, she was advised of current events.

The Fey Inspector had contacted the Twilight Court from which Dahlia had originated. They were only too happy to offer a helping hand to their brethren, and Dahlia was far too fragile to object. She would be met in Rouen by an escort of her own people, then taken to their lands for healing and recovery. No one wanted Dahlia to die of a broken heart, not even Dahlia it seemed. She agreed to go with her people, choosing life over following Charles into death. Gillian spoke to her and praised her choice for living. It was what Charles had wanted, after all.

Helmut had to return to London's IPPA offices temporarily but promised to be in touch and to visit Gillian in Romania soon. He would accompany Brant and Claire on their drive back to the Yard. Jenna and Pavel were going back to Castle Rachlav with her while Trocar was going off to do whatever it was Trocar did. Gillian didn't press the Dark Elf. He had situations of his own to attend to and, like the rest of his species, was enigmatic at best when it came to any sort of unwarranted self disclosure.

For herself, Gillian was both happy and apprehensive about returning to Romania. Daed Aristophenes called her to offer congratulations on avoiding an assassination attempt and to remind her that he still had her back. Gillian wasn't amused but accepted his compliment graciously, for her. She was to go back to Sacele, resume her cover and continue working with the Rachlavs and local authorities to uncover what she could about Dracula's plans. There wasn't anyplace else for her to go. Technically and officially, she was still on assignment, in the midst of a mission. That detail had not changed.

The IPPA set Jenna, Pavel and herself up in a hotel in Rouen to allow her time to fully heal. Daed sent a handpicked squad of Marines down to guard the hotel, something which annoyed Gillian immensely but she could see his point. Jack had not been caught, despite an intensive Vampire hunt in the area, and was still at large. Interpol and the military had a better description of him this time since no one had been Pixie-bit, but any detail involving Jack was a little fuzzy, given his ability to blur and muddle his image.

After a week of lounging around the lodge, Gillian was thoroughly sick of being coddled and wanted to get back to work. She was also contemplating killing Jenna since the tall brunette spent most of her time gushing over the salacious and sordid e-mails that she was exchanging with Tanis Rachlav.

Gillian wasn't at all jealous; Tanis was her friend and

she wanted him to be happy as much as she wanted Jenna to be happy. She just didn't want to examine her own feelings for Aleksei too deeply at that particular time and Jenna's single-minded sexuality toward his brother wasn't helping her keep her own thoughts in check. Grateful beyond measure best described her mood when the doctor IPPA sent over to examine her pronounced them fit enough to travel.

THE flight back to Romania was uneventful. They picked up her car in Brasov and drove back to Sacele. Gillian found her way easily without the map, much to her surprise. It was still fairly early, around nine o'clock, when they turned up into the drive at Castle Rachlav. Driving through the lower guest house area, Gillian could see Cezar's pack pacing the car and covering their arrival with excited barks, yips and an occasional howl.

In Gillian's pocket was Dante, still encased in his rocks, and in a bag Pavel carried was Grace, the other Ghost, still spelled in her stolen demi-Fey body. Gillian felt a little guilty at keeping them both in there all this time but she didn't want to bother with either of them tonight. Tomorrow was plenty of time and daylight would make it to their advantage in dealing with the errant Ghosts. Trocar had given her specific instructions on how to release Dante and revive Grace. She'd take care of it. She'd promised.

Castle Rachlav loomed before them, light gray, shingled

roof, imposing but beautiful, like its owner. Gillian parked a respectable distance from the door and they all piled out. The pack swarmed over Pavel, some in Human form, some in Wolf form—sniffing, nuzzling, with an occasional nip or protesting yelp when one trod on another's toes. Pavel was glad to be among his own kind and clearly relished the attention. Jenna was laughing and introducing herself to the group via Pavel and his lupine communication skills.

Cezar, their Alpha, came toward them from the Castle itself, followed by Tanis, the Egyptians and Aleksei. Pavel pushed through the puppy pile and went to his Alpha, kneeling before him in a submissive gesture. The older Alpha raised him up to his feet and embraced the younger man. "It is good to have you back, Pavel." He glanced over at Gillian and shook his finger in her direction. "You have done your pack proud. You kept her safe and returned her safely."

Gillian followed Pavel and hugged the older man, who scolded her a moment before handing her off to the Egyptian Vampires, who practically broke her ribs in jubilation at her return.

"Gillian! We are so glad you are back, little sister," Sekhmet cried, sweeping Gillian into an embrace then allowing Anubis to take her for another crushing hug. Gillian stopped a moment to introduce them to Jenna, who was a bit awed and amazed by the glorious Egyptians before spotting Tanis coming toward them. With what could only be described as a fangirl "squee," Jenna pounced on him while Gillian was still being Vampire-handled by the Egyptians. Tanis was a bit taken aback but he caught her and hugged her warmly, clearly glad to see her.

"We are glad you are safe, little warrior." Anubis's smile

was warm and reached his eyes. Maybe they all weren't pissed off at her after all. Noph and Montu had relaxed a bit, and hugged her boisterously, spinning her around until Tanis plucked her from their arms, Jenna still at his side.

His kiss was innocent, brief and said more than his words. He knew they were both getting on with their lives. Hugging her tightly, Tanis whispered, "Thank you for my life, Gillian. I cannot repay you for the risk you took."

She hugged him back. "No worries, Tanis. You would have come for me too."

"Indeed I would but Aleksei would have beat me to it."

Releasing her, he turned her around toward his brother, who had quietly approached, waiting until he could welcome Gillian personally. Silvery-eyed Aleksei stood in front of her in all his male glory. Tall, breathtakingly lovely, his sculpted face's harsh beauty surrounded by waves of long ebony hair, his frame large and powerful; he was clothed in knee-length black leather boots, black silk shirt, very tight black linen pants and a fitted jacket. A heavy black cape was fastened at his throat with a large ruby. The icy gray eyes settled on her own and warmed to pools of mercury, hot and burning. He looked like the lord of the manor. What he did was take her breath away.

"Good evening, *piccola*. It is good to have you home." He stood there, arms at his sides, afraid of frightening her with the intensity of his feelings, letting her choose. It was Gillian who closed the gap between them.

What the hell, she figured. She wanted to explore the possibilities as much as he did. Time to stop being a chickenshit and see where this might lead.

She stepped up to him, green eyes bubbling with warmth, her arms opening, and Aleksei swept her into his own powerful embrace, protectively, warmly, gathering her to him like a precious treasure. His mouth found hers naturally, and she was lost in the heat of his kiss.

Time stopped. There was no reality except Aleksei's arms and mouth, no feeling except what was arcing between them like an electric current. Gillian forgot herself and was soon where she'd wanted to be since she'd met him over two years before, wrapped around him like a coat.

There was a delicate cough from Tanis and a derisive snort from Jenna, who obviously sheltered no unspoken thoughts. "Get a room, you two. Good grief, now I'll have to scrub out my skull with bleach to get that image out of my head."

Gillian giggled against Aleksei's mouth and broke the kiss, turning in his arms and realizing she was clinging to his large frame like a monkey. "Dignity, Jenna, always dignity." She dissolved into laughter.

Aleksei's hot breath was on her cheek, his long black hair tickling her neck. "I do not think a room will be necessary." He chuckled softly.

His voice was pure seduction. Black velvet, it burned with a heat that had nothing to do with the blood he had consumed earlier.

Gillian turned to meet those molten silvery eyes, "Really? And why is that?" she asked mischievously.

"Because we are going to need absolute and complete privacy, *carissima*. A room would keep us far too close to the others."

Shifting her in his arms, he unwrapped her legs from his waist and scooped her up, bridal style, holding her against his powerful chest, his heart pounding in time with her own. "If you all will excuse us, Gillian will be available, tomorrow." With that, he strode off with her into the night, Gillian waving and laughing over his shoulder.

Laughing, the rest of the group shrugged, then meandered back into the Castle to get acquainted with one another. There was a little time to rest and welcome old friends home. One night was not so much to ask for those who had been long separated.

Aleksei moved swiftly through the dark forest. The stars were twinkling, the moon was at the three-quarter mark, enough light for Gillian, but he didn't need it. He needed one thing, the woman in his arms.

Looping her arms around his neck, Gillian relaxed against him, inhaling his scent, cardamom and nutmeg. She knew Aleksei and knew he meant her no harm, far from it. Where he was taking her didn't matter; they needed to examine their relationship and the Castle wasn't the place to do it. Not tonight. Tonight they needed to be as wild and free as they could be, lost in each other, enjoying their reunification.

He bore her up into the mountains, finally stopping at the edge of a remarkable glade, where he set her on her feet and turned her to look at what he could see so clearly. "Look, *carissima*. Look at the night."

She looked. The glade was silvery under the light of the moon and the stars. Soft grasses and moss covered the area, an inviting carpet of platinum for them to be lost in. Trees shimmered as the wind rippled their leaves and needles. They were high enough up to get evergreens but they were interspersed with the deciduous growth. Nighthawks circled and called, crickets chirped, and Aleksei was warm at her back.

Reaching back, she took his hand, felt the large warmth of his engulf her own. Not speaking, not wanting to break the spell, she moved into the glade. Aleksei's breath caught in his throat as he watched her walk before him. She was so small, so dynamic. Her hair shimmered with silvery iridescence and golden highlights that he could see but she could not. When she turned and looked at him finally, her eyes were fresh green pools, inviting him to cool the heat raging through him.

Aleksei needed to hold her, needed to feel her against him, needed to calm the fear that he had for her safety when she was away. Lifting her again, he kissed her, gently at first then with more passion as she responded, once again wrapping her legs around him, feeling him pressed against her body. She could feel every tight, thick inch of him, knew it wasn't simple lust that was bringing them together. He cared for her. Cared for her in a way no one else ever had. More importantly, despite her ongoing misgivings about commitment, she felt she could trust him.

Aleksei carried her swiftly to a fallen tree partially braced against a large, ancient oak. He set her down on it, bringing her eye level to him, his hands moving quickly to remove her clothing as he continued to kiss her, building the heat between them.

Leaning back against the oak, Gillian surrendered to her own needs, desires and fantasies. Aleksei was driving her wild, his kisses moving over her mouth, her neck, down her chest after he'd paused a moment to remove her shirt. Her own hands were unbuttoning the black silk shirt he wore, unfastening the cape, pushing it back from his broad shoulders, her own mouth moving over his chest, teasing his nipples and nipping him playfully.

Groaning mentally, Aleksei managed to get her belt undone and her pants down. When he found she wasn't wearing any underwear, he growled and moved farther down her abdomen, his lips teasing her flesh, his tongue making a hot trail down her stomach to the surgical scars she now bore. His heart twisted in his chest. She'd said she'd been injured. In her unique way of leaving out the important parts of a story, she hadn't told him how close she'd come to death. With an effort, he forced his mind away from the "what-ifs" and focused on the "right now."

They'd discuss her adventure in its entirety later. Right now he had her where he'd wanted her for two years. Right now was what mattered. If he broke the spell, questioned her, let his fears for her safety override the mood . . . No, it could all wait. Her scent, her flesh, her warmth was his. Now was for making her feel pleasure, making her feel loved.

Gill tangled her hands in his long, thick black hair, encouraging him along. Dropping to one knee, Aleksei parted her auburn curls and took a long, slow taste. Her gasp was his reward, and he delved into her with his tongue and two fingers, teasing her, enflaming her, opening her for him.

Reaching one hand back, Gillian popped the strap on her bra, and stripped it off. She didn't care, her body was too hot, her clothes were constrictive. Arching against his mouth, she let him plunder her body, losing herself in the sensation as she knew he wanted her to. He was in her mind, she could feel him; knew what her taste and scent was doing to him, how much pleasing her meant to him.

"Aleksei, stop. I think I already owe you one." She tried to sound lighthearted but the reality was she was very close and felt a little guilty about his selflessness.

The dark head rose to look at her, his eyes were molten metal in the moonlight. "Let go, *carissima*. Let go and let me bring you pleasure. Let me have this. There is no scorecard. Let me make love to you, Gillian."

Dammit, he was doing things with his voice that other

men couldn't do with their bodies and a whole armament of sex toys. She nodded. "Okay." Her voice sounded breathless and shaky.

He returned to his task, seemingly feeding at her font until he took her careening over the edge into a blinding orgasm. Listening to her cries, he hardened further, needing the warm depth of her body to ease his own discomfort.

Stripping off the rest of her clothes, Aleksei shrugged off his own shirt next, gathered her in his arms again and laid her on the cape beneath the tree, stretching out beside her. In the moonlight, he could see the rest of the scars that she bore from her time in the Service. Tanis had been upset with her having been hurt in the past and Aleksei was no exception. Tracing the edge of one that cut across the muscles of her arm, he looked into her eyes with a thousand questions before he moved a hand over the ones his mouth had grazed on her abdomen.

"You were nearly gutted." His voice was harsher than he intended.

"Yes, but I survived. Isn't that what is important?" She pulled his face to hers and kissed him, hard and deliberately, her own small tongue plundering his mouth.

Aleksei moaned and moved over her, his knee parting her thighs until he rested in the cradle of her hips. His powerful arms took his weight off her while he kissed her back, his canines descending. A fang nicked her tongue again, whether on purpose or unintentionally, neither of them knew or cared. With her blood in his mouth, on his tongue, he was back on the edge of her mind again. Interestingly she felt a measure of comfort rather than invaded.

"Nothing can happen to you, Gillian. You cannot be harmed." Having him in her mind again only intensified her feelings. He was hot, hard and ready for her. He could

have rolled over her mind, but he didn't; he wanted her passion to be as real as his. It was.

"*Take. Your. Pants. Off*" was her mental command to him.

Aleksei rolled off her and divested himself of his boots and pants. Like her, he wore nothing underneath and his desire for her was painfully obvious to both. Damnation, apparently both the Rachlav boys were gifted in the length and breadth department. Gillian reached out and stroked his rigid sex, watching him shudder and wondering why Vampires didn't look awkward taking off their clothes like normal people.

"Because we have had centuries of practice, *bellissima*." He chuckled, reaching out to tuck an errant hair behind her ear. When she would have moved forward to taste him, he held her back. "In time, *piccola guerriera*, in time, but now . . ." His voice trailed off as he kissed her again.

Gillian responded and rolled into him, pushing at his shoulder, surprising him with her strength and pinning him beneath her. Breaking the kiss again, she rose above him, positioned him carefully and sank down on his hard length slowly until he was firmly seated within her silken sheath.

Aleksei thought he had never seen anything so beautiful in his life as when Gillian started to ride him. Cupping her breasts, he lay back and watched her move. Her own hands were busy, one on his stomach, one scratching lightly over his thigh, driving him wild until he growled, grasping her arm and pulling her down to his mouth. Gillian sank into the kiss again, Aleksei's tongue hot and wet delving into her mouth in time with his thrusting body.

As aggressive as he was, Gillian matched him. Her passion was natural and rivaled his own metaphysically enhanced prowess. Feeling her body responding, her silken channel gripping his like wet, tight bands, brought him fuller, harder into her. Rolling suddenly, Aleksei never missed a stroke but pinned her beneath him, pushing her arms up so he could get to her succulent breasts, tease her nipples to taut peaks, without breaking their shared rhythm.

Gillian writhed against him. Her body was on fire, beginning to tighten. His mouth was everywhere; one of his hands held hers above her head while the other worshipped her breast with his mouth. The feel of him moving in and out of her, touching her deeper than she'd been touched, made her lift her hips, wrapping her legs around him and pulling him deeper into her. At once, he shifted his body to keep his main weight off her, catching her hips in his hands, tilting her body to give him a longer line, a deeper reach. He felt her reach for him in his mind, a tentative touch, questioning, and he opened for her.

"Tell me what you need, carissima, *tell me,"* he whispered urgently.

"Harder, Aleksei, I won't break." She sent him erotic images that nearly sent him over the edge. Her voice was breathless with passion; her cries were music to his soul.

He never paused, never stopped moving, but pressed deeper, reaching the point within her he sought—a silken place, past the tight bands of her canal. As he hit her squarely on the g-spot, she bucked against him. Relentless, he held her at the point of orgasm; his pace increased his own need to the same fevered pitch.

"Kiss me again," she asked and he complied.

This time, she did deliberately slide the tip of her tongue across his elongated canines. The razor-sharp edge nicked her again. The sweet spice of her blood was enough to break his concentration as once more he tasted what he craved. His hips reflexively thrust deep and Gillian arched backward into a titanic orgasm.

Feeling her body clenching and milking his, combined with the taste of her blood, sent him over his own precipice, his body gathering and pulsing its own fluid upward and out. He lifted his head to cry out his own release, his lower body driving into her then pressing tightly, welding their bodies together. He felt his own empty into hers in hot jets and Gillian's pulling him in deeper.

He waited until the last shudders ran through him, the last of his seed being pulled into her with her own sucking caress. Both trembling with aftershocks, he eased down beside her, unwilling to separate their bodies, and looked into Gillian's dancing eyes.

"Jesus. I can't believe we waited two years." Gillian smiled and traced the harsh lines of his mouth as they softened suddenly into a grin.

"I cannot believe we waited two moments." Aleksei's chuckle sent heat racing through her system again. He gathered her to him again, stroking her hair, enjoying the scent of their bodies and her own unique scent of snow-covered meadow and clover. When she moved against him restlessly, silvery eyes swept down to find hers watching him. "Yes, *piccola*?"

To his delight, she blushed. "Er . . . never mind. It's too soon."

An elegant eyebrow arched. "Really? You think so?" As he flexed his hips gently, she could feel him, still hard and thick and growing harder and thicker in time with his heartbeat.

"My Gawd." Gillian gaped at him. "How does an old guy like you do that?" She giggled as his eyebrows both shot up.

"Old, *cara?*" He swatted her lightly on the bottom in mock punishment. "I was thirty-five when I was reborn, about your age now, I believe."

"Nope. I'm thirty, genius. I'm well preserved from all the booze I drank in college."

That brought a chuckle from him. "I believe our age difference is exactly right, Gillian."

A wicked gleam came into her eye. "So you prefer generationally differential relationships?"

Aleksei's smile was positively lethal as he drew her to him. "I always prefer to have the upper hand where you are concerned."

Gill stopped him, still grinning madly. "You seem to be sexually focused, Count Rachlav."

He looked puzzled and stopped his progress toward her mouth. "I beg your pardon?"

"It means you're a horny Vampire."

Aleksei's rich laughter combined with hers and carried into the night. Just for tonight, Gillian would allow herself the luxury of loving him. For tonight they could belong to no one but each other. Tomorrow. Well, tomorrow was soon enough to take on the evils that plagued all of them now. Tomorrow night was soon enough to let everyone back in and focus on the need to defeat Dracula and drive his influence from the Realm of the Vampire for all time.

Tomorrow.

CHAPTER
14

This document shall serve to bind the alliances of: Humans and their respective Courts; the three known Vampire lineages; all Lycanthropes and their various Councils; The Realm of Fairy and The Fey, inclusive of the Elven Courts, Light, Dark and Twilight Courts and the Sluagh, who for the purposes of this document will be counted as a separate entity.

The three Vampire lineages include but are not limited to those who hold their loyalty to Lord Osiris, Lord Dionysus, and Lord Dracula. For those whose loyalty is commanded by the Dark Prince, but who wish to declare sympathy and recognition for this document, we will turn none away.

We, the aforementioned, declare that with good intent toward all and with harm to none, do put into the written word these truths:

That we recognize the sovereignty of each governing body to deal with their people by reward, endowment or retribution in accordance with the laws of each. Heretofore:

1. That we will not seek to hinder, withhold or obstruct the justice or compensation of an allied governing body if a member of such is found guilty of a crime against one of their own or of an allied group.
2. That we, the Paramortals listed herein, shall not by hand, word or deed commit harm or bring true death to a Human through pleasure, feeding or other dealings.
3. That we the Humans listed herein, shall not by hand, word or deed commit harm or bring true death to a Paramortal through pleasure, hunting or other dealings.

The term "other dealings" shall include all manner of magic or contract which the Fey or Humans may employ. The term "feeding" shall include all manner of blood-taking, blood play or sexual endeavors which the Vampires, Lycanthropes and several species of Elf or Fey may employ.

Drawing from the Human document "The Declaration of Independence," all listed herein declare these truths to be self-evident, that Human and Paramortal are created equal in accordance with their own beliefs; each with their own purpose; that they have a right to share all domains and realms: Sun, Shadow, Twilight, Shade, Dark, Blessed or Cursed, freely; with mutual respect and trust, and the goal of a peaceful existence to all.

"Damn, that boy may be older than the gods themselves, but he does know how to write," Gillian stated, her Nile green eyes taking in the Doctrine that Osiris had drafted to support their joint cause of peaceful coexistence. "I think the various factions might just go for it."

"I hope they shall, *piccola*," Aleksei said softly. Gillian nearly groaned. Even deep in intent thought, Aleksei's voice was black velvet, caressing inside her skull and down her spine. He didn't have to try to be seductive. He was sensuality itself. Standing next to him as he sat at his desk reviewing Osiris's words, she noted the calming scent of cardamom and nutmeg that seemed to emanate from his large powerful frame. She absently smoothed her hand down his long wavy black hair to rest on his shoulder. It was an impromptu gesture but one not missed by the Vampire.

Gently, raising his hand, he engulfed hers in the large comforting warmth of his own, never taking his eyes from the paper. "Of course, some may use it as a means for subterfuge but that is unavoidable."

Cronus on a cracker, his voice was devastating; reverberating through her, pooling heat in her pelvis. Gillian's head lifted away from the scrumptious scene of Aleksei in the chair, one long leg extended, the other knee bent and pulled up closer to the seat; flat stomach, groin tight and heavy . . . "*Stop it,*" she ordered him through their mental link and was rewarded by him bringing her hand to the warmth of his mouth, his tongue playfully caressing her knuckles.

Gillian jerked her hand back, meeting his amused ice gray eyes with impunity. "Stop that! We are supposed to be focusing on distributing this document. In fact"—she snatched it out of his hand and retreated to a safe distance— "I need to fax this to Gerhardt at the IPPA, and to Daed and Kimber. I'll just go do that now."

Watching the sensual shift of her hips as she stalked away from him, Aleksei smiled without realizing it. They'd had two nights with each other since she had returned from

France. Two glorious, steamy, passionate nights when they'd kept the world at bay, electing to get to know each other in every sense of the word. His body tingled at the memory of her luscious form making demands on his own.

Moments after Gillian disappeared, Tanis wandered in. Platinum eyes widened at his brother's disheveled state. Tanis's long straight hair was mussed; his burgundy shirt was tucked in but unbuttoned, exposing his broad chest. Tight black pants fit him like a second skin but only one foot was booted; Tanis held the other knee-high black leather boot in his hand. He waved a deferring hand at his brother, golden eyes flashing a warning.

"Do not say it, Aleksei."

He said it anyway. "You are looking . . . fatigued, Tanis. Is everything well?"

Tanis flopped down in a most un-Vampire-like manner on the couch, the booted leg cocked up on the couch, the other still on the floor, an arm thrown across his eyes, head nestled between the back of the couch and the armrest.

"Truly, Aleksei, I am happier than I have ever been these past two days with Jenna, but by all that is holy, that woman is lethal." He sat up and, with the ease that comes with centuries of practice, slid the boot into place before lying back on the couch, his arm again covering his eyes.

"She appeared to be very passionate." Aleksei chuckled.

One golden eye peered out at him. "She had some erroneous notion that men cannot last beyond four and one-half minutes. I demonstrated that was not the case, particularly with a Vampire lover."

"Demonstrated?" Aleksei echoed, his eyebrows lifting.

"To coin your lovely Gillian's turn of phrase, all freaking night." Tanis stretched like a cat, and winced. "If I were Human, I would need an ice pack."

Aleksei was still chuckling over that when Gillian breezed back into the room. "I just realized I am going to need Trocar to release Dante and Grace. I don't think I have the magical skills to bind him back to his own castle. And I may wind up packing Grace in a cooler and sending her back to England if her release doesn't go well." Her attention swerved to the tall Vampire draped over the couch. "What's wrong with you?"

Tanis graced her with a golden glare. "Your friend is quite enthusiastic."

She looked puzzled for a moment then a grin lit up her face. "Jenna and her sensual world of wonder?" Her giggle earned her another glare.

"I wonder if I shall survive."

Aleksei gave an inelegant snort. Gillian didn't bother to cover up her laugh. "Jenna is all woman, Tanis. Just don't piss her off."

"I do not believe I will have time to irritate her. Most of our time seems to be spent—"

"Never mind, Tanis. I'm just happy you're happy." Gill grinned at him then rounded on Aleksei again. "Can you get an international line for me? I need to get hold of Kimber or Daed and have them track down Trocar before he gets too far."

"Certainly, *piccola*." Aleksei reached for the phone to make the necessary connections while Gillian stood, absently looking toward the window across the room.

"Are you all right, *sorella piccola*?" Tanis asked quietly. He gave voice almost as good as Aleksei's. He was still her friend, after all.

"Yeah, just trying to figure what our next move should be," she responded.

"Dante . . . is that not the Ghost who molested you?"

"Shh!" Gill whispered, hushing him, glancing back at Aleksei, who was occupied with getting her an international connection and not paying attention to them. "Yes, but I still have to release him. There's no Ghost Council to turn him into and I can't keep him locked up forever, spelled in those rocks. Plus Grace hasn't done anything, not really." She tapped her front teeth with a fingernail, thinking.

"Gillian, she was planted as a betrayer. You cannot release her. She will lead Dracula here whether she intends it or not." Tanis half sat up on the couch, his eyes warm on his former lover and friend. "I do not want you and Aleksei to suffer as I did."

"Tanis, I—"

She was interrupted by Aleksei calling her to the phone. With an apologetic look at Tanis, she took the phone and found Kimber on the other end. "Hey, Kemo Sabe, what's up?"

"I need Trocar. Can you guys track him down before he gets back to the Doorway?"

There was a pause and muffled conversation, then Kimber's voice again. "You got it. Daed is sending out a chopper with one of the Brownie Mystics in it. They'll find him."

"Thanks, babe! I need him back here ASAP. That whole thing with Dante."

"No worries. I'll be in touch." They said their good-byes and hung up. Gillian turned to find Aleksei's simmering gaze on her. "Stop that."

An elegant eyebrow rose. "Stop what, *cara*?"

"Looking at me as if I'm edible."

Deep chuckle. "Well . . ."

"Never mind," she snapped, but her eyes were shining and she couldn't suppress a grin.

"I'm going to read over my e-mail and call Helmut. You boys play nice while I'm gone," she tossed over her shoulder as she left.

Ice gray eyes followed her departure, and Tanis watched his brother with a critical eye, finally saying offhandedly, "She is still a spitfire, Aleksei. I am glad it is you and not I who has to deal with her."

Those eyes flashed at him, molten silver. "I did not intend for this to happen, Tanis, truly." Aleksei's strikingly handsome face flickered with a moment of imagined pain. Tanis saw it and sat up, leaning forward, elbows on his knees.

"Gillian is a force of nature like the tide, Aleksei. She will what she will, you cannot fight it. We were not right for each other, she and I." Tanis's golden gaze met his brother's silvery one. "If I caused you pain due to my relationship with her, it is I who owe you an apology."

Aleksei rose and paced the room to stand by a window, looking out into the night. "No apology is necessary, Tanis. The two of you needed the time and the chance. I wanted you both to be happy." He turned back to look at his brother. "I waited for the time on her oath to expire, for you to make your relationship more permanent. When it became apparent that you two were over, only then did I truly consider a relationship with her for the first time."

"I realize that. Gillian and I were over by the time I was taken, Aleksei. We knew it even then. Whether I had been here or not, the two of you would have come together. I am not saddened nor angry. Truly, I am happy for you both." Tanis's voice was warm and full of caring for his older brother. Aleksei was the younger Vampire by only a few months but Tanis loved and respected him for the man he had always been.

The two embraced, glad to have cleared the air between them. Glad that the two of them, in very different ways, cared for a certain woman and that she would be their friend and in their lives for a very long time.

Meanwhile, Gillian was multitasking; she was on the phone with Dr. Gerhardt, reading her e-mail and trying to line up a few more local patients to have something to do while they waited for Dracula's latest atrocity.

"Honestly, Helmut, it's been bad around here while we were gone. Most of Eastern Europe has numerous disappearances, murders; one town in Hungary was completely spelled by some faction of the Fey. They haven't figured out how to undo it, let alone who is behind it."

"That is what concerns me, Gillian. This document you faxed to me, Osiris's work, will be helpful in delineation of loyalty but so many of the Fey, and the Vampires for that matter, use deception as a way of life. How will this hold anyone, truly?"

He was right, dammit. "All I can tell you is that the intent is to draw a very large line in the sand. If any group signs that document and then violates it, it will be considered the same as a violation of a treaty. Every other hand who has declared that document valid will be turned against them."

"That could lead to open war, Gillian. Very open war."

"I'm a soldier, Helmut. I am aware of what it means." She sounded distracted and very blunt.

"You are a healer. Do not forget that part of yourself."

That got her attention. "Healing what? What exactly have I done? Helped a Werewolf with a mild neurosis? A Vampire or two with fangxiety? Oh, and let's not forget the Ghosts. Let me see, the last two Ghosts wound up with one molesting me and one being a spy for the enemy. Yeah, I'm doing just great with that healing thing."

Now she sounded bitter and her agitation was enough to get Aleksei's attention from downstairs. *"You are an angel, piccola. You have helped me more than you will ever know."*

"Quit eavesdropping," she shot back, meaning it. He flooded her with warmth, then withdrew, understanding her need for privacy but not before receiving her brief thanks for his consideration.

Gerhardt interceded on his end. "Gillian, you are one of the most gifted and brilliant psychologists I've ever known. You have a flawless track record and an outstanding relationship with your clients. Some of these issues we could not have foreseen nor prevented. Paramortal psychology is still very new—in its infancy. *The Diagnostic Manual of Paramortal Disorders* is only in its first edition. You cannot fault yourself for what many so-called experts still do not fully understand."

Gillian flopped back against the pillows of the bed she partly shared with Aleksei, and sighed. "I know, I just feel sort of useless. I can't fully be a soldier and I can't fully be a psychologist. I feel torn between the two, Helmut, and I don't want to get anyone killed, mostly me, by not being fully aware of which side of me should be at the forefront at any given moment."

Her mentor sighed as well. There was no way to fully help her with this. She was doing the best she could in the field like so many others in their profession were, but would it be enough? He was consigned to the administrative level of the IPPA and could only give her the best advice and research that was changing on a daily basis as information flooded in from a myriad of sources.

There had always been a complete separation between the various Paramortal communities and a curious combination of disbelief and hope from Humankind. Everyone was learning about everyone else's culture, good and bad attributes, belief systems and societies, and the learning curve had gotten very high. No one wanted to screw up. Gillian and her fellows couldn't afford to.

"Gillian, listen to me. You may unofficially be the poster girl for paranormal psychology and the darling of the Paramortals for making them look good again in the eyes of Humans, but you are setting a very high level of expectation on yourself. You haven't failed anyone. Not your patients, not your friends. Stop beating yourself up and get back to work. We need you." He paused, holding his breath. He didn't want to hurt her feelings, but he wanted her to stop feeling as though her skills were in question, and kicking her a little in the proverbial butt was the only way he knew to get it.

There was a pregnant pause, then: "All right. You're right. Do you have any more patient referrals for me besides what you've already e-mailed?" Gillian was gliding over the issue, not a good sign but it meant she was ready to pick herself up and move forward. They'd examine her feelings of failure later.

"Yes, there are one or two more." Quickly he communicated the information to her, then remembering an earlier question, he added, "By the way, I think your idea to start a Ghost Group for Shattered Spirits is a good one. Some of them need to vent more than we can deal with due to time constraints on sessions. Hooking them up to have meetings several times a week might help ease their distress."

"Great. As soon as I get my former lieutenant back here to help release the two Ghosts he spelled, I'll get on it."

"Be careful, Gillian. He is a Grael."

"He is also my sworn friend. Blood oath, Helmut. He will do what he can."

"I have no doubt. Just be careful. I will contact you soon."

They concluded their call and hung up. Gillian focused back on her computer screen, pulling up a mapping site and mentally detailing a route to encompass her new local patients. It was difficult to find one which would afford some level of safety and keep Aleksei from bitching or having someone accompany her.

Aleksei had offered the smaller guest house where she had originally stayed as her temporary office. Gillian could see most of her newly acquired clients there but a couple of them were Ghosts who were bound to specific hauntings and she had to go to them. That didn't sit well with Aleksei but the Egyptian Vampires had offered to bodyguard her when he was busy.

Reluctantly he had agreed, with Gillian gnashing her teeth over controlling Romanian nobles who were still living in the Dark Ages. He responded by sweeping her under his arm protectively, silvery eyes full of amusement, and kissing her senseless. Instead of blistering his ears with a barrage of inspired rhetoric, she'd let him have his moment of feeling in control. Maybe she was going soft. Nah.

Suddenly her e-mail beeped, bringing her back to the present. It was from Kimber, reporting that they had found Trocar and he was willing to spell himself there if she was intending to release Dante. He sent his apologies for not realizing what she intended; otherwise he would have returned to Romania with them in the first place. Kimber also mentioned that the instigator for the pedophile ring had been caught and was facing trial if they could keep him alive long enough. Gillian chuckled, happy that one more scumbag had been removed from society.

After shooting off a response to Kimber for Trocar to come as quickly as possible and thanking her for the update, she flipped her computer shut and set it aside, stretching and rubbing the back of her neck to clear the tension that had gathered there. At least their mission to Russia was something she could feel positive about. Everything else, well, she just didn't know. This was the first time since she'd been a raw recruit that she'd felt so insecure about herself and her abilities. Irritated, she rose and paced the room for a moment. *I'm a good psychologist,* she thought. *I can handle this. I can put things in perspective again.*

She thought briefly about another woman she'd heard of in America: a legendary zombie raiser from Saint Louis who kept company with another Master Vampire. Gill wondered if that woman ever had doubts about herself and her abilities. Somehow she didn't think so.

Wishing she could shake the feeling of dread that was creeping over her, she dressed to go out. If Trocar was as good a wizard as he claimed, he'd be there before too long. Catching a glimpse of herself in the full-length mirror Aleksei kept in the bedroom, she eyed herself critically.

Same long blond hair, same green eyes that Aleksei and Anubis said were the color of the Nile, peaches and cream complexion despite her thirty years. She filled out the black sweater and olive green fatigues admirably for a woman on the back side of thirty. For the life of her, she couldn't see what Aleksei saw in her. Gillian had no false modesty, she knew she was pretty enough. But her knowledge and experience with the Paramortal world told her that he had plenty of choices for stunning beauty. What he wanted with a short blonde with an equally short temper was puzzling.

"Perhaps it is your short temper which intrigues me and your lovely petite body which I desire pressed against me, piccola." Aleksei's voice stroked her soul and tightened her body through his mental link to her.

"Shut up," she said affectionately, unconsciously straightening her sweater before grabbing the bag that held Dante and Grace, then heading out the door. Aleksei was one of the things she worried about. Now that she was back, in his home, in his domain, and in the beginnings of a relationship with him, her fear of commitment was a shadow in the back of her mind. What if it was like Tanis? What if they were bound together only because of circumstance? What if she got in too deep, then discovered she didn't want this?

"You are thinking too much again, bellissima. We will get through this together but you will not run from it." He sounded very dominant, very sure of himself, very male.

"Stop being bossy or I will walk out that door." Her counterstatement was just as dominant, just as aggressive, and she pushed the heat of her irritation through it. His voice was so pure and wonderful she half wanted to give him her word but his alpha nature grated on her equally alpha nerves.

Aleksei fell silent. Not necessarily a good sign, but she ignored it and went down the stone stairs toward the foyer to see if Trocar would show up. Along the passageway a painting caught her eye. It hadn't been there earlier, she was sure. Frowning, she drew closer. Eyes widened in surprise as she saw the subject matter.

It was a painting of herself, in the green dress she'd worn her last night in the Castle as she left to go rescue

Tanis. The detail was incredible, the image lifelike and warm. What pissed her off was that the image was lying on the bed in the master suite she'd just vacated. The eyes were liquid and filled with need, legs bare of hosiery or shoes, skirt almost indecently draped over her thighs. The painting was of her, of a woman waiting for her lover and knowing beyond any doubt that he would come.

"Aleksei is quite talented, is he not?" The new deep male voice startled her, and she spun to find Anubis admiring the painting with her.

"Goddammit, I have told you people not to sneak up on me like that!" Gillian shoved the Egyptian Vampire hard enough for him to step back.

Black eyes crinkled at the corners and the breathtaking Lord of the Underworld laughed in his remarkable voice. "Little sister, you are not angry about the painting, you are angry about your insecurity in your feelings for Aleksei."

"Is that so?" Gillian practically snarled. She was damn tired of everyone who was older and possibly wiser than she was telling her what she was thinking and feeling. "Maybe I'm just pissed off that he's got me looking like . . . like . . ." Words failed her and she gestured at the painting. "That!"

Anubis chucked her under her chin. "You look like a woman in love, Gillian. That is what bothers you. That it is obvious to everyone but yourself." Still chuckling, he left her fuming in the hallway.

CHAPTER

15

DEEP breaths, that was the key. Breathe and focus. There. That was better. Gillian leashed her anger with effort. In love? With Aleksei? Desire, definitely; lust, oh hell yes; but love? Not even going to go there. She stomped down the rest of the stairs, laid the Ghost sack next to the door, then grumpily crawled into one of the window seats to simmer and wait for the Grael Elf.

"Gill?" Jenna's dulcet voice sifted through her chaotic thoughts.

"What?"

The warmth of Jenna's hand moved over her shoulder, "Thanks for bringing me here. I really like Tanis."

"I'm delighted."

"Gill, it's not a problem, is it? I mean, me and Tanis together?"

Gillian turned to look at her. "Of course not. Why would that be a problem? You and Tanis are grown. He's just really old, that's all." She grinned at her friend, not wanting to take out her mood on others.

Jenna grinned back. "Okay, I just wanted to make sure." There was a moment's pause. "Aleksei is really good to you too. I've watched him, and it's nice to see you really happy."

With a final pat, Jenna sauntered off to find Tanis. Gillian was left with her insecurity until she felt Aleksei's presence in the hallway.

"Not now, Aleksei. I need to think."

Ignoring her, he moved to wrap his arms around her smaller form, pulling her against his chest and lightly kissing the top of her head. "You need to stop being afraid, *piccola*."

She turned and shoved him back, giving her room to hop off the window seat and poke him in the chest. "Afraid of what? I have been in situations all my life that were frightening, Aleksei. I don't need some wiseass fossil from the Old World to tell me what to think or feel."

Something flared for a moment in his ice gray eyes then it was gone, replaced by a simmering anger that he let her see. An eyebrow rose. Fossil? The little twerp had just called him a fossil. And here he'd been prepared to be understanding and patient.

"Fossil?" he repeated. "Perhaps Tanis was correct about you being in need of better manners." His voice dropped an octave, reverberating through her, making her shivery and damp. She was half his size and was tilting her head back to meet his metallic gaze. Unfortunately she didn't look very intimidated.

"Really? I would like to see you try," she snapped.

Aleksei moved forward, crowding her, intending to kiss some sense into her, when the front door unceremoniously slammed open. Aleksei moved with blurring speed, putting Gillian behind him as she struggled to do the same for him. He was bigger and stronger so he won. Gill settled for swearing at him as his arm held her back.

A familiar tall, dark and amazingly beautiful Grael Elf glided through the door, brushing sparks and ash off his cloak and cursing, from the blistering tone in his voice, in some unknown language. Iridescent colorless eyes, like living diamonds, lifted to meet Aleksei's stormy gray ones, then dropped to the small blonde who was attempting to strong-arm the Vampire into letting her around him, knife drawn.

"Good evening, Count Rachlav and the fair Gillyflower." The Elf's voice was lovely but carried irritation. "How nice of you to invite me for a visit." Now he was being sarcastic.

"Welcome, Elf," Aleksei politely offered. "I trust you will keep this young lady out of harm's way when you go with her to release the Ghost." The Vampire thought this was a routine release. Gillian hadn't enlightened him as to Dante's sexual escapades.

Trocar's eyes widened and he looked at Gillian, who shoved Aleksei again. "Goddammit, *move!*" She gave up trying to get past Aleksei's arm and simply ducked under it, moving to Trocar and pinning Aleksei with a furious glare.

"Of course, with my last breath, I will protect her. Not that I have noticed that she needs protecting, mind you," Trocar said, quite seriously.

Gillian shot him a grateful look and gave Aleksei another scathing one. "Let's go, Trocar. The sooner we get this over with, the better." Snatching up the bag with the two Ghosts, she marched out the door without so much as glancing at Aleksei, looking very much taller than her five foot two inches, all fire and fury.

Aleksei's eyes followed her as he said half to Trocar, half to himself, "I love her and want to understand her, but I find myself torn between wanting to cherish her such as she deserves or simply putting her across my knee for how she behaves." He raked a hand through his long hair. "In a manner consistent for a fossil of my time period," he muttered as an afterthought.

Choking back a laugh with an undignified cough, Trocar replied, "She has been known to bring that type of confusion to males of many species, Vampire. It is a gift of hers, really." Trocar flipped a mock salute toward Aleksei, then with a swirl of still smoldering cape, was gone out the door after Gillian, leaving Aleksei swearing eloquently under his breath.

Trocar caught up with Gillian as she reached the car. Beside them and in the woods surrounding the property, Cezar's Wolves kept watch. The Elf's outstanding arrival had been enough to convince all of them that he was a force to be reckoned with; seeing him with an obviously annoyed Gillian clarified that thought further.

Pavel loped up to greet Gillian, who discovered that Werewolves didn't come with brakes as accessories, as Pavel squished her against the car. "Down boy," she groused, grinning a little, unable to keep her thoughts in the dark and angry range with the sight of the pony-sized Wolf backpedaling so he didn't crush her too badly. Pavel bounced away in a very unscary-like manner, earning him a nip on his flanks from Cezar for his antics.

Gillian called to the Alpha Wolf. "Cezar, we're going to a client's home. Trocar here is a friend and with me. Please don't shred him if he is out alone." Still grinning, she got into the car, waving cheerfully, and drove off with the Dark Elf.

The ride went smoothly. Trocar wasn't much for small talk and confined himself to noticing the countryside and the beauty of the little village by night. Gillian chatted a bit about how she wanted to handle Dante's release but he wasn't really listening. He was looking for signs of magic—of Fey, Elf or Fairy influence. Gillian's questions to him in Russia had left him wondering who or what could be behind the creation of a dampening field. The wizard in him was simply curious. The friend in him wanted to make sure it wasn't switched back on if there was going to be a fight. He noted some things near the castle that he intended to investigate later. For now, he turned his mind back to releasing the Ghost and deciding how to punish him for what Dante had done to Gillian.

Boganskaya Castle loomed dark and foreboding as they pulled up in front. There was an uneasiness in the air as if it missed its resident haunter. Arkady Boganskaya, the owner, greeted them at the door. Gillian briefed him on Dante's activities and broke the news that the Ghost needed to be reunified with his haunt. Arkady looked so sad for a moment that she wanted to hug him but checked herself and patted his arm instead. "I'm sorry, Arkady, but Dante belongs here. If we dissociate a spirit from their haunt unwillingly, it's the same as murder."

The viability of Ghosts had been established through years of research by the Institute of the Ectoplasm and they were viewed as still living, noncorporeal organisms. Unfortunately most of their research had been centered around whether or not a Ghost constituted a living being. There still wasn't enough research being done on the things a Ghost actually could or couldn't do if it chose.

Arkady agreed with minimal argument. He'd missed Dante a little and his guests complained about staying in a falsely advertised haunted castle. He was afraid that Dante would be vengeful after leaving then being held in stasis and didn't want them back to square one on the Ghost's therapy. On that, Gillian agreed but they had to release him so they had to take their chances with Dante's not-so-forgiving nature.

Trocar followed Gillian to Dante's hallway. The Italian mercenary swordsman had been murdered here, six hundred years before, in an ambush. His Ghost had inhabited the stones of this castle ever since, and not pleasantly, until Gillian had been called in as his therapist.

Dante had been seemingly making progress, while concealing his growing obsession with Gillian. He had sexually used her more than once, leaving his haunt to track her to Castle Rachlav and beyond, an ability unknown to Ghosts but due to his inherently magic Grael Elf heritage. It was only Pavel's intervention that had brought Dante's duplicity to her attention and stopped it with Gillian's, then Trocar's, binding of the cunning Ghost.

Trocar helped Gillian prepare a makeshift altar on the small table she used whenever she needed to call Dante. White cloth, a copper plate, incense, willow oil; Trocar added his own implements: crumbled nettle, fennel and garlic, all for protection and banishing. He also slipped in some dragon's blood and yarrow to increase the power of what he was about to do and to effectively put a stop to Dante's sexual predation. After they released the Ghost, he would have seconds to bind him.

As a Grael Elf, Trocar was honor bound to put a stop to this abomination. He would have destroyed Dante outright but Gillian had intervened, insisting that the Ghost needed further therapy and the opportunity to get past his crime. Trocar thought he needed to be castrated at least. Gillian wanted restitution. Small difference of opinion.

Taking the stones that contained the Ghost out of the bag and brushing the salt from them, Gillian placed them toward the end of the hallway and away from the two of them. She had some skill as a minor spellcaster, like calling, binding and some healing, but she was nowhere in Trocar's league.

A full Grael wizard, the Dark Elf was a force to be reckoned with on anyone's terms. He had a deeply rooted streak of pure malice; all Grael did. But like all Elves, Grael were people of their word: honorable, noble and lawful. Serving with Gillian and her multicultured detachment had given him a deeply rooted respect for his former Captain. They were "declared friends" via a Blood Oath, which was the closest translation from Elvish in regard to a lifelong vow of friendship. So they would remain until her death or unless she betrayed him, which Trocar found to be unlikely.

He waited until Gillian placed the stones then walked back to stand next to him before beginning. "Trocar, just what we spoke of, no more." Her voice sounded loud in the deserted, cold hallway.

Iridescent, crystalline eyes riveted her way and soft layered waves of wondrous crystal white hair shifted over his shoulders as he looked down at her. "Gillyflower, I swore to assist you. I shall do what I came here to do." He gave voice almost as well as Aleksei. Too bad she knew he was full of shit.

Gillian sighed, knowing she would get no more assurances from him. "Okay, just don't destroy him."

A brilliant smile lit his perfect ebony features. "You are learning."

"Yeah, that you're an asshole when you want to be,"

she grumbled, folding her arms across her chest in an unconscious defensive gesture. "I mean it, Trocar, don't make me shoot you."

He chuckled as he made arcane symbols in the air in front of them. The incense smoldered, the herbs flared, essence of willow oil and burned landscape filled the small hallway; the stones containing the Ghost trembled then everything went to hell.

While Gillian and Trocar were headed off to do some Ghost busting, Pavel had shifted back to his six foot three inches of blond, blue-eyed, gorgeous Russian male. He wanted to chat with Kimber online since she was still in Russia handling the orphan situation and Aleksei had promised to show him how to use the computer.

Happy and energetic in either form, thanks to Gillian's perceptiveness to his former counseling needs, Pavel walked quickly in long, exuberant strides to Aleksei's library, where he found the Vampire going over some papers and visiting with his brother and two of the Egyptian Vampires, Anubis and Sekhmet. All eyes lifted at his approach and he blushed.

"Now, Pavel, you know we are going to look at you when you enter a room," Sekhmet purred, causing Anubis's eyebrows to rise at his mate's tone. She continued, teasing the young Wolf, "You cannot help but look beautiful. Enjoy our admiration."

He blushed even more but smiled as the astonishingly beautiful Vampire snuggled closer to her equally beautiful mate. Anubis chided her, "You have been around Gillian too long, Sekhmet. You are picking up her mischievous behavior." She giggled and kissed him as the others chuckled.

"Come, Pavel." Aleksei's voice was black velvet and sensual to anyone's hearing, but Pavel was more used to it and it didn't make him blush. Well, that and the fact that Pavel was straight. Sekhmet and even Maeti when she was there had teased him about his purely physical reaction to the female Vampires' inherent sensuality. The males just didn't have the same effect.

Pavel moved to where Aleksei sat and watched as he flipped open Gillian's laptop and taught him how to access an instant messenger program that Gillian had shown him the night before. Vampires that had lived any real length of time were intelligent and could pick up new skills with ease. Aleksei remembered how everything worked from one session with Gillian and now passed on his knowledge to Pavel so the Werewolf could contact his lady love as he wished.

When he had the program up and had demonstrated it, the other Vampires rose to leave to give Pavel some privacy. Aleksei leaned over the back of the chair, showing him the "talk" feature, and handed him a set of headphones, should he be inclined to use them. Aleksei started to leave only to be brought up short by Pavel's next comment. "I am glad Gillian is getting rid of that creature."

The tall Vampire paused and half turned back toward Pavel. "The Dark Elf?" Aleksei asked, puzzled.

"No, the Elf is fine. It is because of him that creature is bound. I am speaking of that foul Ghost. After what he has done to Gillian, I am surprised that she is asking for him to be released and not destroyed." Pavel's tone was of pure disgust.

"What has he done to Gillian?" Aleksei's voice was soft but so menacing that the other Vampires turned and waited for Pavel to answer.

Pavel's cerulean eyes met Aleksei's and were confused then frightened, realizing that he had revealed something Gillian may not have wanted shared. "She did not tell you?"

"You tell me." It was not a request.

"He . . . he . . . molested her, Aleksei. I thought you knew." Pavel couldn't have looked more terrified if he had molested Gillian himself.

The Vampire seemed to grow taller than his six foot seven inches, more muscular, more ethereally beautiful before all of their eyes. Aleksei's eyes went to a shade of glowing platinum that none of them had ever seen before, and within the dark ring of pupil, a red flame flickered.

Sekhmet gasped and Anubis tucked her under his arm protectively. "It is no problem, my love. Aleksei has come into his full power. He will be fine once he knows Gillian is all right."

Carefully to Aleksei, Anubis said, "Go, my friend. Use what has come unto you. Fly to her side and see that she is well." His voice was soft as if he feared triggering an explosion.

Aleksei turned at his words, his great body trembling with barely controlled rage. "She will be fine." His voice, purer and more beautiful than it had ever been, sent shivers down Sekhmet's spine; even the males longed to hear him speak again. He did. "She has to be all right or I am lost." There was such a myriad of emotions conveyed in his words that even Tanis couldn't discern his brother's state of mind.

"Aleksei," Tanis began, his own power beginning to burn in concern for his brother and Gillian.

"Stay here." Aleksei left the room, his speed increasing as he sought to close the distance between himself and Gillian's location.

"Shit," Tanis muttered, uncharacteristically swearing, and following him as best he could.

Once outside, Aleksei didn't think; his mind was a haze

of fury. Gillian had been touched by that noxious spirit. That damn Ghost should be burned out of existence.

"My friend and ally, hearken to me."

Osiris. The voice of his mentor and friend crackled through him like an electric current, warm and empowering. *"You have come into your own power, Aleksei. Use it. Shape it. Become what you need to be. You have my gifts, though you are not of my Line. Take the image in your mind, shape it as I hold it for you and go—she is safe but you must see it with your own eyes."*

Aleksei allowed Osiris's mental direction to sift through the rage that was engulfing him. Power beat through him, fueled by Osiris's command. There was a wrenching twist and shift then his vision straightened. The ground dropped away and Aleksei nearly fell out of the sky in surprise. Only the automatic beat of his wings kept him airborne. Wings?!

Moonlight cast its sheen on his newly changed body, though he didn't need the illumination to see. Above the skies of Sacele, Romania, for the first time in seven hundred years of memory, a dragon flew.

There was another voice that splintered through his head, distracting him so much that he almost lost control of his new shape and phased back to his original form. It was a scream of absolute rage from his oldest, deadliest and most hated enemy.

"Rachlav!" Dracula's voice didn't shimmer through his mind like Osiris's, it rammed in like the force of a freight train. Aleksei didn't bother with insults or niceties. Barriers he never was able to erect before slammed home, cutting off his former Master and Lord, severing their link, forever.

He didn't stop to contemplate the physics or the logic of the shift. His thoughts were on Gillian and that damned

Ghost whom he was going to put an end to. In what seemed moments, thanks to his powerful body's abilities, Boganskaya Castle was in his sight. The great beast circled, leathery wings spread wide to bank downward. The thick neck bent and legs extended for landing. Backdraft from the wings caused a minor dust storm and frightened the Fairies inhabiting the gardens around the castle. Squeaking indignantly, they flitted off to take shelter under the bushes.

Once again, he heard Osiris through their link. *"Well done, my friend. Now . . . you know your own image. Become who you are."*

"Thank you, Osiris. I owe you much." Aleksei started toward the Castle, shifting back to his own form.

"Nonsense. You owe me nothing. A new Lord has arisen, metamorphosed from the chrysalis of a Master. You are now the foundation of your own Line, Aleksei. Examination of your newfound power can wait until a later date." There was warmth, absolutely no censure and a great deal of pride in Osiris's voice. *"I am proud to have you as an ally, an equal and a friend."*

"I am honored," Aleksei sent back, then broke the connection as he reached the entrance to the castle. He had other things on his mind. Things like how to murder a Ghost and how to handle a certain woman. One thing was certain, Trocar had better be keeping her safe or he was going to be one very dead Elf.

When Arkady opened the door and found Count Rachlav standing there, he couldn't have been more shocked.

"Good evening, Arkady," Aleksei's pure, beautiful voice rumbled.

After stumbling between Romanian and English, Arkady managed to get out, "Please come in."

Aleksei swept past him, now unencumbered by the

Vampire requirement of invitation, already mounting the stairs as he tossed back, "I must see to the doctor's safety from your Ghost," by way of explaining his abrupt entrance into the other man's home.

A blood-chilling shriek rocked the walls of the Castle and he blurred with speed to get to Gillian's side, his heart in his mouth. He skidded into the hallway, drawn unerringly by her light scent. He was unprepared for what he found. Gillian and Trocar were standing practically nose to nose apparently yelling at each other. It was hard to tell since there was a grotesquely bleeding Ghost standing a few yards from them and a demi-Fey flattened up against the wall, screaming her tiny but powerful lungs out.

"What in the name of all the Realms is *that* doing here?" Trocar was pointing at Grace, the Ghost in the demi-Fey body.

"She was in the bag!" Gillian yelled back.

Trocar slapped his forehead in frustration. "You left a spelled Ghost next to another spelled Ghost that you wanted me to release?" He glared at her, ignoring the bleeding, screaming Ghosts and the Vampire who had just slid into his peripheral view.

"How the hell was I supposed to know you put extra juice into your magic?"

"Ever read *Magic for Dummies*, Gillyflower?" Trocar was digging around in one of his mysterious pouches. With a flourish he tossed something toward the screaming demi-Fey. Suddenly she looked like a Fairy mime. She was still screaming, still plastered back against the wall in horror, only now the noise had stopped.

"Thank the gods." Gillian relaxed visibly. "Remember when you put her in that pouch, you arrow-twanging dumbass?"

"Remember when I used to have superior hearing?" Trocar snapped, rubbing his ears gently upward to the pointed tips. "Besides, I believe you would say, 'I have slept since then.'"

"How could you forget something like that?"

"How could *you* forget that magic spills over anything in the vicinity? Really, Gillian, you must spend more time on your spell studies." Trocar was clearly annoyed, hands on his hips and staring her down.

"What the hell is going on here?" Aleksei wanted to know, striding forward purposefully. He took Gillian by the arm and pulled her to him. She was too surprised by his appearance to struggle, letting him tuck her against his side.

He dipped his head, brushing her hair with a kiss. "We are going to have a talk, later," he said softly, sending heat curling through Gillian's soul. She stared up at him, noticing the implacable set to his mouth and the chill in his icy eyes.

Since Grace was busy being terrified and Dante was loose again but spelled in place, Trocar and Gillian took a moment to fill Aleksei in on what the hell was going on. Aleksei listened but was not amused. "I am furious with you for withholding this information from me, Gillian. You are supposed to tell me when you are in danger, upset or harmed. I am not so much of a fossil that I do not have the first inklings about how contemporary relationships work. You are supposed to share your feelings with me. Not just your body."

He had her by both arms and his reproving tone was enough to shift the focus of her anger. "So you could do what, exactly? Hurt Dante? He's already dead! Get all overprotective on me again? Why, Aleksei? Why should I tell you anything that is going to push you over into Medieval Testosterone Land?" Gillian shook free of his grasp.

"You don't get it." She glared at him, her normally cool green eyes positively shooting sparks. "I didn't tell you because I knew how you would react. Once and for all, I am not too proud to ask for help when I need it. I do know how to gauge a situation. I can't do this on my own. That's why Trocar is here." She gestured back at the Elf, who was circling Dante. The ghost had stopped bleeding and was alternatively watching the Dark Elf and the newly arrived Vampire warily.

"If this situation were something you could have helped me with, I would have welcomed your help. As it is, I am now violating confidentiality . . . Hell, I'm violating a lot of things right now. I am trying to help my patient, Aleksei. Just let me do my job. Trust in *me* for once." She covered her face with her hands, then looked at him again, exasperated.

"He molested you." There was a wealth of fury and tenderness in that statement that Gillian couldn't fight. Aleksei's eyes were still silvery but were smoldering as he looked down at her. Her face softened as she looked at her Vampire hero. Poor guy. He meant well and she did take some getting used to.

"Yes, he did. He's going to pay for that; Trocar will see to it. Dante didn't hurt me, Aleksei. He used fantasy and his own powers against me. He is part Grael Elf. That's why Trocar is the best one to help."

"I cannot understand why you would hide this from me."

"Because I didn't want you to worry about it. I'm fine." Puzzlement clearly crossed his breathtaking features.

"Gillian, how does a man not worry about the woman he loves?"

Shit. Shit. *Shit.* He said the "L" word. Gillian stiffened, "Loves?" she squeaked, hoping she'd heard wrong.

"Do not talk, Gillyflower," Trocar interjected from across the hallway. Dante was now flattened up against the wall in front of the Elf, abject horror on his face, but he wasn't screaming. Trocar continued calmly, "Mellina, if you value my friendship, do as I say, and for once, just shut up."

Turning to stare at the Dark Elf, Gill opened her mouth to say something scathing but Trocar cocked an eyebrow at her. "Stop. Talking."

She closed her mouth and managed to look indignant. Trocar inclined his head toward Aleksei. "Go to him."

Turning back toward Aleksei, she looked into those glorious silvery gray eyes. He looked utterly stunning, powerful and very, very vulnerable. A light smile curved his sensual mouth and he held out his hand toward her—a composition of beauty, elegance and strength. Irritation melted from her and she put her hand in his, almost shyly. Aleksei drew her to him, gently, not for a kiss but to embrace her against his hard chest, feeling her mold her body to his. He lowered his head to inhale the scent of her hair—snow on the meadow and clover—letting it fill his lungs.

"Gillian." Trocar's voice made her turn and Aleksei look up. "You feel safe with him, and yes, it really is that simple. There is no shame in wanting to feel secure. Go. I will finish here."

Gratefully, she nodded. She'd have to come back and finish with Dante. Trocar wouldn't hurt him. Much. Grace was another matter. She looked at the demi-Fey crumpled on the ground, but Trocar was ahead of her. "I will look after her. Take her out of here, Vampire."

As they turned to leave, Gillian's arm slipped around Aleksei's waist, unbidden. He pulled her tighter against him, holding her close as they went down the stairs together. Gill yelled to Arkady that Trocar was finishing with Dante and walked out into the night with Aleksei.

CHAPTER
16

WHEN they left the castle, Gillian paused in the parking area, her hand on his chest. "How did you get down here so quickly?"

His smile was devastating and a little sheepish. "I have discovered some new abilities."

Gillian looked skeptical. "Really? You mean besides the long-distance mental link?"

Aleksei briefly worried that he would be unable to repeat his earlier performance if he wasn't consumed with anger, then he rallied, scooping Gillian up in his arms. No, he could do this. He would do this. The power was there; he just had to wield it. Determination flooded his features and Gillian glared up at him.

"Hey! None of this caveman shit!"

He kissed her to shut her up and formed a clear picture in his mind, then in a running leap, while she gasped from the intensity of the kiss, phased into the dragon form. A powerful thrust of his newly acquired wings and they were airborne.

"Holy shit! Would you look at this! This is so cool! Did you know you could do that?" Gillian was entranced and not the least bit worried. Trocar was right. She did feel safe with Aleksei. Safe with a Vampire. How far had her standards fallen?

Since Aleksei couldn't kiss her in dragon form, he settled for listening to her happy voice and feeling her hands investigating the scales, his neck, his jaw with the daggerlike teeth, his neck again. Better land, she was wreaking hell on his concentration. He took a lazy circle down toward Castle Rachlav. The Wolves barked an alarm and figures appeared on the yard below. Swirling down, he landed, shifting as he did so, and set Gillian on her feet.

Tanis and Jenna reached them first, "My, my, brother, you seem to have acquired a myriad of powers that we were unaware of. But I wish you had refrained from being a dragon in full view of the castle," he said reproachfully, his golden eyes twinkling.

"Why is that?" Aleksei asked.

"Because now everyone will want a dragon."

"That was so cool!" Jenna squeaked. Grabbing Tanis's arm, she asked, "Can you do that? That would be so cool if you could do that."

"See?" Tanis sighed.

Everyone laughed, thankfully, releasing some of the tension they'd been dealing with. Tanis had tried to follow Aleksei but found that he had vanished when he'd gotten outside. When he detected no distress from his brother other than his concern for Gillian, he'd left him alone but had worried. Now, Tanis, Anubis, Sekhmet and the other

Egyptian Vampires congratulated Aleksei on his elevation in status. Aleksei even received a mind touch from Dionysus, also filled with warmth and congratulations. He hoped that their combined abilities would shut down Dracula's threat at least in his village and his Country.

Right now, however, he had a matter to attend to. "Gillian." One word in that deep, soft, velvet, magical voice and she felt heat race through her, pooling in various parts of her anatomy.

"Yeah?" she gulped.

"We need to talk."

"Okay."

He stared at her a moment in disbelief. "Now."

"I said okay."

"Good evening," he said to no one in particular, shackling her arm and moving toward the castle.

Gillian spoke up. "Don't ever say that again."

He glanced down at her without slacking his stride. "Why not?"

"Hello? Hammer Horror Films? B-movies? Bela Lugosi? Dracula?" She sounded annoyed.

Aleksei couldn't help it; he laughed, feeling a tremendous weight lift from his chest that he hadn't been aware of. He had frightened her by saying "love," but she was trying. Trying, exasperating, frustrating, maddening—a powerhouse of a woman whom he was finding he did not want to exist without.

Pausing to scoop her up again in his arms, he tossed her over his shoulder, then walked unhurriedly into the castle with Gillian alternately laughing and swearing all the way, up the stairs and into their room, booting the door shut, then tossing her unceremoniously onto the bed.

Gillian bounced and rolled away from him, coming up on all fours, then watched as he slowly unbuttoned his shirt, his eyes never leaving hers.

"Did you have something in mind, Count Rachlav?"

He moved toward her like a stalking panther, watching as her breathing sped up and her heart began to accelerate. "Perhaps." Aleksei always was a man of few words.

He closed the gap between them and she didn't pull away. Their lips met; he flicked his tongue over hers, encouraging her to open her mouth for him. Tongues danced together and Gillian's hands pushed the silk shirt from his shoulders, straightening until she was kneeling on the bed. Even sitting on the edge next to her, he was taller and she had to reach up to gather his long hair in her hands, pull him deeper into the kiss.

Aleksei divested himself of his boots, never breaking the kiss. He reached for her and pulled her close, pulling her sweater up and over her head, delighted that she wasn't wearing a bra. Gillian pressed against him, skin to skin, chest to chest. She couldn't get close enough and straddled him where he sat, reveling in the feel of him, long, thick and hard, still encased in the black velvet pants he wore. Aleksei leaned back, taking her down with him, loving the feeling of her smaller, softer form fitting so perfectly against his own hard frame. When she slithered backward and off him, he reached for her but she stopped him, smiling. "No, this time is my turn."

Her husky voice tightened him further. Raised up on his elbows, he watched her as she kicked off her own boots, then slowly slid her fatigues down her hips, letting them puddle on the ground as she stepped out of them. Aleksei waved a hand, and candles sprung to life. Gillian's delighted smile was his reward. Her attention turned back to him and she motioned for him to move back. He did as she asked, sliding back against the headboard as she crawled up onto the huge bed, pushing his legs apart so she could kneel between them and unfasten his velvet pants.

Aleksei reached down to help her, but Gillian grinned wickedly, pushing his hands away—"Not a chance, Fangboy"—and slid them down his narrow hips, letting him spring free to her hungry gaze.

Dropping his pants to the ground, she crawled back up, kissing her way up one leg then back down another, her breasts brushing his aching arousal as she moved over him. She paused over his hipbones, running a hot, wet line with her tongue to the light brush of dark hair running down his flat abdomen. Fingernails lightly raked his hips, her warm breath caressed his velvet tip. Leaning back, eyes closed, Aleksei thought he would explode when her mouth closed over him.

Gillian felt his pleasure through their link and increased her efforts. She teased him with her teeth, raking gently over the sensitive head before soothing it with her tongue, gently plying the slit before sliding him into her mouth. He was too large to take too deeply but she did what she could, applying a glorious suction as she pulled up, keeping her mouth firmly around him, her hand moving on his shaft in perfect synchronicity with her roving mouth.

Twining his fingers in her hair, Aleksei flexed his hips involuntarily and groaned. She was going to kill him. That had probably been her plan all along. He just knew it. His heart was beating like a jackhammer; his body was on fire. The things she was doing with her tongue and her hands were driving every sane thought from his mind. Swearing in several languages, he dragged her up his body, trying not to be brutal as he fastened his mouth on hers, lifting her bottom and opening her thighs to settle her over him. His breath hissed between his teeth as he probed her heated entrance, slick with her own need.

Gillian shifted restlessly as he moved her slowly down, inch by gratifying inch, feeling him stretching and filling her. Aleksei was trembling; the velvety caress of her, the tight wet bands of muscle that gripped him as he entered her were winding his body tighter. He fed his feelings to her, his heightened senses, let her know what she was doing to him. As their bodies met, he pressed against the back of her canal, making her shudder. He fit inside her as though he were made for her.

Fangs broke through the soft tissues in his mouth, lengthening, demanding; the need to penetrate her in every way was hard on him, but he held back. Gillian felt the razor points with her tongue and knew what he needed, knew what she wanted to give him. She broke the kiss, feeling him seated as deeply as he could be, and pressed her hand to his chest so he would look at her. Pushing her own apprehension aside, she wanted to give him this gift.

"Aleksei, I know you've fed tonight so I am not food." Lazily, she reached up, her green eyes warm with welcome and passion, her lips moist and a little swollen from his kisses, and moved her hair away from her neck. "I want this tonight. I want to know what it's like to really make love to you, the way you would have all along if I'd let you."

Molten silver eyes searched her face. He saw she meant it, but he had to give her a chance. His honor demanded it; his respect for her compelled it. Cupping her face with his large hands, he spoke softly, his voice dropping to a lower register, setting deeper fires within her. "Do you understand what you are asking, Gillian? Truly?"

Goddess, his voice, his amazing voice. He made her

wetter just saying a simple sentence than anyone else had during the throes of passion. "Yes, I believe I do."

"It means that you will truly be mine if we exchange blood, *piccola*. There will be no going back." Right now, he was struggling not to roll her under him and plunge into her furiously as he felt fresh wetness bathe him.

"You're not going to drain me, are you?" She straightened a little to look at him skeptically, but it made him move inside her in such a way that she couldn't think straight and she clutched his arms for support.

Aleksei's great strength came into play. He gathered her to him and shifted up on the bed so she was more firmly positioned. His body pulsed at the thought of tasting her, of having her with him, and she moaned, moving on him. If she kept that up, he wouldn't be able to think. He grabbed her hips to hold her still. "It is not draining, Gillian. It is an exchange. A commitment."

Oh. That. A commitment. The "C" word. "Er . . . couldn't you just take my blood?"

He chuckled, making her squirm harder on him, and his breath slammed from his lungs at the sensation. "No. I do not want to merely taste what you are offering, *piccola*. I want to be with you. Now and when this is all over. I want you."

"Like a servant?" Her eyes narrowed.

"Never. I want my partner, my mate." He stroked her hair back. "Love, Gillian. I want love in my life. You bring that to me along with a renewed joy and interest in the world. Let me give it back and enjoy the giving." He was so earnest, so sincere, so vulnerable. There it was again. This powerful being, this Vampire, was allowing himself to be as vulnerable as she was. That made up her mind.

She looked at him, wonderment plain on her face. If he

was willing to open up like that to her, it was the least she could do to trust him. "Well, since you put it that way."

He watched her smile and it lit up his heart. This time his kiss would have melted metal. It definitely melted Gillian. She started to ride him, his fingers tightening on her hips and his arm locking her against his body as he pressed up to meet her. Somehow he shifted her on his cock and drove up and deep. The orgasm slammed into her, and she bucked as he swallowed her moan, her inner muscles clamping down and pulling him in farther.

Aleksei took over, rolling her under him, sliding effortlessly into her mind as she welcomed him, pouring his own desire and need into her. He brought her quickly up again, her passion mirroring his own as his hips drove into her. Gillian arched upward, welcoming every deep stroke. His mouth moved over her jaw, her chin, feathered down her neck, sending flames and chills through her body. The rough velvet of his tongue stroked over her pulse and she stiffened just a little.

Aleksei lifted his dark head and looked at her, never breaking his rhythm. "Gillian, I will be yours too, *cara mia*. This goes both ways." He gathered her tighter to him, still moving relentlessly inside her. "Give yourself to me, *bellissima*. This night, let me have all of you."

Consent formed in her mind, her eyes; she lay fully back, exposing her throat, fingers tight on his arms, her legs wrapping around his hips to pull him in deeper. Aleksei shuddered. The sight of her in complete surrender turned his heart over. His dark head bent, their hair, gold and black, intermingling on the pillow and at the juncture of their bodies as he brought them together over and over. Gill felt his teeth scrape gently, his tongue smoothing over her pulse, then fangs pierced deep.

Intense pleasure, so close to pain that she gasped, roared through her. The deep pulling at her throat as he drank echoed the thrusting into her body and she careened over the edge of another explosive climax, crying out against his shoulder, biting him as she tried not to scream. Her teeth weren't sharp enough to pierce him but Aleksei jerked, his pace increased, his body moving faster and harder. The taste of her danced on his tongue, sweet, hot, a soul's addiction. He swirled his tongue over the tiny holes, sealing them.

Reaching up, he slashed a small opening in his throat, then cupped her head, turning her mouth toward him. Gillian was too far into the seemingly endless climax to think, her body clenching over his, releasing, then grasping again. Aleksei supplied the illusion of need, her mouth fastened onto him and she took what he offered. She felt a brief moment of surprise when his blood flowed into her mouth. Realizing at once that he was making it pleasant for her, she relaxed and drank from him, thinking this couldn't be worse than anything else she'd ever swallowed in her life.

Instantly she felt him harden further, thickening, lengthening in anticipation of his climax. They were spiraling up together this time, but he held them at the pinnacle, increasing their pleasure to a fever pitch. She bit down, hoping to provide what he needed. Aleksei reacted, his hands tightening on her as he began almost frantically plunging into her, driven to the edge of his control by her attempt at Vampire Sexuality. Holding Gillian as tightly as he dared, he softly commanded her to stop before he lost his careful inhibitions with her completely. He moistened his finger with his saliva and sealed the small opening in his neck, then bent to take her mouth as he dropped his control and let them both fall into a glorious, explosive void.

Both of them cried out into their kiss, Gillian pouring over him and Aleksei pouring into her. Their bodies were welded together as he strained at the apex of his final thrust, throwing his head back. She watched the tension flow over his face, then relax as the rush came; felt his deep heat bursting inside her. She couldn't pull him in deep enough, get enough of him within her, though he was buried to the hilt. The waves kept coming in another endless climax and left them clinging to each other for stability.

Immediately he rolled to keep his weight off her and pulled her bottom tightly against him, not wanting to relinquish a centimeter of her warmth. Gillian ran a finger along his chiseled jaw, and his silvery eyes swept down to meet hers. He was smiling with contentment. The woman he loved was in his arms, and he was deep within her body.

"Did I hurt you, *bellissima?*" he asked gently. Gods above, his voice nearly made her climax.

"Of course not." Gillian smiled, shivering. "I love your passion, and I love making love with you." Oh no. That breathy voice again. What the hell was wrong with her? Jesus, she sounded like a soap opera heroine.

"But?" he pressed her.

"I think I love you, but I'm not sure," she said in a small voice, quite unlike the Gillian he knew. A faint blush rose to her cheeks and she looked away. Dammit all to hell, he did make her feel safe. Fine. She'd go with it. She let herself snuggle closer against his hard chest.

Chuckling, he cradled her head to his chest, letting her hear his rioting heartbeat slowing to a normal level. She loved him. She was just too scared and too stubborn to admit it. That was all right. He could live with things the way they were until she was ready to tell him and to admit it to herself.

Gillian fell asleep in his arms. Aleksei watched as her breathing changed to the deep, slow respiration of sleep. He stayed to watch her for a while, wanting to let this moment go on a little longer. When he finally disengaged from her body, he felt deprived of her warmth. Their combined scents lingered in the room and he began to harden from the memory. Watching her, he knew she was too tired for anther round of lovemaking so he tucked her in tenderly and let her sleep, brushing a kiss over her forehead as he gathered his clothing and left without a sound.

Gillian woke late in the afternoon the next day as the sun was descending. She stretched and immediately wished she hadn't. Every muscle was wound tight and ached. Gingerly she set her feet on the floor and wobbled toward the shower. Standing in the steaming water, she felt her muscles relax. Well, most of them anyway. Thank all that was holy, she wouldn't have to walk much or ride horseback. Aleksei's and her combined enthusiasm the night before had left her a little tender. Tanis's similar predicament with Jenna flashed through her mind. Karma. Definitely karma. This was what she got for snickering at the Vampire's situation after Jenna had worked him over.

Dried and dressed, she appraised herself in case of inspection by her sharp-toothed friends. Who was she kidding? She'd be inspected all right. Neck check. Hmmm, no marks. How did he manage that? Lips, a little puffy, can cover with light lipstick—nope, a dead giveaway; she rarely wore it. Eyes bright and clear, complexion normal, not pale or flushed. Hair, damp but otherwise manageable. Experimentally she walked away from the mirror, then turned and walked toward it, a smallish figure in her cargo pants, hiking boots, brown short-sleeved shirt and safari vest. *Ack!* Even to her eyes her walk was careful. Good Lord, she couldn't go downstairs yet. Trocar was probably there and Tanis, not to mention the Egyptians.

A soft knock on her door startled her, "Yes?"

"May I come in, *cara*?"

Aleksei. Hooray for early-rising Vampires.

"Sure."

He moved into the room with that mesmerizing grace only a Vampire or Elf could manage. Goddess, he was gorgeous. Black velvet pants again but these were laced up the front, tucked into calf-high velvet boots. His shirt was dark burgundy, no lace, but silk. It had no collar and allowed his hair to shift in a most becoming manner over his broad shoulders. Smiling, he bent to wrap her in his arms and kissed her. Gillian started to protest then relaxed into his embrace. Pressed against him, she could feel the strong demands of his body, smell his comforting scent, cardamom and nutmeg. Hell, he was hard already. And now she was wet. Wonderful. They had to get this out of their system or they'd be crawling all over each other everywhere.

"That is a delightful thought, piccola," he murmured in her mind, making her breasts ache and her pelvis clench. Her scent called to him and he released her with effort, knowing she had other things on her mind besides him, regretfully.

Laughing, she turned away, grabbing her backpack and notebook. Aleksei immediately noticed her stiffness and careful walk and swore, *"Dio, innamorata,* I have hurt you." He was at her side instantly, caressing her back, turning her face up to him. "Gillian, I am sorry if I was too rough with you."

She smiled up at him and turned her mouth to kiss his palm. "No, we were both a little enthusiastic. I'm just a little tender. It's no problem."

Heart melting at her defense of him, he bent to lift her and sit her on the bed. "Take your pants off," he ordered her.

"What?" she snorted. "You and I just got up. You need to feed and get to your meeting and I have got to go back to Dante's and get a situation resolved. Oh, and I will take Trocar with me, so don't worry." Scooting forward, she tried to move around him, but he held her shoulder and pressed her gently backward until she was flat on her back, her butt on the edge of the mattress.

"My saliva has healing properties."

Shocked, she looked up at the most wicked smile she had ever seen on anyone grace his sculpted face.

Embarrassed, she covered her face with her notebook. This was just mortifying. Here he was offering to . . . She suppressed a shriek when he stripped her pants down to her ankles and pressed her legs apart, opening her fully to his scalding hot gaze. He knew she was wet and ready prior to looking at her. Before she could smack him with her notebook, he knelt; his hot mouth fastened on her and she stuffed her fist in her mouth to stifle the scream that rose in her throat at the first touch of his tongue.

Aleksei held an arm across her pelvis, holding her still when she would have wriggled away. His tongue stroked and caressed, covering every soft, delicious fold and every sweet valley. His other hand held her open, her flesh deep pink, swollen and tender. The taste of her and her small cries hardened his body to a painful ache but he pushed his own need down to attend to her.

The orgasm jolted both of them. Gillian lifting her hips,

instinctively pushing against his tongue, Aleksei making a guttural sound in his throat and clutching her tighter to him. He let her go after the quaking in her body stopped, then rocked back on his heels and took her hand to pull her up.

"Better, *piccola*?" His eyes glowed with male satisfaction but his smile was soft and gentle.

Blushing, she nodded an affirmative. "Uh, yeah, thanks, Aleksei."

What did one say when one's Vampire lover just blew your mind with the best oral sex of your life because he could heal you with his magical saliva? Hopping off the bed in front of him, she yanked up her pants, fastening them with an ease born of long practice. She glanced at him, his arousal very evident against his thigh. "I can't leave you like that." She started to remove her pants again but he stopped her.

"No, *bellissima*. I have not yet fed and it would be dangerous for you." Gently he closed her fatigues, tucking her shirt back in and kissing her head affectionately. "We will let my healing abilities do their work, and later tonight, you can do as you wish. I am yours."

Sweet Hather, his voice was incredible. She wanted him all over again just looking at him, smelling him, seeing her effect . . . She jerked her mind back to reality and laughed, knowing he knew. He found it charming that he could make her blush, and chuckled with male satisfaction. Her hand covered her eyes, and she shook her head, feeling unsure.

Enjoying her normally confident persona's journey into unknown territory, he said teasingly, "Do you think once was enough?"

"Bite me." Realizing what she said, she clapped her hand over her mouth, eyes wide. "Shit! I didn't mean . . . !"

Smiling, he rose, towering above her. He snaked an arm around her, pulling her against his heavy erection, leaned in and whispered warmly in her ear, "Later, *bellissima*." He popped her on the butt before taking her hand and, ignoring her blistering diatribe about chauvinism in sexual situations, led her downstairs. Gillian was halfway down before she realized her delicate bits didn't hurt anymore. His saliva really was healing. Hell, who knew?

Trocar was lounging in the library, leg over the arm of a chair, seemingly engrossed in a book. "Are you two quite finished?" he asked without looking up.

Aleksei raised a hand to hide his smile, chuckling, and Gillian thought she just might shoot herself and spare everyone the embarrassment. "Hera's hackles, Trocar, have you no sense of decorum?"

The crystalline-haired head rose that time as he snapped the book shut. Laying it on the table next to the chair, he stood, fluttering his cape over his shoulders. "Of course, Gillyflower. I am the soul of discretion." Icicle eyes raked over both of them. "I see you are well. Are we ready to go?"

"Yes."

The tall Elf mirrored Aleksei on one side of her, grinning to beat hell. "You are certain."

"You are expendable, you realize that, don't you?"

Ruffling her hair, he winked at Aleksei. "She is crazy about me, you know." As he walked past the pair, he said to the Vampire, "I grow on you."

"I can see that." Aleksei returned the smile. Though ethereally beautiful and close to Gillian, the Elf was no threat to him. He'd been in her mind and knew the Elf regarded her as an attractive Human, even teased her about sex with him, but his loyalty to her was absolute. That trust would not be broken.

Trocar shooed Gillian out the door as she swept past him. Aleksei headed out to check the village as he did nightly. He visited with the local Humans and checked on the Vampires in his immediate territory to ensure no more murders had taken place. He'd called a meeting for that night with the local Fey, hoping to solidify some alliances. He knew Trocar's intent was to diffuse the dampening fields since the Dark Elf had asked him to inquire about the area Fey's assistance before he'd gone up to get Gillian.

Back at Dante's abode, Gillian and Trocar entered the hallway. Without her compulsion or calling, Dante shimmered into view, dressed and whole. "*Dolcezza*, I humbly beg your forgiveness for intruding on your life," he said with head bowed and his hands in front of him as if in prayer.

"Intruding? That's a nice euphemism for sexual assault," Gillian said harshly.

To her surprise the Ghost nodded; his clear turquoise eyes held shadows. "Again, I insult you. I am a monster, Gillian. What I have done, I have never before done in all my years on Earth, both dead and alive." He seemed sincere but Gillian wasn't buying it yet.

"What did you do to him?" she hissed at Trocar, who gave her an all-too-innocent look, his hands out and open as he shrugged. "Sonofabitch," she whispered, turning back to Dante.

"I don't believe you," she said flatly.

Dante visibly cringed. "*Dolcezza*, what can I do to make this right? I need your help. I know this now."

Tapping her forefinger on her teeth, Gillian thought for a moment. Her mind drifted back to her conversation with Dr. Gerhardt. "I tell you what you're going to do. You are going to help rally all the agonized spirits in the area for some group therapy. Maybe a little peer pressure will help you mend your ways."

He floated a little closer to her, nodding. "*Sì*, yes, *grazie*, I will do this for you."

Gillian held up a hand, her eyes narrowing. "That's close enough and you bet your ass you'll do it. A rapist anything is at the top of my 'Needs Killing' list. You pull that crap again with anyone, and I will have you exorcised and destroyed, is that clear?"

She'd gotten word from Dr. Gerhardt that since Ghosts didn't have a governing body, per se, there was an old obscure law that, while never written down, was accepted by most religions. A hostile-acting Ghost like Dante could be deemed a menace by any religious authority and a healer and be summarily banished, exorcised or destroyed, if possible. Gillian was the "healer" and Trocar, while a wizard, was a sort of cleric in his own society—something that she found interesting, but it did explain his healing abilities. Dante had two willing votes to nail his ectoplasmic ass to the wall. He damn well would cooperate.

"*Sì, dolcezza*, very clear." Her empathy flared. Dante wasn't lying but he didn't like it. Tough tombstones. He'd do it.

Another thought occurred to her. "Where's Grace?" she asked Trocar, while Dante wrung his hands and looked convincingly sorry.

"She wanted to go outside into the garden." The Elf pointed at Dante. "He was glad to see her go. The noise, you see."

"There are Fairies in the garden, Trocar!"

The Dark Elf had the grace to look sheepish. "I shall go retrieve her. After you finish with the Ghost, I am to meet with Aleksei and some of the local Fey so please do not dawdle." He swept from the hall.

Dante's richly accented voice got her attention again. *"Dolcezza?"*

She rounded on him. "Back off, Dante."

His hands came up in a reflexive gesture. "I truly mean you no harm. The Grael explained the ways of our people and I am forbidden to touch you ever again."

"Or what? You're already dead." That was mean as hell, but she felt better for saying it. Plus he paled and his eyes widened in fear.

"No, Gillian, you do not understand. For the Grael, and I am one, if only a diluted bloodline, there are worse things than death. I do not wish to contemplate where Trocar would send me should I break my vow."

"I see." She watched him critically. "I can't see you anymore as a therapist, Dante, you know that." He nodded and kept his eyes averted. "I will make sure you get appropriate help but you compromised our relationship the first time you took advantage of me. If I had known you were behind it, I would have stopped seeing you long ago." Her voice was positively chilly. He got the message.

"Again, I am sorry. I know it is not enough, but it is all I can give." Dante finally looked up at her, studying her face. "In all my years, I have never done such a thing. It was as though I were being influenced, controlled."

Gillian cocked an eyebrow at him. "Don't even start with the 'voices in your head,' Dante. You're a Ghost. And we are done. I wish you the best and hope you can heal."

She started to turn away to leave when she stopped and turned back to him, fishing a business card out of her notebook. "Dante, you need to know that bringing Trocar here last night, then Aleksei storming in, was a violation of your confidentiality. That was my fault. If you wish to file a complaint against me, here's my card with the IPPA's number on it. Call them and file a complaint with Helmut Gerhardt if you wish." She laid the card on the table near the Ghost.

Dante denied that he would file anything but praise on her when Grace fluttered in, followed by an annoyed Trocar. "She insisted on speaking to you, and I could not convince her otherwise."

"Gillian, please, miss. Can I . . ." Grace's voice trailed off as she looked at Dante, who was standing in all his male glory and not bleeding all over everything. The swordsman Ghost's eyes flicked up toward her, and she was caught by their turquoise regard.

Dante even seemed to see her for the first time. "You are not a demi-Fey, *piccola*." He was puzzled. His inherent magic allowed him a multitude of abilities. Dante knew magic when he felt it. There was magic here but it wasn't Grace herself; it was around her and in the body she occupied.

Suddenly there was the distinct feeling of sex in the air and Grace's noncorporeal eyes glazed. Shit. Dante apparently either had Ghost attention deficit disorder or he was still heavily into denial about his sexual predation because he was just moving along, turning on his charm and sex appeal for Grace as if he hadn't just nearly had a Grael wizard's metaphysical boot up his transubstantiated ass for assaulting Gillian.

Grace shook her head as if to clear her thought and shared with Dante how she wound up in the hands of Gillian and her crew. Gillian pulled up a chair to watch.

Ghost peer therapy, Goddess, she didn't see this coming. She felt Trocar move in behind her, his hands beginning to absently rebraid her hair while they both waited for the Ghosts to stop talking.

Trocar's hands were gentle and soothing. Gill felt herself drifting a little and paying less attention to the Ghost's discourse. Lost in thought, she jumped when the Dark Elf cleared his throat meaningfully. Looking up, she saw both Dante and Grace in front of her.

Yup, Dante had swept all of yesterday and today into some dark corner of his twisted psyche, ignoring the fact that his ego was what had gotten him into trouble in the first place: narcissistic personality disorder. That was going to be fun to work with. Gillian didn't envy his next therapist. Dealing with Dante was seriously a bitch. He was staring at Grace as if he'd devour her. Grace was blushing. Holy Revlon. Ghosts could blush. Who knew?

"Miss? I want to ask, can I go back to what I was?"

It was Trocar who answered, "You want to again be a spirit? Out of this body you now inhabit?"

Grace nodded solemnly. "Yes, please. I am a simple lass, flitting and fluttering around in this small body. I can't see Tanis anymore anyway." She sounded sad and a little lost.

"Grace," Gillian began, "you can go back to England, close to where we found you if you wish, and you don't have to stay in that body if you don't want to. You're here because we brought you. I will be happy to take you back there if it is what you want." As an afterthought, she added, "No, I'm afraid you can't see Tanis anymore. He is still healing."

That was a small white lie. Tanis was fine, but he wanted nothing to do with Grace, who had been a spy, a plant, for

Dracula and was meant to lead the Dark Lord to Aleksei. Gillian saw no reason to hurt the woman's spirit further.

"If it pleases you, miss, I would like to stay here." Grace flitted a little closer to Dante. "That is, if it is all right with Sir Montefiore?" She made it a question and looked at Dante.

"It is all right if you wish to remain here, in my hallway with me, *piccola*. I would enjoy getting to know you." Dante smiled brilliantly. "I would like to see your true form as well."

Grace blushed. "Then I will stay." She looked at Trocar. "Can you undo this thing you have done?"

The Dark Elf looked impatient, then murmured a few words, which they all heard but which seemed to melt away into the air, not to be remembered. He made several runic gestures. There was an audible "pop" and the demi-Fey body crumpled to the ground, lifeless. Grace swirled up and away toward the ceiling, spinning and expanding until she floated down, formed as tightly as a normal Ghost could be.

She was actually very pretty, Gillian noticed, fairly tall, about five foot six with a slender build and small, shapely breasts. Curly brown hair pulled back in a Victorian hairstyle, a dress which was modest but nicely made in dark blue with lace at the cuffs and throat. Her eyes were a warm hazel surrounded by dark brown lashes, her mouth generous and full. Grace was staring unabashedly at Dante, who was turning on the charm.

"Why, you are lovelier in your own form, *dolcezza*, than in that Fairy body." He took her hand and kissed it while Grace giggled and blushed, then curtsied to him. Dante tucked her hand in his arm and began to walk with her toward the end of the hallway, speaking softly to her. Wherever he touched the lady Ghost, she seemed more solid, more like him. *Interesting,* Gillian thought, glancing at Trocar. She saw he noted it too.

She gathered their things then followed the Elf downstairs to ask Arkady's permission to let Dante have his Ghost Group somewhere on the premises, twice a week. Arkaday was accommodating as always, believing that he would attract more tourists with the show. Then she dialed Helmut Gerhardt at the IPPA, explained the situation and how they had handled it, and about the confidentiality issue. He made note of it but felt that there was sufficient reason for caution after everything that had happened owing to Dante's molestation of her. The reason for the wizard's involvement was an ethical and legal one to determine Dante's fate. Since her own personal safety concerns were at the crux of that involvement, he saw no reason to sanction her, especially since she was hell-bent to get the Ghost help rather than opting for revenge, though she had a right to request it.

Gillian was grateful, acknowledged that she had his list of new clientele then requested a new therapist for Dante and Grace, who would need some adjustment counseling. Feeling satisfied that she'd covered everything as best as she could, they drove off to the places Trocar had marked to investigate the dampening fields Aleksei felt had been in place.

CHAPTER
17

PULLING over to the side of the road where Trocar indicated, Gillian flipped open the trunk and took out a non-UV flashlight, glancing at the moonlit meadow they paralleled. Trocar, like most Paramortals, could see just swell in the dark. The moon was almost at three quarter, but it was dark enough for Gillian to break her leg if she stepped in a hole or tripped over a tree root. He waited for her, impatient to know who or what had put dampening fields up around the village and the surrounding areas.

Just for shits and grins, she'd also brought her gun. No sense in being stupid was her thought as she hurried to catch up with Trocar. The tall Elf strode noiselessly through the field, elegant, noble looking. Gillian tried to match his stealth; for a Human she was quiet. She'd had to stalk living prey before on Black Ops missions. To the Elf's ears, she was going to alert everything in a three-mile radius to their presence and he shushed her.

Gritting her teeth and swearing silently about all pointy-eared beings of note, Gill focused on being lightweight and at one with her environment. When Trocar didn't turn again and smirk, she felt redeemed. So she was a little out of practice, she could slide right back into her profess—*branch!*

There was a loud crack as the bit of old tree limb, concealed by dirt and grasses, was destroyed under her boot. Trocar whirled and the stiletto he snapped toward the unknown enemy who was obviously sneaking up behind Gillian whizzed by her ear to embed in a tree some distance behind her.

To her credit, Gillian didn't shriek at the sound of a needle-sharp blade whirring by in close proximity to her face. She did pale a bit and glare reproachfully at the Dark Elf, who looked both disgusted and relieved that he hadn't just killed her inadvertently. There was a sudden crack of thunder and the smell of ozone in the air as lightning scored on some unfortunate tree. Trocar had noticed the clouds gathering earlier, but since Human visual skills were more limited at night, Gillian twitched a little at the sound then recovered, moving along toward him. She hoped that the rain would wait until they checked out whatever it was Trocar thought he saw in the field.

"Lower your shields." Trocar's suggestive voice was a musical whisper on the wind. Gill obeyed him, opening herself to her surroundings and clamping a firm barrier between herself and Aleksei should he inadvertently eavesdrop.

Instantly she felt it. Pulsing. First a deep thrumming, then weaker and weaker, then back to a fairly strong pulse again. Magic. Trocar was drawn to it through his sensitivity to magic, and his entire aura vibrated like a tuning fork. Gill was drawn to it through him. But wait, there was something more here. Something that felt anticipation. Felt, eager. It recognized Trocar as a magical force and reached for him.

Trocar went to a small, innocuous-looking pile of rocks. As Gillian approached, she could see they weren't just jumbled together but stacked in a tiny cairn shape. The Dark Elf stalked around the little structure. It was placed up against the hollow of a dying tree, unseen from the road or by a casual walker. They would have missed it if they hadn't been searching with their combined talents. Gillian watched as he held his hands out toward the object. The moonlight, not yet obscured by the fast-moving clouds, glinted off his ebony skin and crystal white hair, giving him an ethereal glow.

Murmuring ancient words of magic, Trocar painstakingly unraveled the spell. It was as he thought. The spell itself was rather rudimentary, not the work of a powerful wizard but rather of several lesser magic users. Careful not to be overconfident, he took his time, dissipating the field, which was already corrupting and weak. As he finished, a wave of his hand obliterated the little structure. He knelt and swiftly rebuilt the stones. The new pattern was subtly different than the old one. Only a true wizard would be able to tell the difference.

Gillian was scanning the area as Trocar worked. She didn't fancy any uninvited entities sneaking up on them. While she was preoccupied, Trocar's hands moved swiftly to place wards over the site. Anyone tampering with it magically would be in for a nasty surprise. He didn't share that with Gillian, though he doubted if she would have minded. If a child or other innocent found the stones, the spell would have no effect. Grael Elves had their own concepts of Karma, and Trocar didn't want any innocent blood on his hands.

When he was through, they headed back toward the car until Trocar caught the sense of more of the fluctuating thrumming of magic gone awry. He moved to retrieve his knife then shifted toward the feeling. Gillian felt it through him again and automatically adjusted her direction to keep up with him. Feeling more apprehensive than she would have admitted, she held the Glock against her thigh as she walked. Something wasn't right. She could feel it but couldn't yet identify what it was.

Big, fat raindrops began to fall on the pair as they crossed the moonlit road and headed up the mountain into the forest. The sharp odor of wet macadam hit the air. Trocar glided smoothly. Gillian paced herself; her legs were shorter and she compensated by zigzagging up after him. Her skin prickled; whether just from Trocar's aura, the chilly rain hitting her, the darkness after the moon disappeared into the heavy clouds or from the dampening field, she couldn't tell. The prickling was familiar somehow. She couldn't quite put her finger on it. Something during her graduate studies on identification and mollification of species via empathy. What *was* it? Irritated with herself, she trudged after Trocar, seeing him stop by a cairn similar to the one below them in the field.

Without warning, the side of the mountain opened with a dull clanging sound. Trocar was faster and moved back, suddenly producing a wicked-looking Elven knife from somewhere in his robes. Gillian barely had time to bring her gun up when she heard a distinctive "flap, flap, flapping" noise.

That, combined with the prickling feeling, snapped her

memory circuits on and she knew. So did Trocar because they both half turned to the other and hissed, "Goblins!" at the same moment before a mass of the underground horde burst out of the opening and were growling and snarling at the pair, complete with armor and very sharp pointy lances all leveled at her and Trocar. An advance guard of Goblins. How festive.

Cronus, they were hideous or they would have been if she could have seen in the dark better. Goblins came in all shapes and sizes, all of them ugly as hell and twice as nasty. It was rumored that Goblin royalty were actually beautiful beings but with the same charming disposition as the rest of their horde.

Bipedal and ranging from about Gillian's height to very tall, the Goblins sported grayish green skin with assortments of warts, pustules, facial anomalies and scars. Their eyes were oversized and would have been luminous except they ranged in color from ragged spider web, a dull corpse gray to the flat matte black of the Abyss. Their eyes were completely uniform in color, no whites showing, and their pupils were vertical slits instead of round as with the rest of Fairies. Ugly as they were, Goblins were card-carrying members of the Fairy Realm and made sure no one forgot that.

Shit, there were about twenty of them, Gillian thought. There was no way in hell the two of them could take them all in a direct fight. Okay, time for diplomacy. Yeah, diplomacy. The art of saying "Nice Goblin" until you found an incendiary device and blew their ugly butts to Kingdom Come. Mentally she shook herself; she was a psychologist, dammit, not a soldier anymore. She would solve this through her professional skills and empathy, not firepower.

"Greetings, dwellers of the deep places," she began, trying like hell to remember cultural diversity with regard to Goblins who had a mind-set toward potentially gutting someone. "To what do we owe the honor of a Goblin Guard?"

Pouring her empathy toward them, she reflected a non-hostile attitude and concern for their collective welfare, with a bit of badass thrown in. No sense in seeming defenseless. She carefully kept her face and tone neutral, not wanting to belie the feelings she was projecting. It wasn't easy. The Goblins were ugly as vultures on a manure cart and smelled about as enticing.

There was an icky-sounding collective grunting and chittering among the unsightly assemblage. The shortest, thickest and ugliest one spoke in a voice that was deep and gurgling. "Why does a Human and an Elf come near our doorway?"

Goblins. Why did it have to be Goblins? She liked them about as well as she liked Pixies. Not! At least they spoke Common English because her Goblinese sucked. "Well, we were just . . ." Gillian began, frantically thinking about a plausible excuse for them to be there. Trocar's silky arm and silky voice surrounded her.

"I think that the reason would be obvious to such connoisseurs of Human delicacies." Trocar leered at her suggestively as she pondered whether to be a good bitch and cooperate or a bad bitch and shoot him in the knee again. Diplomacy. Right.

She decided to cooperate and leered back at Trocar for emphasis. "The Dark Elf made me an offer I couldn't refuse," Gillian added helpfully, wondering just how deep in shit they were at the moment.

The Goblins decided for them. "You lie!" gurgled the

short one, who appeared to be the leader, rattling his spear and repositioning his crotch. Goblin weenie grabbing must have been a signal of some kind because they collectively yelled and rushed the pair. Twin knives leaped into the Elf's hands.

How the hell did he do that? Gillian wondered, crouching slightly and rapid firing with the Glock at anything ugly that moved. The Dark Elf always appeared unarmed, producing weapons of deadly force in a heartbeat. It was one of the reasons he was so effective as an assassin. No one noticed that he was literally bristling with hidden weapons until they were looking down at the bleeding wounds or felt the garrote tighten about their throat. Any further pondering about Trocar's abilities would have to wait; they had problems.

The Goblins were vicious, heavy-handed fighters who tried to surround you before they sliced you up into snack-sized bits. Trocar and Gillian fought back to back, knowing each other's style from years spent together in the Marines. They stayed out of each other's way, fighting silently and with deadly efficiency. Gill did a quick mental assessment. Goblins: five down, about fifteen to go. Bad, very bad. She and Trocar: still standing, fighting and uninjured at this point. Good, very good. Her gun clicked empty and she dropped it, snatching a spear from one of the dead Goblins and wielding it like a quarterstaff.

Swinging upward with the business end of the spear while bracing the haft against her thigh, she managed to tear the throat out of the closest Goblin warrior. He gurgled and went down but she was already stepping over him to block the hacking blade of another one who was going for Trocar's back.

An unearthly howl sounded and was echoed around the

valley. Everyone froze for a heartbeat, then resumed hostilities in earnest. Trocar was swearing in High Elvish, or at least that's what it sounded like. Gillian added her own voice when a spear nicked her arm as she was blocking a particularly strong thrust. It was too dark for her to see anything clearly so she was operating on instinct and her slightly enhanced senses. Aleksei's blood must be responsible for that. She'd thank him later.

Trocar managed to gain enough space for the few seconds it took him to throw a spell. Lightning crackled from his fingertips and took down several other Goblins, leaving smoking holes in their bodies. The rest of them, including Gillian, shrieked at the sudden burst of light that unfortunately illuminated the mountainside for a brief second. Dead Goblins were under her feet and around them, counting the pile of bodies that Trocar had just contributed, but more were pouring out of the hole in the mountain. This was very, very bad.

Temporarily blinded by the flash of white light, Gillian was swinging frantically with the spear, hoping to nail something by sheer luck if nothing else. Fortunately for her, the original Goblins who had been in close proximity to them were also blinded by the white flash and were staggering and swinging, much as she was.

Unfortunately, the new Goblins had no such problem and were swarming over their fellows to get to the Elf and her. The howl sounded again, very close now, and Gillian had a brief joyful thought that they might just live through this.

Sure enough, moments later Cezar's pack descended on them, snarling and snapping. One Werewolf against twenty Goblins is not a fair fight. The Werewolf always wins. An entire pack of them, about twenty-five to thirty Wolves, against a hundred was a slaughter. Crunching, snapping and ripping sounds clashed with howling, barking, screaming and yelling for supreme sounds of the night. The mixture of dialects was confusing: Goblinese, Elvish, Common Tongue or English and deep guttural Wolf noises filled the air. Thunder, lightning and the pattering sounds of rain on the forest floor added to the cacophony.

Part of the pack inserted themselves between Trocar and Gillian, forming a tight circle with them in the middle, surrounded by furry butts and tails, jaws and teeth toward the Goblins. Each Wolf weighed between four and six hundred pony-sized pounds; a circle of teeth, muscle and bone kept the Goblins from reaching them. The rest of the pack was driving the Goblins back into the dark hole in the mountain. It didn't take long. Goblins were ugly, foul-tempered beings, but they weren't altogether stupid. Most of them high-tailed it back into the hole in the ground, leaving the dead and injured to the jaws and claws of the Wolves.

As soon as the last mobile Goblin backed into the hole, Trocar snarled something magical in his oh-so-lovely voice and the gate slammed shut with another dull clang. The Wolves swung back and gathered around Gillian and Trocar. Gillian recognized Cezar and Pavel as they shouldered their way to the pair.

Unsure what she should do, she tentatively reached toward Pavel's neck ruff and patted him. "Thanks, Pavel." She turned to the pack Alpha. "Thank you, Cezar." The massive head dipped once in acknowledgment then he moved back, barking sharply at the others to give them room. Werewolves weren't mindless killers as everyone thought. If they were young or new, there was a lack of control at first. An Alpha like Cezar and a budding Alpha like Pavel had more control than most, but the pack attended to their leader and moved away, positioning themselves to scan for any further threats.

Trocar wiped his knives on the nearest Goblin carcass and went to finish what they came to do. Again, he unraveled the spells then rebuilt the little cairn, warding it as he did so. When he was finished, he turned to Gillian. "You are undamaged?"

"Yup. Just fine."

"Good. Then let us go to your Vampire's meeting and inform the Fey that the Goblins have grown bold." He moved as gracefully as ever, no hint of the exertion from fighting a bunch of Goblins, Gillian noted ruefully. She was going to be sore later; she just knew it. She followed him, but at a slower pace, the Wolves flanking them even after they got into her car.

She drove slowly, letting the pack keep up, until they reached the meeting hall in the village. Once they were at the door, Cezar barked sharply to the pack. With a final nod from himself and Pavel, they melted into the night.

They walked into the large room, bringing gasps and scornful looks from the assembled parties as they collectively turned to see who was entering. Aleksei was seated at a long table in the center of the room. With him was an assortment of Fey: Elves, Fairies—probably from all three Courts—Brownies, Demi-Fey, Sluagh and Shifters of some sort who were in Human form; all seated, standing or hanging from the walls and ceiling. Even Noph and Montu were there, standing behind Aleksei. The leaders were at the table, their various entourages scattered throughout the room. They all looked clean, lovely or unlovely, depending on species, composed and shocked.

Gill and Trocar looked each other over. The Dark Elf

looked fine. Not a hair out of place, only a small tear in his cloak and some Goblin goo on his boot. He smiled at Gillian and she knew she must look a tiny bit worse than he did. Oh well. Glancing down, she saw blood spatter down her shirt and pants, she had defensive cuts on her hands and arms and mud up and down one leg where she'd slipped during the fight.

"Bellissima!" Aleksei's marvelous voice crawled up her spine.

The voice sounded horrified. Still deep and black velvet but horrified. Shit. She looked up and watched the tall beautiful Vampire leave his place at the table and cross the room toward her in moments in the gliding, graceful way only a Vampire or some of the Fey could have managed.

"Hi, Aleksei," she began. "I'm fine. We just ran into an unfriendly Goblin group." She brushed ineffectively at the mud on her pants.

When he reached her, he held her at arm's length, quickly scanning her with his eyes to determine that she wasn't seriously hurt, then gathered her to his chest and hugged her tightly. Gillian made an "oof" sound as he squashed her against his hard frame.

"Aleksei, you're breaking my ribs," she pointed out with a squeak. He released her enough so she could breathe and she hugged him back.

Ice gray eyes met hers as he pulled back enough to look at her. "Truly? You are uninjured?"

"I'm fine. Just a little muddy and have a few scrapes. Nothing major." Looping her arm around his waist, she let him tuck her under his shoulder and lead her back to the table with Trocar following. Montu, one of the Egyptian Vampires named for the ancient God of War, brought them chairs, winking at Gillian as he went to seat her. She was too tired to argue about chauvinism in multispecies assemblies and sank into it gratefully.

"Goblins! Their stench covers you!" one of the Fey hissed at her.

Gillian couldn't tell if he was Light Court, Dark Court or Twilight Court. He was about six foot two, very slender, ethereally beautiful with shimmering blue-white skin, hair that was so dark a purple it looked black and sparkling with violet highlights. His eyes were the glittering midnight blue of the Aegean shot with silver sparks. He looked delicate, almost feminine in his deep purple, skin-tight, velvety togs. His slender hand caressed the jeweled sword on his hip. The entire picture was deceiving. All of the Fey were much stronger than their fragile appearances often belied, and Gillian had no doubt that he would be counted as a badass among any company.

The Courts of Fey and Fairy were also very class conscious among themselves and outsiders. Problem was, their differences weren't always obvious nor was their class structure. Since blood feuds had begun due to an unrealized insult, she didn't want to offend him by saying the wrong thing so she nodded.

"And Wolf," one of the Shifters announced, sniffing Gillian. She couldn't tell what he was, but he moved with the springy confidence of a Lycanthrope.

She batted at him. "Stop it!" He receded, smiling with a toothy grin.

Trocar apparently had no problem distinguishing between Fey varieties. "They are overseeing the dampening fields which have been placed around this village, dweller of the Twilight Court," he said, casually stretching booted legs out in front of him. He was the very picture of contempt and let it show.

The tall, purple-haired Fairy became paler. "And how might we have prevented this, Grael?" he sneered back at Trocar. No love lost between the Fey and the Elves.

Aleksei and Gillian exchanged a brief glance. This wasn't going to go well if they couldn't keep The Purple Prince and Trocar from sniping at each other.

"Enough," Aleksei ordered, in his marvelous, magical voice. "We are not here to cast blame nor fight among ourselves."

There were nods of assent from all the beings. Purple Hair suddenly yelped and jumped backward. "Do you seek war with the Twilight Court?" he snarled, reaching down to rub his foot.

Gillian, Aleksei and Trocar couldn't see what was happening, but the rest of the Paramortals snickered and a tiny, accented voice shrilled, "Fairy Big will not insult Gillian Big!"

"Shit, now the horror is complete," Gillian moaned, her hands covering her eyes. Afraid to confirm what her ears were telling her.

Aleksei looked at her anxiously. "Are you all right, *piccola*?"

Something occurred to her and she rose to walk round the table, ignoring Aleksei, and glared at the Brownie who had stuck his small sword into the purple Sidhe's foot. "You can't be the same Brownie Clan from Russia!"

"No, indeed, Gillian Big. We are not. The Brownies have a most complex system for information sharing," the little being said proudly.

Prince Purple Hair sniped to Gillian, "You consort with this vermin?" His tone was venomous. Great, now she was pissed but she bit back a smart-assed retort and looked the Fey straight in his gorgeous eyes.

Gritting her teeth, she focused on psychology, logic and being rational. All this fighting and stress had been refocusing her in the wrong direction. She let out the breath she'd been holding, and aimed for polite.

"The Brownies stepped forward without question to save over a hundred Human children in Russia, before the need for an alliance had been realized. This Clan is here to show support and are valued allies, as are you all. They will not be referred to in any derogatory manner." She took the two steps that closed the gap between herself and Prince Purple. "Have I made myself clear?"

There was a collective intake of breath at this scruffy little Human facing down an obviously Titled Fey. Before he could answer, she turned on the Brownie. "And as for you, don't start arguments with the others. They are here to help all of us so no more sticking people, understand?"

The tiny figure nodded sullenly and drew back. Gillian resumed her seat wearily. "Look, we all have got to cooperate, pool our knowledge and resources. We are fighting a common enemy, everyone. Fighting each other isn't going to accomplish anything."

"Well said, *piccola*," Aleksei said.

"I'm getting too old for this shit," Gillian groused under her breath, bringing a chuckle from Aleksei and the Egyptian Vampires. Trocar bothered to cock an eyebrow at her.

"You are a mere babe in arms, Gillyflower." The dark silken voice shimmered over all of them.

Gillian was about to say something nasty when, glancing around the room, she realized he was right. Every single being in the room was a Paramortal but herself. All of them, even the Lycanthropes, had some kind of extended life span. She literally was the baby in the room. Oops. Time for diplomacy again.

Dropping her shields, she projected warmth and understanding. "You're right, Trocar. To all of you, I am young. Too young to understand the thousands of years of history that all of you have amassed." There. Let them know that she knew big words too. "However, I am a target, just like you. I have military and diplomatic experience, just like you. We are here to stop the spread of an evil together, so let's not lose our focus, shall we?"

There were nods of assent around the room. "How is evil defined, Human?" a growly, raspy voice asked from somewhere in the dark corner to Gill's left.

A Spriggan stepped forward, out of the shadow, and most of the Paramortals winced. Spriggans were ugly. There was no room for middle ground here. Their shapes shifted slightly as you looked at them, so you were never quite sure *what* it was you were looking at. Basically they looked like walking cow patties with eyes and mold. Ugly, short-tempered, they were capable of growing to a huge size when threatened, provoked or in battle. Part of the Sluagh Court of the Fey, Spriggans—like Nightflyers, Goblins, Jack in Irons, Hags, Red Caps, Trolls, Phoukas, Glaistigs, and a dozen other similar beings—had little love for any of the other beings in the room, Humans least of all.

Gillian swallowed hard and tried not to look repulsed. "Evil is defined by thoughts or deeds that threaten our individual cultures' freedoms and liberties." She had paid attention during Diplomacy 101.

It, for it was impossible to tell a Spriggan's gender, looked at her for a moment, considering. Finally it replied, the voice now clogged with thick things but still raspy, "Very well. We will listen." It faded back into the corner with its fellows.

Aleksei and Gillian quickly outlined Osiris's Doctrine

and the plan for unification among the Paramortals. Aleksei explained that those assembled were free to advertise the document, to encourage recruitment and to hold meetings such as this one, in order to have an organized, united front.

Gillian also pointed out that they were free *not* to sign the document if they were afraid of reprisals from their various cultures or communities. "No one is going to force anybody to sign this or to join this Alliance." Her eyes locked with each of them as she scanned the room. "What we are essentially promising is to be supportive and protective of each other and our interests. This is not an anti-Dracula document. This is a pro-unification document."

Trocar rose and, to Gillian's and Aleksei's surprise, produced an elegant quill from his robes and signed it. Noticing their astonishment, Trocar smiled. "I do not speak for all the Grael, but I speak for myself."

There were nods and murmurs of assent from around the hall. One by one, either in groups or singly, the varied beings came to put signature, paw print, mark or seal on the Osiris Doctrine. Watching them, Gillian felt a swell of pride. The idea had been hers and Aleksei's, but Osiris had come through with the diplomatic eloquence needed to reach this variety of creatures.

The door swung open suddenly, making everyone startle. Three tall, cloaked and hooded figures strode into the hallway, bows slung over their shoulders and quivers bristling with arrows, clearly visible. The lead figure reached up a gauntleted hand and shoved back its hood to reveal long glowing hair that was golden but shot through with orange, blue and violet, the colors of the setting sun, tucked back in a warrior's braid from an elegant and heartrendingly beautiful face. He smiled at the assembled as he moved toward them. To Gillian's surprise, the purple-garbed Fey gave a slight bow, which the approaching Fey returned.

The purple-garbed one spoke. "We are honored, Prince Dalton, Son of the Light. Why do you travel with the brethren of the woods?" he asked, gesturing toward the two remaining figures.

"Finian!" Dalton's voice was cheerful and made the air shimmer with warmth. Gillian's mouth went dry and her palms felt damp. Glamour. Yeah, that was it.

Gillian didn't look at Aleksei but she could see he was watching her reaction to the approaching trio with interest. *Shit,* she thought. After all her training and exposure to the Fey, she thought she'd be immune to their magic. Apparently not.

"Think nothing of it, piccola,*"* Aleksei murmured in her mind. *"I feel it too, as do they all."* His black velvet voice negated anything the Fey could throw at her.

Dalton stopped next to her and Aleksei, the two figures mirroring him, their hoods and cloaks still up. "Greetings to thee, Prince Finian, Lord of the Twilight Court. I am pleased to see thee here." Dalton said formally, giving sort of a half bow and sweeping back his cloak to reveal a jeweled sword on his hip, just as Finian wore. Gillian wasn't sure if it was a gesture of respect or a veiled threat.

Turning, the Fey prince motioned to his companions. Slowly, the two raised arms to their hoods and pulled them back. Twin Wood Elves, male and female, stoically regarded the room. Dalton introduced them. "Please welcome Aisling and Gunnolf Crosswind. They have been my traveling companions of late and wish to offer the services of the Woodland people in this momentous endeavor."

Gillian felt the familiar wrench at her heart whenever she

met one of the Fey or Elves. Trocar, she was used to. He was no less heartwrenchingly lovely than the newcomers or the Vampires but he was familiar and didn't have the same effect when she saw him daily. The newcomers were breathtaking. Their hair was a rich chestnut brown, shimmering with light. Their eyes were as crystal gray as Aleksei's but sparkled with starry iridescence. She gave them all greeting, right arm diagonally across her chest and a slight nod of the head. They were there to offer their services, and it never hurt to be polite.

Since Dalton's and the Elf twins' minds had been made up before they arrived, the rest of the signing went smoothly. Aleksei offered accommodations for the Elves and any of the Fey who wished to stay on his estate. The meeting wrapped quickly with plans for everyone to scout, recruit and report at regular intervals. The Egyptian Vampires offered to coordinate the various Teams and to keep track of everyone's progress on weeding out Dracula's supporters and the gaining of new allies.

It was late or early depending on whose body clock was being referred to. Gillian just wanted a hot shower and bed. Aleksei would have liked an intimate moment with her but he could sense her weariness and settled for escorting her back to the Castle, laving her defensive wounds with his healing saliva, then tucking her in after she'd bathed.

"We may have made some progress tonight," Gillian said, her voice husky from tiredness. Reaching up, she smoothed her fingers through the handsome Vampire's hair.

"Indeed, *angelina*, we seem to have awakened the need for solidarity," Aleksei murmured, stroking her hair and pitching his voice to calm her further. He removed her hand from his hair, kissed her fingertips, then slid her hand beneath the covers. Gillian smiled tiredly and snuggled down farther, then went to sleep.

Aleksei remained sitting on the bed watching her for some time. He wondered if he would ever get used to her independence, the chances she unwittingly took, her determination to protect and soothe everyone. She was an amazing, interesting woman. He knew she was restless to get back to being a therapist and was annoyed when her soldier side asserted itself. Gillian believed that she could separate one from the other—her nurturing side and her confrontational side. Aleksei understood better than she did that she needed both sides equally. Gillian wasn't domesticated; she was restrained for the moment by her own volition. When he left her, she was muttering in her sleep— growling orders to someone or something.

Meet Gillian Key. She's a Paramortal psychologist
who can treat the mental distress of non-Humans.
And she's a Marine Special Forces operative who
can get physical with them when the situation
calls for it...

Key to Conflict
By TALIA GRYPHON